THE ROAD TO JUSTICE

by Tamara Lyon

The third installment in THE Ugly TREE series

THE ROAD TO JUSTICE

First printing

Cover design
By Julie Nor of Flair Studio

ISBN: 978-0615937540
Lyon's Novel Books

For my family and my fans

CHAPTER ONE

Late September 1998

Not that I have a watch, clock, or anything else to tell me what time it is, but I'm guessing it has to be near midnight, because the programming quality has tanked. Lounging on my sleeping bag and cramming ketchup-riddled microwave popcorn into my mouth, I channel-surf. Since I've managed to misplace the remote to my barely nineteen-inch television, circa 1988, and am too lazy to get up every time I want to change the channel, I'm using my big toe. Had I taken Grandma Betty's advice and used Velcro to adhere the remote to the side of the television like she's told me to do multiple times, I wouldn't be in this predicament. My toe accidentally grazes the power button. The screen makes an electric snapping noise and goes black.

Spectacular. I'm going to have to get off my butt.

Setting my snack aside, I army-crawl over to the television, push the power button, and change the channel the old-fashioned way. I land on an infomercial where a slick con artist named Lester Stanford tells me that I can make millions buying real estate even if I have poor credit and no money. Apparently intelligence is not a prerequisite. Easing myself backward, I resume eating as Lester promises that I can quadruple my wealth in a matter of weeks. If I mail him $59.99, he'll send me a booklet and CD that will explain the simple process, and I'll be well on my way.

Sold! Let me get out my checkbook and run to the post office to overnight the money!

Who actually believes this crap?

Extending my big toe, I'm about to ax Lester and his empty promises when I hear a musical chirping. With surprising toe dexterity, I mute the television.

What is that? It sounds like a small bird trapped in a closet. Oh, wait! It's my new cell phone. Only I have no idea where it is. Leaping up, I spill my popcorn all over the top of the television. A few kernels with ketchup stick to the screen, one landing right on Lester's head. From this angle, it looks like he shot his brains out.

Racing around my new apartment and hurdling over stacks of boxes, I discover my phone in the bathtub. I must have left it there when I was hanging my new frog shower curtain.

Bending down, I grab it and answer on the last ring. "Did you survive the trip?" I ask breathlessly.

My best friend, Caprice, emits something of a growl. "Holy. Shitty. Balls. That was the longest drive known to mankind. The longest. Do you know how many miles it is from Colorado to Illinois? Too many."

"You could have spared yourself the misery. My suitcase isn't that big—you could have brought it on a plane." I'd spent the summer out in Briar, Colorado, with Caprice, helping her build her cleaning company,

2

Maid Hot, the Hooters of the cleaning industry, where the maids are required to wear bikinis. In my haste to start my new marketing job at Schaeffer Dairy back in my hometown of Savage, Illinois, I inadvertently left behind a suitcase filled with the majority of my business clothes. Because I'm excessively thrifty and only buy things when they're on clearance or in a second-hand store, I've been rotating three dress shirts and two skirts for the past two weeks.

"Obviously that would have been easier, but I didn't want the hassle or expense of renting a car once I got here. Never mind that I don't know how long I'm going to be stuck in Chicago dealing with my family. My cousin's upcoming wedding? Absolute nightmare. Turns out there are dozens of events planned. Since I'm the oldest, I'll be expected at all the showers, parties, fittings, all that shit. Besides, if I'd flown, I wouldn't have been able to bring your present."

Caprice has been mysterious about the housewarming gift she's bringing me. "You don't have Nikeo stashed in the trunk, do you?" I ask half jokingly. It's occurred to me that Nikeo, her handsome and antagonistic cousin, might also be attending the wedding. Nikeo and I'd had a summer fling that flung my life into the gutter. Two months later, I'm still trying to crawl out.

"Don't panic, I left him back in Briar. Although what I brought you does resemble him," she says enigmatically.

"Come on, you have to tell me what it is."

"No hints. It's a surprise. Did you get everything moved in?"

"Justice and Samson are bringing the furniture tomorrow, but all the boxes are here. Lots of unpacking to do."

"I can help when I get there."

"You won't have to. Grandma Betty will be here in the morning, and she won't let us go to bed until everything is cleaned, unpacked, arranged, and put away. She abides by the a-place-for-everything-and-everything-in-its-place rule."

"My kind of lady. Maid Hot could use a woman like her. Think she would wear a bikini?"

"Hot pink isn't her color."

Caprice laughs. "Too bad. I bet she would be popular with the senior set."

Fist planted over my mouth, I stifle a yawn and sit on the edge of the tub. "So when are you getting here?"

"Tuesday night, and I can't stay long. Probably just a night."

"I wish I didn't have to work—"

"I wish you would ditch your job and come back to Colorado with me," she interrupts.

Ever since I left Colorado, she's been hounding me to return. "Not possible. I signed a six-month lease on this place. The job at Schaeffer Dairy is going well. Not to mention that Justice is here. I need to be where he is."

"And how are things with him? Good?"

Good? Try the antonym of that. Because of what happened with Nikeo, my relationship with the love of my life, Justice Price, isn't on the rocks, it's buried beneath the rubble. Our interactions, once loving and playful, have become frosty and formal. I would prefer to spend every second together, moving forward and planning our future. Instead we have scheduled dates, every Wednesday and the occasional Friday night. This was his brilliant idea. It feels like we're a couple on the verge of divorce, trying to give it another go and acting all fake and upbeat. It's thoroughly depressing, especially since I'm doing everything in my power to make it work.

In the four weeks since our pseudo-breakup, when he said we needed to slow things down and put our future into an indefinite holding pattern, I've sent him flowers, surprised him with the fancy fishing rod he's been wanting for two years—obscenely expensive, by the way, and not even on clearance—written him a two-page love poem, and treated him to a candlelit picnic in the woods.

The picnic was memorable but not exactly successful. Justice was about to kiss me when one of the pillar candles somehow tipped over, rolled down an incline, and landed under a pine tree. The brittle dead branches at the bottom burst into flames, an event that seemed more like an omen than an unfortunate accident. Once we were sure there wouldn't be a forest fire and Smokey the Bear wouldn't put us on any Wanted posters, we packed it up and packed it in.

Justice, though politely appreciative of my wooing, hasn't been over the moon about it. I fear it's only a matter of time before he signs his walking papers. Worst of all? I'm positive he has his eyes on someone else, and I'm hoping that's all he has on her at the moment.

Clamping the phone between my ear and shoulder, I ease myself backward into the claw-foot tub. My legs dangle out over the edge as I weave small sections of my hair into scalp-hurting braids. "We're making progress," I respond generically, sparing her the less-than-stellar details.

After twenty minutes of conversational nonsense, I disconnect but stay planted in the bathtub, gazing up at the plaster ceiling and running my hands over my half-plaited head until I doze off. When I wake up, my bony butt has gone completely numb, and my neck feels broken. Sore and groggy, I climb out of the tub and shuffle into the living room.

Collapsing onto my sleeping bag and mound of pillows, I stare dumbly at the ketchup-and-popcorn-garnished television. It's quite a mess, and I can't make out what new infomercial is airing. I should clean it properly before it dries and gets crusty, but I don't have the energy to find the paper towels and cleaning supplies. They could be in any one of the boxes strewn around the room.

My eyes are drawn to the lower half of the screen, where an advertisement for a psychic hotline scrolls by.

The purple words emit a smoky haze. "Our certified psychics will tell you everything you need to know about your life. We have the answers you seek. Find out your destiny. Only $1.99 for the first minute. Call 1-888-550-5000 right now!"

I didn't like what Lester was selling, but this concept appeals to me. My life would be so much simpler if I knew what was going to happen. I don't even have to mail a check and wait for a booklet and CD that will explain everything; I can charge $1.99 to my credit card and hear everything I need to know straight from a psychic's mouth. Instant gratification—the one thing Americans can agree on. I bet Lester would be rolling in even more dough if he set up a hotline.

Where is my wallet?

Thirty minutes later it's nowhere to be found, and I'm entering full-blown panic mode. Then I remember the last time I had it: when I came home from work, carrying a gallon of Schaeffer Dairy Cow Pie ice cream. I yank open the freezer door, and there's my wallet, sitting right on top of the ice cream. Perfectly illogical, just like the rest of my life right now.

Now that I have my credit card, I've forgotten the stupid phone number. I sit, eyes glued to the television, another ten minutes before the advertisement comes on again. Cell phone at the ready, I punch in the numbers, read the operator my credit card number, and impatiently wait to be connected to psychic extraordinaire Rhonda Riddle. I'm already skeptical. The name suggests a stripper more than a psychic.

"Hello, this is Rhonda Riddle," drones a nasal voice. "Thank you for calling. What's your name?"

"Cane Kallevik."

"Ohhh! That's a pretty name. How old are you, sweetheart?"

"I turned twenty-two on August fifteenth."

"Such a young thing! A Leo, which means that you are enthusiastic, faithful, and loving."

Enthusiastic and loving? Maybe. Faithful? Up to a point. "I don't know about that."

"The stars tell me that you are all those things," she states emphatically.

"What would you like to know about your destiny?"

What don't I want to know? If she could hand over a detailed outline of the next year of my life, that would be ideal, but it boils down to one thing. "I want to know if I'll end up with Justice."

"End up with justice? Something happened to you. Someone hurt you. I'm sensing an assault, a robbery, a horrible crime, a murder."

"Go fish," I mumble under my breath. I'm quickly losing faith in Rhonda's ability. "I'm not talking about justice as in legal justice, I'm talking about the man I love, Justice Price."

"Is he a lawyer? Because it would be perfect if he was. The price of justice? Justice Price! Get it!"

I would have done better to flush two bucks down the toilet and spare myself the humiliation of this call. I flick my credit card at the television. It knocks off one of the kernels. I wait to see if she'll say anything else.

"You're deeply upset right now. You love Justice. You want to know what's going to happen with him."

Not exactly intuitive, since I've spoon-fed her this information. "Rhonda, can we cut the crap? You and I both know that you aren't psychic."

"I am," she insists, employing a mystical tone of voice.

Give me a break. She doesn't have a psychic bone in her body, but I desperately need someone impartial to hear my story and give me feedback. Since I don't feel like cruising any more channels looking for a therapy hotline, though I'm positive I could find one, I'll settle for the nonpsychic.

"Here's the deal, Rhonda. Four months ago I graduated from college, and when I came home, Justice popped the question in front of a hundred friends and family. I said yes. After that he drove me to my surprise party, where he proceeded to show me the dream house he was building for us. Then at this very same party, in a very public and humiliating way, Mikayla, my best friend from childhood, found out the secret I'd been keeping from her for years: while we were still in high school, Mikayla's mother cheated on her father, not with a man her own age but with Mikayla's boyfriend. To make matters worse, she got pregnant and had his love child. Mikayla was furious at me for keeping this from her, and then she dropped her own bomb. She told me she was in love with Justice, and that she'd made out with him!

"It was all too much. Graduating college? Getting married? Building a dream house? Finding out Justice and Mikayla had kissed, and that she loved him? I needed time to process everything. I took off for the summer, met this guy named Nikeo, and fell for him. Things got complicated between us—more than complicated, actually—but in the end I knew it was Justice I loved and wanted to be with.

"Just when I figured this out, I got this cryptic message that said Mik and J were getting married! I assumed that it referred to Mikayla and Justice. I rushed home to stop the wedding and ended up crashing the end of the ceremony. But it wasn't Mikayla and Justice, it was Mikayla and Justice's cousin Jeremy. I felt like the biggest jerk. I was hoping that Justice would be ready to move forward with our relationship, but then he told me that he needed time to think things through.

"To make things more problematic, I'm working at Schaeffer Dairy for the owner, Samson Schaeffer, who just so happens to be Justice's uncle, and Justice also works for the company. And so does Samson's son Jeremy, who's now Mikayla's husband. One big happy family. It's been a bit awkward and tangled, to say the least."

After that verbal purge, I need a gin and tonic, heavy on the gin, light on tonic. Unfortunately, the only liquid I have in this apartment comes from the tap.

Rhonda lets out a low whistle and abandons the mystical tone of voice. "Wow, it's like a storyline from *General Hospital* or *The Young and the Restless.*"

"Not a soap opera, just my life." I snatch a kernel off the top of the television, throw it in the air, and catch it with my mouth. "So, what's going to happen?"

"Sweetheart, I have absolutely no idea, but I'm dying to find out! I'll give you my home number. I want you to call me back!"

CHAPTER TWO

Grandma Betty, punctual to a fault, pounds on the door at ten in the morning. "Cane! Cane! Open up. Are you awake? It's me! I'm here!" she trills excitedly.

When I open the door, she drops her suitcases at her feet and gives me the biggest hug. When she finally lets me go, she holds me at arm's length. "No more hotel living! It's your first place! You must be so happy."

I'm not sure if I'm overcaffeinated (I drank six cups of coffee, and I should really be more mindful of how much I ingest; once I ended in the emergency room from caffeine overload), or overtired (I barely got five hours of sleep and then decided to tackle the day with a six-mile interval run), but as soon as she says this, I burst into tears. Fat, gulping, unattractive sobs. The kind of crying that's unacceptable for a twenty-two-year-old independent career woman.

"I'm okay, I'm okay," I squeak during my outburst, but clearly I'm not. My face probably looks like a terrifying Picasso rendering. Snot trickles out of my nostrils. Tears fly every which way. My lips have gone all Muppet-like. And my lungs are huffing and puffing, only there's nothing to blow down. My long auburn hair, still wet from my shower, sticks to my freckled face. Not wanting to risk being seen by the cute, geeky guy that lives next door, who I spotted carrying a large coffee this morning as I was leaving for my run, I slink backward.

"Sugar Cane!" Grandma guides me over to the only chair in the apartment and sits me down. She peels my hair off my cheeks, holds her hands on my shoulders as if to steady me, and gives me delicate kisses on the faint cross-shaped birthmark on my forehead. "It'll be okay, sugar. It'll be okay. I know it will."

I've cried so violently and purged so many emotions that it feels as if the only thing left is my skeleton. Grandma opens her purse and pulls out her ever-present package of tissues, stowed in a plastic container. She yanks out a handful and gives it to me. I pat my swollen face and attempt to blow my nose, but it feels like I've got concrete in my sinuses. Nothing's coming out. I sprinkle the used tissues on the floor.

She kneels in front of me and pats my knees. "Feel better?"

"You look beautiful," I tell her. "You've gotten tan. It makes your eyes stand out." I've missed everything about Grandma, from her cute face to her predictable wardrobe. She owns hundreds of sensible belted pantsuits in many styles and colors. Claiming they disguise her big bosom and accentuate her small waist, she wears them constantly. Today she's sporting a ribbed cashmere suit that I haven't seen before. It's a deep rose color, and it contrasts nicely with her cornflower-blue eyes. Since she takes color schemes seriously and will go to any length to match, her blush, eye shadow, lipstick, handbag—even her shoes—are all some variation on pink.

"Oh, honey. I've been waiting for that for weeks now."

"For me to say you're beautiful?"

"No—I've been waiting for you to break down and have a good cry.

I've been wondering when it was going to happen. You've been bottling it all up inside for weeks, and it was bound to come out sooner or later. I'm just glad I was here when it did."

"This is all so hard. I want Justice back. I want to marry him. I want to be living in the house that he's building for us."

She nods sympathetically. "I know you do, but it will take time. He asked for space, and you need to give it to him."

"It doesn't feel like he wants space. It feels like he's only interested in punishing me for what happened between Nikeo and me."

Crisis or not, Grandma Betty can't stand messes. She reaches down and gathers the used tissues. "Do you think that when you told Justice you needed space and left for three months, he might have felt like you were punishing him for what happened between him and Mikayla? Which you and I both know was nothing. I mean, look at her now. She's married to Jeremy."

Leaning my head back, I indulge in a sigh-slash-groan. "I'm not in the mood for a game of devil's advocate."

"How about we start the day over again, shall we?" she asks.

"Good idea." I stand up and reach out my hand, and Grandma Betty takes it. I help her off her knees. "Welcome to my new apartment."

Stuffing the tissues into her coat pocket, she looks approvingly at the living area and kitchen. "The hardwood floors are beautiful, and the woodwork is stunning. So are the copper ceiling tiles in the kitchen. I love the original detail."

"There's even a claw-foot tub."

Her cheeks stiffen and rise upward. Blinking back tears, she presses a hand over her heart. "Oh, honey. Being back in this building? It's quite something. Your dad and mom sure loved this place. I remember how proud they were of it. I came for dinner the week they moved in and helped your mom roll out dough for an apple pie she was making while that adorable son of mine couldn't unstick his nose from the newspaper. He was reading an article about the Cubs and griping about their horrible season." She tucks her lower lip under her upper teeth and shakes her head. "Funny what you remember. It's always the small things."

When they were first married, my parents had rented a third-floor apartment in this very building, which had been an old sewing factory back in the 1800s. Six years ago, after a major tornado ravaged downtown Savage while I was in high school, there had been a major and necessary remodel. Instead of keeping retail and office space on the first two floors, all levels were converted into apartments. There are six apartments total, and I'm in the two-bedroom unit on the first floor. "Is it hard being here?" I ask her.

She frowns thoughtfully. "Not hard. Strange. And, also in a way, wonderful. If your mom and dad were alive, they'd be tickled that you were living in the same place where they started out."

She surveys the room. Her furrowed brow and the determined set of her chin are dead giveaways. She's done with nostalgia; she wants to attack this mess and establish order.

"We've got a lot to do," she remarks. "We're going to be busy."

"Frank doesn't mind that you're here, does he? I know that you had to push back your trip to New England."

"I'm not leaving one second sooner than I have to!" She pinches my cheek. "I've missed you. I haven't seen you in more than three months!"

Grandma Betty and my step-grandfather, Frank, moved to Florida this past June, trading a house that overlooked amber waves of grain for a condo overlooking Pacific blue. "It feels like longer," I muse.

"I know, which is why I'm staying until Tuesday morning. Besides, we only pushed back our trip by a few days. We'll still get to see all the glorious fall colors. Living in St. Petersburg is lovely, but I do miss the change of the seasons. By the way, I'm desperate for you to visit. Frank is too. He wants you to bring the video camera so that you can go through all the footage from Colorado. He thought that maybe you would want to make a highlight video or something." She chuckles. "Although I have no clue how he would go about doing that! I don't understand that blasted equipment at all, much less his fascination with it!"

A technology and gadget aficionado, Frank gave me a video camera for a graduation gift. Every time we speak on the phone, he's eager to discuss what I've been filming. "I'll make it down to visit soon. Promise."

"You better." Grandma Betty unzips her coat, the same rose hue as her pantsuit, and tosses it onto the chair. "When's the furniture arriving?"

"Samson and Justice will be here after lunch."

"That doesn't leave us much time. Let's get started! We need to clear the area before the big stuff gets here."

Grandma Betty, who would have made an excellent drill sergeant, barks out orders, and I follow them. We organize the boxes into piles, carry them to the appropriate rooms, and begin the tedious unpacking process.

While we sort through my belongings, Grandma Betty peppers me with questions.

"Has your schedule at work still been reasonable?"

"Yeah, usually nine to five, but Samson's really relaxed about it. He doesn't mind if I take off early some days. As long as I make headway on the projects."

"And the website you're helping design? How's that coming along?" she asks.

"It should be up and running by next week. Just a few things to tweak. We're waiting for the photographer to finish up with all the different ice cream flavors so we can link those with the descriptions. The more visual, the better. Samson is excited about the idea of people being able to order products and gift cards online, and customers having twenty-four-hour access."

"Frank is so excited about this whole internet thing. He drives me crazy talking about it! He can't wait to see what you've been working on. I was thinking, how about a visit at the end of October, maybe close to Halloween? Does that work for you?"

She nails me with a make-a-decision look that I know all too well. If I don't commit, she's not going to be happy. "Sure. I'll talk to Samson on Monday and see what days I can get off."

Pleased with this, Grandma Betty gives me the biggest smile I've seen since I walked across the stage at graduation. "And how are things with Jocelyn? Have you spoken to her yet?"

"No. I sent her a birthday present last week. I've stopped by the house twice, but Jenny Ryanne wouldn't even answer the door."

My history with the Schaeffer family is complex. I've been working for them since I was eleven. Samson, my father's childhood best friend, adores me. His wife Jenny Ryanne despises me. I befriended their only daughter, Jocelyn, when she was eleven and I was sixteen, and we've had a sisterly relationship for years. Needing to get away from family drama, Jocelyn came out to Colorado this past summer and stayed with me for a few weeks. She happened to catch me kissing Nikeo. It wasn't the kissing that bothered her so much as the fact that I was cheating on her older cousin, Justice. This devastated her, not only because she adored Justice and wanted me to marry him but also because she had recently discovered that Jenny Ryanne had been cheating on her father. Instead of hating her cheating mother, she hated cheating Cane, and she broadcast my indiscretion to everyone back home, including Justice. I don't blame her at all. I've been trying to reach out to her for weeks so that we can patch things up, but she hasn't responded.

"She'll come around," Grandma assures me. "It's just going to take time."

That seems to be a recurring theme in my life lately. I don't have time for time. Let's get on with everything already. Enough of this limbo crap. I punch the top of a box; the tape busts open, and so does the ridge of one of my knuckles.

Grandma gives me the stink eye. "You could have used the scissors. There on the floor. Right next to you," she adds pointedly.

From the second I was born, she's been telling me to slow down and take my time. But those ants in my pants she's always accused me of having haven't slowed down over the years. They've multiplied. And they aren't run-of-the-mill friendly ants. The way I always feel, this burning inside me, I'm convinced that they're fire ants. "Punching is faster."

"And more dangerous. If you don't slow down, you're really going to hurt yourself."

Too late. The damage has already been done. If I hadn't bolted for the Rocky Mountains this past June, I'd be sitting on the back deck of my new house looking through bridal magazines and playing footsy—or something more provocative—under the table with Justice. Instead, I'm playing the role of a semi-single girl (if that's even a label) in farm city USA, setting up her new apartment.

This unpacking business is taking forever, because everything I do, Grandma Betty undoes. I stack my favorite romance novels in a pile in the corner, and she rifles through them, organizes them alphabetically, and then places them against the opposite wall. I remove all the towels from a box, fold them, and put them in the linen closet. I leave to get another box, and when I return, Grandma Betty is refolding the towels in thirds, the way she prefers, and putting them on a different shelf. "See," she says, pointing. "This makes more sense. They're at a better height for grab and go."

I love her to pieces, but she's already driving me crazy. Grab and go sounds good right about now. I grab my wallet, which is no longer in the freezer but logically sitting on the kitchen counter next to my keys, and head out the door to pick up lunch at Savage Suds Bar and Grill, less than a block down the street. By the time I return with the food, the big Schaeffer Dairy truck loaded with my furniture is parked on the curb, and Justice is pulling up in his own truck.

I wave at Samson. Justice parks and hops out of his pickup. He smiles at me. "Ready to get started?"

Even after all these years, my heart still flutters at the sight of him. He's your classic superman: tall and lean, strong jaw, gorgeous eyes under a pair of perfectly arched brows, a pair of the most delectable dimples, and a kissable mouth. He's wearing worn jeans and a faded gray sweatshirt that makes his aquamarine eyes more noticeable. He has a sprinkling of dark stubble on his face. "Guess so."

He kisses me chastely on the cheek. I'm dying for a real kiss. Some tongue. Some heat. Some passion. But this is all I get. Maybe if the pine tree hadn't burst into flames last week . . .

"Grandma Betty make it okay?" he asks.

"Yes, and she's making herself right at home. This will be her place in no time at all."

He smiles. "I wouldn't expect anything less. Want me to carry the food upstairs for you?"

"That's okay." I smile back at him. "I've got it. You and Samson have done too much for me already."

Even though I initially hired movers, Justice insisted I cancel, saying that he and Samson were happy to help. They've spent the morning at my storage unit, breaking their backs loading all the hand-me-down furniture that Frank and Grandma Betty gave me when they moved to Florida.

"Thank you again, by the way." I go up on my tiptoes, intending to show him my appreciation, but he turns suddenly and walks toward the back of the Schaeffer truck.

Deliberate avoidance? I'm not sure. Justice unlocks the latch and rolls it up, revealing cargo space that's filled to the gills. I didn't realize how much stuff was in that unit.

Samson, who's been talking on his cell phone, turns it off and shoves it into the front pocket of his flannel shirt. He climbs out of the truck. "How's the new place looking?"

"A mess at the moment, but Grandma Betty's straightening it out for me. Thanks so much for helping today." I give his arm an affectionate squeeze.

"No problem, kiddo."

"How's Jocelyn?" I ask. "Did she like the gift?" I got her a gift certificate to an athletic store, remembering that this summer she'd been eyeing a pair of pricey running shoes.

"She loved the gift. It was too generous of you."

"I'd like to try to stop by again. Do you think Jenny would mind that?"

He takes off his well-worn Cubs hat and folds the bill. He lowers his head, and his eyes skirt to the side. "I don't know what she'll do." He turns and reaches for the dolly that Justice hands him.

Grandma Betty, who has spotted Justice and Samson through my bedroom window, rushes out and smooches Justice so many times it's embarrassing, and then makes a similar fuss over Samson. When she's finished loving on them, they start the tedious unloading process. I offer to help, but they tell me to go inside and enjoy my lunch. I try to do as I'm told, but as a rule, I'm not a good spectator or listener. While Grandma Betty munches on her turkey club and uses my cell phone to call Frank and check in with him, I help Samson and Justice carry in chairs, dressers,

18

tables, box springs, and mattresses.

We make fast work of the truck and soon come to the last piece of furniture, the one that I love the most: an antique armoire. It was Grandma Betty's wedding gift to my parents, and when they died, Grandma Betty stored it in the downstairs office, promising that someday it would be mine.

It's solid oak with hand-carved detailing, and it weighs a ton. Justice frees it from the protective blankets, and Samson chuckles. "I helped your parents move this into the very same building years ago." He looks at me. "I'm glad you live on the first floor and not the third."

It takes the three of us to wrestle the unwieldy antique off the truck. We make it into the building and to my door—but that's as far as we get. We set it down and try to figure out how to get it inside.

"They've narrowed the doorways," remarks Samson. "This might be tricky."

The three of us pick up the bulky piece and maneuver it through the doorway, failing once, then again. On the third attempt we make it through.

"Where's it going?" Justice inquires breathlessly.

"The big wall."

While I have faith in my muscles, Grandma Betty doesn't. She hovers and frets as Samson, Justice, and I shuffle sideways and situate the armoire against the wall. "Careful now, Cane! You'll get squashed! I'll be taking you to the hospital before this day is over."

"I'm not going to get squashed. See?" I step back and admire the effect. Angled in the corner of the living area, the armoire makes an amazing focal point.

"As beautiful as I remember." Samson takes off his hat and wipes his brow with his shirtsleeve. "Suppose I should be going. Jenny Ryanne wants me to do some work at the house this afternoon."

Grandma Betty and I thank him profusely. After he leaves, Justice carries in some smaller items from his pickup truck while Grandma Betty and I put the legs on the kitchen table.

"This is the last of it." Justice places a piece of my metal bed frame on the couch. "I can help set everything up if you want."

Justice always goes the extra mile to make things easier for me, and I'm trying to spare him the trip lately. I'm out to prove that I'm an asset, not just a pain in the ass. "No. I'll take care of it. I'll do it."

"Yes, don't you worry, we can manage," says Grandma, who's begun scouring every surface in the kitchen.

"You sure?"

"Yes. But you could stay if you want, hang out."

His eyes dart away from me. I follow his line of vision. He's looking out the window at his truck. "Um, I have some things to take care of at the office."

"It's Saturday."

"I have to go over a financial plan for the new Aurora branch this weekend."

"Do you really have to go in?"

"Yes, I really have to go in." He walks over to Grandma Betty and gives her a hug good-bye.

"You'll be back later, won't you? We want to treat you to dinner," she says.

"Wish I could, but I'm busy tonight. Can I take a rain check?"

Busy doing what exactly?

"I'm holding you to that, young man."

"I'll walk you out," I offer. "Be right back," I tell Grandma Betty, who's sitting on the floor in front of the dishwasher.

She holds a sponge up in the air, letting me know that she's heard. "Take your time. I'll be scrubbing."

Justice and I walk out to his truck.

He tweaks the end of his nose. "She's going overboard with the bleach. I don't have any nose hairs left," he says, immediately following up with, "I should get going."

In a hurry to leave, which seems to be his modus operandi lately, he bends down and pecks me on the cheek.

Not so fast, buddy. Before he can open his door, I place my hand against it, lean into it, and cross my ankles, making it clear that I'm not letting him go anywhere. "Can we talk for a second?"

He tucks his keys into his palm and inhales through his bleach-burned nostrils. "Sure."

"I called a psychic last night. I saw the ad on TV, and I called," I announce, like it's something to be proud of. Only now that I've said it aloud in the light of day, I'm embarrassed. Mortified, actually.

A pragmatist to the core, Justice smiles dubiously. His adorable dimples appear. "Are you being serious? Please tell me that you didn't do that."

"I did."

He looks genuinely perplexed. "Why?"

"Because Lester didn't win me over with his get-rich-quick scheme, so I went with something cheaper and more appealing."

He gives me a have-you-lost-your-mind look. "What are you talking about?"

"I was watching infomercials last night," I explain. "Lester was selling how to get rich in real estate, and that's when I saw the ad for the psychic number. She was nice, not much of a psychic, but I might call her again. She gave me her home number."

"Come on—she did not give you her home number. It's probably a scam."

"It isn't a scam, and yes, she honestly did give me her number."

"You're not going to call her back, are you?"

My desperation is impressive enough that I'm contemplating it, but I'm not going to tell him that. I clear my throat and respond to his earlier question. "I called because I wanted to know what's going to happen with us."

He runs his hand through his fresh crew cut. "You do realize how nuts you sound?"

"No one ever said I was normal."

"You've been pushing me hard, Cane. Please don't. It's only been four weeks."

I'll admit that I have been pushing, but that's what I do. It's who I am. Why nudge when you can shove? Why take time to find scissors when you can punch? "I'm not pushing. I'm just making conversation."

He raises his shoulders, holds them for a second, and then drops them. "That's not what you're doing."

"Then give me something to go on, something to let me know this is going to turn out well."

"You need to be patient."

"I don't have the patient gene. It's missing."

"Tell me about it," he grumbles.

"I thought by now you would have figured things out. I mean, the house is close to being done. I only signed a six-month lease, so when that lease is up . . . I'm trying to plan ahead."

He settles his eyes on my face but remains mute.

I focus my eyes over his shoulder and stare at the heartbreaking cobalt sky. "Why are you going in to work today?" I ask. "And why can't you have dinner with us tonight?"

He gives me another one of those ridiculous cheek kisses. "The apartment looks awesome," he says. "I can help you move furniture around later if you want."

I stare him down in a way that lets him know he still hasn't answered my question. I reluctantly back away from his truck, even though I want to push him, this time in the literal sense.

I give a verbal shove, just a small one. "Justice. Come on."

"I already told you why," he says as he climbs into his truck. "I have a meeting."

He said he had to go over the financial plan—he didn't say anything about a meeting. He drives away with a cursory wave out the window. His truck roars down the street, smoke curling out of the exhaust pipe.

I should have pushed him while I had the chance. Not only did he not tell me what he was doing tonight, but this meeting of his? I bet anything it's with her, the one he has his eyes on.

CHAPTER THREE

"I don't know if this is going to work out." I stand in the middle of my living space and critically stare down the pull-out sleeper sofa, which weighs only slightly less than the armoire. "It takes up the whole living room!"

A total exaggeration. It's the perfect size.

I'm just looking for a tenable excuse to kick it to the curb. It's ugly and outdated, a country-plaid nightmare in hues of raspberry and hunter green with tufted cushions and a crocheted white doily that Grandma Betty made herself and lovingly spread across the top. It gives off an old-lady vibe that doesn't suit my feisty persona.

I walk over to it, push my knees up against the rolled arm, and nudge it so that it's centered under the abstract painting that Grandma Betty and I hung only twenty minutes ago. The plaid monstrosity slides a fraction of an inch across the hardwood floors. I appraise the position. I'm a stickler for symmetry, and it's still not centered. A nudge isn't going to do this. I squat down and prepare to give it a good shove.

"Here's what I think," Grandma Betty says from the kitchen as she sets the Pledge bottle on the countertop.

About time she's finished with the Pledge. For the past hour she's been crawling around on her hands and knees, squirting every baseboard and buffing it to a high sheen.

She reaches for the last box of dishes, opens it, and starts removing gobs of crinkled-up newspaper. She's so intent on her work, I think she's forgotten she was going to tell me what she thinks. "You were saying?" I ask as I start to heave the couch with all my might.

"Oh, yes. Sorry. Here's what I think. You shouldn't have had sex with Justice before you got married! That's where you went wrong," she exclaims, holding a glass up in the air and inspecting it for dust.

I'm mid push when she says this. Without warning, the couch hits a slippery patch of floor. I lose my balance but maintain my forward momentum. I topple gracelessly forward, smashing my chin and then nose on the sharp piece of metal bed frame that's sticking off the end of the couch.

I fall to the floor, barely having enough time to brace myself with my hands, and look at the ever-expanding red puddle beneath me. My nose and chin have exploded all over the place. Once I realize what has happened, the pain registers at once. Woozy and seeing stars, I ease myself into a sitting position, which intensifies the throbbing, burning, stinging sensation.

I hold my hands under my chin to try to catch the red waterfall, but it's no use. Pawing blindly at the couch, I grip one of the arm covers in my hand, but it's so stiff with Scotchgard, the blood would probably bead up and roll right off.

I need a fluffy, absorbent towel. Thanks to Grandma Betty, they're in the linen closet at just the right height for grab and go. I try to stand, but

I'm too dizzy. I sit back on the floor. The effort has made the bleeding worse.

"Cane! What was that noise? Where are you? Are you okay?"

I hear her footsteps getting closer. You're getting warmer, Grandma Betty. Keep coming.

I want to yell out for help, but my jaw feels broken too. What if I've mangled my face permanently? What if I end up with a bulbous, leaning nose, a crooked jaw, and a scarred-up chin?

"Oh, my word!" She rushes over to my side.

I try to look up at her, but my eyes, like the rest of my face, have turned into a leaky faucet. At least they're not leaking blood—that is, I hope not—but the tears have nearly blinded me. "I burt my bace."

Grandma Betty enters calm crisis mode. "I'll be right back."

Seconds later she returns with one of those fluffy towels and a roll of paper towels. She unwinds the paper towels first. "Put these up against your face to soak some of it up. We need to see how bad it is. Here now."

She helps me take hold of the white paper towels, and we both gingerly press them against my face. The white quickly becomes saturated with blood. We repeat the process with a fresh bunch.

"Okay, now, let me have a look." She pulls it away. A sharp intake of breath and then, "Hospital it is. Take the towel and press it gently. Now that's a good girl."

Grandma Betty puts her hands under my armpits and helps me to my feet. "Now sit on the couch and don't move."

Fat chance of that happening. I lean back into the cushions and try not to cry, because that would only make things worse. I'm in so much pain, I'm breaking out into a cold sweat. I need drugs. Or a few gin and tonics. Or both in successive order, preferably through an IV. I wonder if they offer bar service at the hospital.

"Almost ready, Sugar Cane. I'm putting on my coat, getting your purse and keys, and then I'm going to come over there and get you off the couch."

Seconds later she helps me off the couch and out to my car. She buckles my seat belt for me, making sure it's nice and snug. "We'll get there in a jiffy. Promise."

She rushes around to the driver's side and starts the car. I moan as she steps on the gas.

"Oh, honey. It'll be okay." She pats my knee consolingly and eases off the accelerator.

"Brugs. I need brugs," I mumble through the towel.

"A bug? You saw a bug, and that's why you fell?"

I shake my head and move the towel away from my face. "Brugs. I want some."

"Oh, yes, you'll get some."

Guess she wants me to get those drugs sooner than later. Because when we're stopped at the stoplight, and it turns green, for the first time in her life Grandma Betty burns rubber and cruises five miles over the speed limit.

Sixty minutes later I have an IV in my arm, a glorious injection of I-don't-care drugs, packing shoved up my nose, and six stitches in my completely numb chin, all compliments of Dr. Gettinger.

"I bet I look like Frankenstein, and I'm sure my nose looks like the Leaning Tower of Pisa."

Grandma Betty, who sits on a stool next to me, pats my hand. "Now stop! You still have the cutest Tinker Bell face ever, even with a broken nose."

"Liar."

Dr. Gettinger holds up a mirror. "I agree with your grandma."

I give him a dubious stare. "At this point, flattery is insulting and absurd. I know I'm hideous. Grandma has to lie to me because she's family. But you should be telling the truth."

He smiles. "You do look a little rough."

"Thank you for your honesty."

"You're welcome," he says.

I cross my arms and give him a level stare. "Now, when will I need rhinoplasty to repair my hideousness?"

"Oh, honestly, Cane." Grandma Betty clicks her tongue in disapproval. "Stop being so dramatic. It doesn't look that bad."

"You won't need surgery. Even though you did fracture your nose, it's barely crooked at all. Nothing to be concerned about," Dr. Gettinger says.

"Barely crooked? I'm not fond of that adjective. I would prefer 'not crooked.'"

"Once everything heals, you won't be able to tell," he assures me. "I want you to take it easy for a few days. No running or biking. No lifting weights. I don't want your blood pressure elevated, because we want everything to clot up and heal properly. I don't want the bleeding to start again. And it would be best to lay off the caffeine," he says pointedly. "We don't want that heart soaring for any reason. No palpitations."

"No running? No biking? No weights? No coffee? Are you trying to kill me?"

Grandma Betty chuckles. "I'll make sure she follows directions."

"That drug you gave me for the pain?" I ask him.

"Fentanyl."

"Yes—it's starting to wear off. You don't happen to have any gin and tonics around here, do you?"

"Hate to break it to you," he says, frowning, "but alcohol is out of the question for at least a day or so, because it thins the blood and—"

"And you don't want any more bleeding," I interrupt. "I get the point."

"I'll be back with your discharge orders. You'll have to follow up with your primary doctor later this week."

"I don't have a primary doctor, and I don't need one. I can handle yanking this packing out myself and hammering my nose back into place. Plus, I have a small pair of scissors that would make fast work of the stitches."

Dr. Gettinger laughs and looks at Grandma Betty. "She always like this?"

"Self-sufficient and with ants in her pants? I'm afraid so."

"I didn't break my eardrums. Only my nose. I can hear every word you're saying."

Dr. Gettinger takes off his gloves and tosses them in the garbage can. "No yanking or hammering or cutting. You'll have to get a primary doctor and get that nose looked at. I'll be back shortly."

He leaves and draws the curtain. I reach up and tentatively touch my nose.

"Cane, leave it alone! You don't want to make things worse."

Sighing, I drop my hand. "Like things could be any worse than they already are?"

"You should thank your lucky stars! It could have been much worse."

"Where's Justice?"

Grandma shifts the coat in her lap and glances at her watch. "He'll be here soon, I'm sure."

"He's taking his sweet old time," I complain. "What did you tell him?"

"I told him you were hurt, not badly, but banged up enough to need stitches."

I pick at the blanket that's on my lap and jiggle my feet until the bed starts shaking. The doctor didn't say anything about foot aerobics, but Grandma Betty's keeping a close eye on me.

"Stop all that shaking. You're making me a nervous wreck." Sighing, she crosses her legs and hugs her pink handbag to her chest. "Didn't I tell you earlier that we would end up in the hospital before the night was out?"

"You jinxed me."

"I did no such thing! You're so impatient. Punching boxes! Moving furniture by yourself! That couch was fine where it was. I mean, honestly, Cane," she chides softly. "You could have asked me for help. I would have gladly helped. I may be seventy, but I'm still as strong as an ox."

Cranky, in pain, embarrassed by my grotesque appearance, and even more embarrassed by how it happened, I'm not in the mood to be reprimanded. I give her the stink eye that she's always giving me. "I wasn't picking it up into the air and trying to be Superwoman! I was only sliding it across the floor. Someone I know got Pledge all over and turned the hardwood floors into a sheet of ice! The couch slid out from under me, so I fell forward and conked myself on the metal bed frame."

"Oh, honey! I didn't even think about that! I should have been more careful. I probably did get quite a bit on the floor. I'm going to give it a good scrub with apple cider vinegar and water. That'll do the trick. I'm so sorry."

She looks miserable and tired, and I feel awful for sending her on a guilt trip. "It wasn't your fault. The place looks great because of you. Although I could have done without the sex comment."

"You should have waited. Why buy the cow when you can get the milk for free?"

If I weren't drugged up, I would probably be mortified that I'm having a conversation about sex with my grandmother. "He was trying to buy the cow, remember? I ran away."

"I suppose."

"Cane!" Justice stands at the door, looking disheveled. His Gap T-shirt is on backward, and one of his shoelaces is untied. "I'm sorry it took me so long."

He rushes over and places a gentle kiss on my forehead.

What am I? His sister? His mother? What is with all this innocent familial affection? Where's the passion?

He inspects my stitches and my nose. "Are you okay?"

I wave my hand around my face and smile. "Never been better! Don't I look great!" Thankfully I didn't fracture my sarcasm.

Grandma Betty gives Justice the details of the accident.

He wipes his face with his hands. "It's my fault for leaving the bed frame there. I knew I should have moved it into the bedroom."

"It's nobody's fault but mine. I was a complete klutz."

Grandma Betty hooks her purse strap on her shoulder and stands. "I'll let you two have a minute."

Justice sits next to me on the bed and takes my hand. He starts stroking my wrist with his thumb. His eyes go all smoky and intent, and he leans toward me. Will he finally kiss me for real? I wonder if making out is forbidden, because I know for a fact my blood pressure is on the rise. He gets closer, but then he takes a detour and kisses the small cross-shaped birthmark on my forehead instead.

Spectacular.

"Are you in a lot of pain?" he asks.

"I am now."

"Why?"

"Justice, why haven't you kissed me?"

"I have."

"Forehead and cheeks don't count. I'm talking about a proper kiss. A melt-in-your-mouth-and-in-your-hands kind of kiss."

He closes his eyes and rests his forehead on my shoulder. "Because if I do that, if I kiss you on the lips, then I won't want to stop."

I give him a quizzical look. "And that would be a problem . . . because?"

"Cane." He gives me a please-understand look.

Only I don't understand it at all.

"Knock, knock," says Grandma Betty as she steps back into the room.

Justice pulls away from me and puts more than a little distance between us.

Grandma waves two slips of paper in the air. "I have a prescription. I thought I could have this filled at the twenty-four-hour Walgreens, and Justice could take you home and get you all set up there. How does that sound?"

I shrug. "Whatever. That's fine."

"Um, I don't know if I can," says Justice at the same time.

I give him an incredulous look. "Why?"

He nervously taps his finger against his knee. "Because I didn't come here alone."

"Is Jeremy with you or something?" He and his younger cousin are best friends.

"No, he's not." His voice is oddly strained. "And I didn't drive."

"I can drop Cane at home and then go get her prescription, if it's too much trouble," says Grandma.

"No, I'll figure something out." He stands rather suddenly. "I'll talk to my ride."

"Your ride? What's with the mystery? Who drove you here?"

He has the look of a trapped animal: dilated pupils, darting eyes, and fidgety hands. "Someone from work," he responds evasively.

I take in his disheveled appearance once again. My fears from earlier are confirmed. He was with *her*. I attempt a snort, forgetting that I've broken

32

my nose. I'm rewarded with an instant headache and nice throbbing pain that shoots all the way to the center of my brain.

"I can't believe you! It's Susan, isn't it?" I yell in a crazy, jealous voice that I didn't even know lived inside me.

Grandma Betty puts a hand on my leg and gives me a calm-down look.

Justice shrugs with one shoulder. "Yes, Susan drove me."

Dumbfounded, I stare at him with open hostility. "I can't believe you!"

"It's not at all what you're thinking. Let me go talk to her. I'm sure she would be more than happy to take us back to your place."

"I don't want her driving me anywhere."

"I can explain."

"I don't think you have to. I think it's rather obvious why you've been kissing me like I'm your sister, because you've been too busy making out with her. Wouldn't want to cheat on your new girlfriend with your ex-fiancée who you're stringing along just for kicks."

"You're being ridiculous."

"I'm being ridiculous?" I narrow my eyes. "That's rich."

"She's a friend. I wasn't making out with her. And"—he lowers his voice—"please keep it down. This is something we should discuss in private."

It's belittling when he tries to get me to mind my manners and behave like someone I'm not. When I want to discuss something, I discuss it. Immediately. "What? You don't want to air your dirty laundry in the emergency room?"

"Stop it right now, you two!" Grandma insists in her no-nonsense voice, giving us both a harsh stare. "Justice, why don't we go chat and come up with a plan," she suggests.

"Sure." He nods and follows her out of the room.

Shortly after they leave, my stomach suffers a series of mini seizures. I swing my legs over the edge of the bed and reach for the pink emesis basin, but it slips out of my hands, somersaults in the air, and lands wrong side up. I try to reach for it again, but it's too late. I start puking. Never mind my aching stomach; the pain in my face is excruciating. I'm pretty sure that my nose has fallen off my face. From the amount of blood, it sure looks like it has.

My retching alerts Terri, the nurse, who rushes in to help. By this time, I've finally stopped—but, I warn her, I may start again any minute.

She helps me back into bed and gets me as cleaned up as she can.

"I'll get the doctor right away. Sometimes painkillers can make your stomach upset. We'll give you some antinausea drugs and see if we can stop that nose from bleeding again."

"My nose hurts."

"I bet it does. How about some more pain meds?"

"Please, can you just knock me out? For an entire day?" I mumble.

"I don't think the doctor would be very happy if I did that."

"But I would be happy, and isn't that all that matters?"

When Dr. Gettinger comes in, I ask him to page anesthesia, but he refuses.

"Why not?"

"I'm afraid it goes against policy. We aim to keep patients conscious," he explains.

I hold my clammy fingers up against my cheekbones, which feel almost as bad as my nose. "That doesn't seem fair to the patients. It's rather cruel, actually."

He laughs, but I don't see the humor at all. They fill my IV with a lovely assortment of drugs, and I tell them I feel much better.

"You hadn't said anything about feeling sick." Dr. Gettinger scribbles a few notes on my chart and looks at me.

"I wasn't, and then my ex-fiancé arrived. Things got worse after that."

He nods knowingly. "Well, that will do it."

Terri hands me the emesis basin again, just in case. They tell me I have to wait a while longer before they'll release me so that they can observe my condition.

What am I? A lab rat?

A few minutes pass, and I get the oddest feeling. I want to crawl out of my skin. I want to tear my flesh off bit by bit. I want to pull this IV out of my arm and run around the earth a hundred times. Those ants in my pants have multiplied exponentially. I have a billion ants in my pants. A trillion, and they're burning and biting and raring to go.

Where is Grandma Betty? Why isn't she back? Why can't I leave? Where is Justice?

I start yelling for Terri, who hurries into the room.

"I have to get out of here now! Something's wrong! Please, get me out of here!" I start clawing at my IV.

She puts her hand on mine. "Don't pull it out, honey. It will be okay. You're having a reaction to the medication we gave you. Hold on one second, we'll get you better."

She rushes out of the room, and seconds later she's back with Dr. Gettinger. He explains that Compazine, the drug they administered, can sometimes have this side effect. Terri pumps me full of Benadryl, and when that doesn't seem to take the edge off, he gives me something called Clonazepam.

"It won't knock you out, but it will relax you."

"I doubt it. There aren't too many things that relax me."

When Grandma Betty returns and finds out what's happened in her absence, she makes a fuss and apologizes for not being there.

Smiley and happy, I pat her hand. "It's no big deal."

And it isn't! I feel blissfully optimistic. My life is easy, breezy, beautiful, and even though I have a broken nose and stitched-up chin, I'm feeling like a cover girl.

I don't care that I can't exercise for a few days.

I don't care that Justice is cheating on me and that we're never going to get married and that I'll never have my happily-ever-after with him in our dream house.

I don't care about any of this right now, because Clonazepam is my new best friend.

The next thing I remember, I'm waking up in Justice's arms. He places me on a bed.

"Where am I?" I ask groggily.

"In your bedroom."

I'm picturing the spacious master suite with the tray ceiling and beautiful chandelier that Justice let me pick out of a catalog a few weeks ago. "At our house?"

"No, in your apartment."

"My mattress is in the hallway."

"I came back here and set everything up while you and Grandma Betty were at the hospital. I also filled your prescription. It's sitting on the counter in the kitchen." He gently pulls off my shoes and socks.

My brain slowly catches up with the situation. "Did Susan take you?"

"She dropped me back at my house. I took the truck."

I prop myself up on my elbows. "I know that you still love me."

"You're absolutely right." He smiles, and those two dimples that I love so much pop into place on his gorgeous face. "I do love you. I'm going to get you a glass of water, an ice pack, and your medication. I'll be right back." He stands and leaves the room.

Regardless of all the issues we're having, and trust me, there's a heap of them, I know that this is indeed true. He takes care of me with such tenderness and always aims to make my life easier.

Every time he drives my car, he fills it with gas, checks the oil, and makes sure that I have windshield wiper fluid.

Because I'm perpetually freezing, he keeps a blanket stashed in his truck for "Cane's emergency freezing purposes," as he calls them.

Three weeks ago, on my first day at Schaeffer Dairy, there was a gift on my desk when I arrived at work. The card read, "It's like a meat locker in this place, and I can't have you freezing to death. Stay warm." I ripped open the box; he'd bought me a fuzzy white blanket covered with cute green frogs, my second favorite animal next to golden retrievers.

He recognizes that I'm a terrible sugar hound and would most likely commit homicide for chocolate, so when we split a dessert, he lets me eat as much as I want and without fail gives me the last piece.

A few years ago on a breezy summer night, we stopped at one of the Schaeffer Dairy stores to get a triple chocolate cone. We decided to eat outside at one of the picnic tables, and I was holding my cone with one hand and keeping my long hair captive with the other. Justice set his chocolate malt on the table and walked behind me.

"I've got this," he said. He took my hair out of my hand, gently raked it into a ponytail, and fastened it with a band.

"Hey!" I reached back and felt the elastic tie. "Where did you find it?" I couldn't keep track of hair ties to save my life. Every few weeks I would have to make a trip to the store to replenish my supply and listen to Grandma lecture me on why it was necessary to keep them in one place.

"I didn't find it." Leaning down, he placed a circle of kisses on the back of my neck, sending a delicious shiver down the length of my spine. "I bought it for you. I know how you hate having your hair in your face. One less thing to worry about."

I turned around slowly to face him. My eyes filled with tears.

He pushed his palm against my forehead and smiled. "You have brain freeze, don't you? Slow down—I can promise you the dairy won't run out of chocolate. Samson would never let that happen."

"You bought a rubber band for my hair?"

He shrugged like it wasn't that big of a deal. "I stopped at the store the other day and got a package of those rainbow-colored ones that you love. I figured I would keep some on hand, since you never have any."

I didn't know what to make of this man who was so faultlessly sweet. I let my triple chocolate cone fall to the concrete, threw my arms around Justice, and kissed him senseless.

He's been nothing but kind and thoughtful for as long as I've known him. Even now, when things are completely crappy between us, he's making me priority number one. I hear him in the kitchen, dropping ice cubes into a glass, turning on the faucet, chatting with Grandma. It's like everything is okay, only it isn't.

I'm experiencing such a strong feeling of disorientation. I'm sure it has something to do with being in my new apartment and the cocktail of drugs that I've had tonight, but it's deeper than that. Rolling onto my side, I open my nightstand drawer and pull out the box that holds the antique silver compass that Frank gave me last June as a graduation gift; he told me that it would help me find my way. I've used it many times over these last months, and I've developed a dependency on it that I can't explain.

I lift the lid off the box. I don't know how it happened, because I've been so careful with it, but the face is cracked down the middle. It's useless. It can't tell me where I am or where I need to go. I'm as lost as I've ever been.

Feeling like I might burst into tears, surely not a good idea given the state of my nose, I drop it back into the box just as Justice returns to my room.

"Take a sip." He holds the water to my lips.

When I'm finished, he places it on top of my nightstand.

"You know that I love you, right?" I ask him.

Does he know how much he means to me? I've taken care of him over the years. I've done his laundry, made sure his preferred wardrobe of plain Gap T-shirts, sweatshirts, and jeans is replenished each year on his birthday, baked him chocolate chip cookies without nuts (he likes his food as plain as he can get it), surprised him with fishing gear, surprised him in fishing gear (I wore his fly-fishing boots, vest, hat, and nothing else), given him hundreds of back rubs, written him countless love notes and poems while away at college, and sang him multiple karaoke songs, most notably a horrible rendition of "I Will Always Love You," executed so poorly that people cheered out of pity.

"Sugar Cane, I know that you love me," he murmurs.

"Then why were you with her tonight?" I ask in a tone as wounded as my face.

He looks up at the ceiling, and then his eyes fall back to me. "We met at work this afternoon and went over the financial plans. We work together. I needed her input. When we finished, she offered to drive over to the house and help paint. I went home, changed into my painting clothes, and she showed up an hour later. We painted. Then I got the call from Grandma Betty. So I rushed to get dressed, and she gave me a ride because the truck was almost out of gas."

"That's it?"

"That's it."

"But you're interested in her?"

"No."

There's something frail about his denial, and I don't believe him. I let my head sink into my pillow. "I don't want to do this anymore, Justice. I don't. I'm not equipped to handle limbo. I just want to move on with things." I swallow nervously. "One way or another."

He looks at me for a long time, and I think about hounding him some more, but I don't have the energy.

He turns off the lamp on my nightstand. "Get some rest."

Like the gentleman he is, he sits on the bed, hand on my arm, and waits for me to fall asleep.

CHAPTER FOUR

"Holy. Shitty. Balls. I didn't think you would look this bad. It looks like someone beat you with a crowbar. And I should know, because two years ago my cousin Vincent got beat with one. Lost all his front teeth, though." Caprice peers into my mouth. "You didn't lose any teeth, did you?"

I give her a jack-o'-lantern grin. "Still there. You should have seen me earlier this week. I look much better now that the packing is out of my nose."

"And you look righteous sexy with those black eyes. It's like smoky eye makeup gone wrong. Makes those hazel eyes of yours pop." She gives me a big hug, and because she's a good eight inches taller, lifts me clear off the ground. "Man, I've missed you."

She sets me back down. "Sorry I didn't make it here yesterday. I was hoping to see Grandma Betty before she left. Did she drive you crazy?"

"Certifiably insane, but I love her to death."

41

"Yeah, well, that's family for you." She gives herself a tour of the apartment. "Fancy, fancy. Hardwood floors. Crown molding. Copper ceiling. Pretty nice place, but you should still move back to Colorado."

"You're never going to stop nagging me to move back there, are you?"

"Not a chance." Making herself at home, she opens the fridge and peruses the liquor that I've stocked in the door. "I'm making us drinks. What's your poison?"

"Gin and tonic."

"Nikeo got you hooked on those, didn't he?" she asks rhetorically.

I sit at the breakfast bar while she mixes up the drinks.

Caprice dumps ice into a glass, pours in the alcohol and tonic water, and gives it a good swirl. "He's still brooding about you. He asks about you all the time."

"He does?"

"That surprises you?" She hands me the drink.

"I thought he would be over me as soon as I boarded the plane and ran back to Justice."

"He's not." She squeezes a wedge of lime into her drink and raises her eyes to mine. "Are you over him?"

"I thought I was. I am, I mean." I shrug. "But lately I've been thinking about him."

"Things are in the shitter with Justice, aren't they?"

"Yep, and I think he's getting ready to flush."

"I still think you and Nikeo would be good together. If you ended up together, we would be family." She grins and raises her brow. "Ideal situation, no?"

"Nikeo doesn't believe in marriage. He's all about unlawful carnal knowledge."

"What's wrong with that?"

I sigh and place my fingers on my temples. "A relationship can't be all sex. Though any sex at all would be good at this point."

Caprice, who's chewing on a piece of ice, spits it back into her glass. Her green eyes, a few shades darker than the lime that's floating in my drink, narrow into slits. "You haven't had makeup sex with Justice?"

"Seeing as how we haven't really made up, no."

Since I haven't been exactly forthcoming with information, I spend the next half hour catching a nice buzz from the gin and tonic and illuminating Caprice on my relationship with Justice, or lack thereof, and everything that's happened over the last few weeks, including the small-scale forest fire and Justice's possible love interest.

When I'm finished, she smacks the countertop with her palm. "Why didn't you tell me it was this bad?"

"I don't know. . . . Maybe because I don't want to face the fact that it is this bad. I'm trying to give him space, but he seems to want more."

"I'll bet he does. Give a man an inch, and next thing you know, he wants a few miles." She tosses her long dark hair over her shoulder and crosses her arms. "What's this Susan like?"

I roll my eyes. "I've dubbed her Susie Homemaker. She bakes constantly. She brings stuff into the office every day. Cookies. Pies. Breads. She's levelheaded, polite, and annoyingly and suspiciously cheerful, like a Disney princess. Oh, and she's also pretty and curvy and doesn't have one freckle on her." I'm most conscious about the physical differences between us. My ability to look like a woman is compromised by the fact that I'm barely five foot three, one hundred and five pounds, sprayed with a zillion freckles, and have a hell of a time trying to fill out a 32A.

Caprice makes a sound like a whale blowing water out his spout. "She sounds annoying."

"Justice doesn't seem annoyed. He said he's not interested, but . . . I'm not sure I buy that."

"Not an ideal situation, seeing as how you three work together," she remarks.

"Not as together as I would like. He's with Susie Homemaker in the financial growth and management department, and I'm stuck in marketing with Trina, my cochair, who's addicted to tanning, idolizes Madonna, and hasn't gotten the memo that blue eye shadow, shoulder pads, neon colors, and high hair have gone out of style. She's sweet, but all that tanning-bed time has turned her brain into a raisin.

"She's chronically late, unable to relay messages, and I don't think she understands a thing I say. We split up tasks the other day, and I told her to research Ben and Jerry's, assuming she would know I was talking about ice cream. She got it a little wrong and researched the old cartoon *Tom and Jerry* instead. Now she's obsessed with it, and tells me about all the episodes she watches every night."

"She sounds worse than Lizzie."

Caprice's cousin, Lizzie, who works for Maid Hot, is a renowned slacker, and also the one responsible for giving me that cryptic message last summer—the one that said Mik and J were getting married. "I think the only reason Samson and Justice haven't canned her is because she's been with the company for so many years."

Caprice gets a funny look on her face. "Holy shitty balls!"

"What?"

"Your present! I left it in the car."

"That's okay."

"No, it's not. I'll be right back." She bolts out of her chair and out the door.

She returns, holding a sinister-looking black cat. She wasn't lying the other night when she said my gift resembles Nikeo; it's his animal doppelganger. The cat has luminous green eyes, jet-black fur, and a smug expression.

"This is Lenny Kravitz." Caprice kicks the door shut with her foot. "Happy housewarming."

"This is my present?"

Lenny meows once and looks at her, and Caprice shifts him in her arms. "He has a slight drug problem."

"How is that possible?"

"Smoked quite a bit of pot. But he's been clean for a week now. Withdrawal was hell. He howled for most of the road trip. It sounded like he was being tortured. I thought about finding a rehab center and leaving him there, but wasn't sure about their policy on animal addicts."

She hands me Lenny and gives me his history. The cat belonged to Zeke, one of Lizzie's pothead friends, who enjoyed blowing smoke in the cat's face every night. Lenny was perpetually dazed and confused and rarely walked in a straight line. Lizzie took pity on him and stole him from Zeke, but since she happens to be slightly allergic, they couldn't keep Lenny at the house in Colorado.

"And you thought I would be the perfect candidate? I can't keep him," I protest.

"He's low-maintenance, and you are keeping him, because I'm not taking him back with me."

I study Lenny, and he stares at me defiantly, yawns, and then leaps out of my arms. Lenny inspects his new digs, and Caprice and I carry in her bag and my long-lost suitcase. While I unpack my skirts, trousers, and dress shirts, Caprice updates me on my former cleaning clients, including the nudists, Arlene and Skeeter, who were arrested last week when they came to town to grocery shop and forgot to pack clothes in the car.

"They decided to give society the middle finger and make a statement by buying their bananas and milk in their birthday suits. They couldn't reach any of their friends, so they called me. I was happy to bail them out. I get a kick out of them."

"I bet they refused to wear the orange jumpsuits."

Caprice laughs. "Probably, but they didn't refuse wool blankets—that's what they were wrapped in when I arrived on the scene."

We're too busy catching up and swapping work stories for a traditional dinner, so we opt for snacks and cocktails. By ten that night, we're starving and decide to break out the Cow Pie ice cream. We shovel the Cow Pie into our pieholes and jam out to the Lenny Kravitz CD that Caprice pops into the stereo. When the song "It Ain't Over 'til It's Over" starts playing, I blast the volume. Caprice and I groove around the kitchen, using our spoons as microphones and sing about tears that we've cried, the pain inside, and how many years we've tried.

Lenny the cat must like either ice cream or his namesake's singing, because he wakes up from his nap, stretches, and staggers over like a drunken sailor.

I dish up a tiny bowl for him, but he seems more interested in the gin and tonic I'm drinking. He keeps dunking his paw in the glass and then licking it. He's enjoying himself way too much.

"You didn't mention anything about his drinking problem."

"Guess the cat's out of the bag now, isn't it?" Caprice observes Lenny and chuckles. "Drinking and pot usually go hand in hand. You would know that if you weren't so straitlaced."

"Do I need to sign him up for AA?" I ask as he bounds around the living and dining area, running sideways and hitting walls. He's either inebriated or the most graceless cat ever.

Caprice sticks her spoon into the ice cream. "Someone's knocking at your door."

"I don't hear anything." I turn down the stereo.

Licking her spoon, she listens more closely. "Maybe it's the bass from the music."

I walk over to the door and open it. Jocelyn, who hasn't spoken to me since she left Colorado in July after catching me and Nikeo in a lip-lock, is standing there, tears rolling down her sweet face.

She startles when she sees my two black eyes, bruised nose, and stitched-up chin. I smile. "I've been wondering when I would get to see you again."

"Dad told me what happened. Does it hurt?"

"It's not that bad anymore."

Caprice, who's still dancing to Lenny Kravitz, boogies over and peeks around the door. "Hey, kiddo, good to see you! You look great!"

"You left Colorado in such a hurry that I didn't even have a chance to say good-bye."

Ducking her head, Jocelyn smiles shyly at Caprice and tucks her brown hair, curled into beautiful spirals, behind her ears. "Yeah, sorry about that."

"No thing." Caprice grins and dances away from the door.

Jocelyn fixes her bloodshot blue eyes on me. "Can we talk?"

I want her to know that there are no hard feelings at all, so I wrap my arms around her and squeeze tightly. "I've been waiting to talk for a couple months now."

"Do you mean that? Because I thought you would hate me and never forgive me for telling Justice and everyone else what happened between you and Nikeo. I mean, you and Justice are broken up because of what I did."

"It's not because of what you did. It's because of what I did, and how I handled things. And we're not broken up." Not yet anyway, but the writing on the wall isn't looking so hot.

Caprice nods. "As Lenny says, it ain't over till it's over. Now, come on

47

in!"

I steer Jocelyn over to the couch, and she sits down heavily.

"Want some ice cream?" Caprice asks.

Jocelyn dries her tears with the sleeve of her hooded sweatshirt. "Just water. I ran all the way from home."

"At ten at night?" I give her a reproachful look.

"I know, but I was careful. See?" She holds up her shoes. "Reflectors on the back."

"Nice new kicks."

"I used the gift card you gave me. Thanks so much."

Caprice hands Jocelyn a tall glass of water. Lenny comes over to inspect the new houseguest.

Jocelyn, who's a sucker for furry things, picks him up and cuddles him. "You got a cat?"

"A housewarming gift from Caprice. Meet Lenny Kravitz. Haven't decided if I'm keeping him yet."

"I already told him you're keeping him," Caprice declares bossily.

"I don't even know if cats are allowed, and I don't like staring at the litter box, let alone smelling it."

"No one will know you have him. It's not like you have to take him for walks. You could move the litter box. It doesn't have to be smack-dab in the middle of the living room."

Jocelyn studies him. "He's cute, but you know what? He kind of looks like Nikeo."

Caprice and I laugh.

"That was the first thing I thought when I saw him," I say.

After Jocelyn finishes her water, we give her a tour of the apartment. We end up in the kitchen, and she sits on a barstool. "Mom and Dad don't know I'm here."

I glance at the clock that Grandma Betty conveniently hung on the wall next to the phone—so I could look and go, she said. Ten thirty on a school night? They aren't going to be happy about this. I'm sure Jelly Roll, the nickname I gave Jenny Ryanne long ago due to her large figure and penchant for glittery clothing, will find some way to blame me for this. She loves pointing all her fingers at me. I hand Jocelyn my cell phone. "Call them."

She rolls her eyes but makes the call. She wanders into the other room while she talks to Samson.

"Wonder what's up?" Caprice whispers.

"My bet? Family drama. They're still dealing with the fallout from Jenny Ryanne's affair."

Caprice dumps the last of her gin and tonic down the drain. "There's never a shortage of that."

Jocelyn returns to the kitchen. "My mom wants to talk to you."

She hands me the phone, and I take it reluctantly. I haven't spoken to Jenny since she told me off in the church parking lot after I crashed her son's wedding. I contract my abdominals as if bracing myself for a blow. "Hello."

"Hi, Cane."

She says this normally. Even pleasantly. Her tone catches me off guard. "Um, hi."

"Jocelyn would like to stay with you tonight. Is that okay?"

"Of course."

"Samson will be by early in the morning to pick her up. Probably around six. Keep her safe. Don't let her run out on you. She's been doing a lot of that lately."

I look over at Jocelyn, wondering what she's been running from. "I can do that."

A harsh, impatient sigh. "I sure hope so."

I hang up, ready to play the role of responsible older sister. "Party's over," I tell Jocelyn. "You have school tomorrow. You need to get to bed."

She ducks her head and scratches at the countertop with her fingernail. "Not like I want to go, but if I skip again, I'm going to get suspended."

Jocelyn, like me, has been a rule follower her whole life. "You've been skipping?"

She slides off the barstool. "I'm going to take a shower."

Caprice rinses out the ice cream bowls and opens the dishwasher. "I wouldn't have pegged her for a kid who ditches."

"She isn't."

Caprice wipes her hands on the dishtowel and hangs it up to dry. "I'm going to get ready for bed."

Twenty minutes later, while Jocelyn's in my room, changing into a pair of my pajamas, I go into the guest bedroom to say goodnight to Caprice, but she's fast asleep. Lenny's next to her on his back, spread-eagled and snoring. Loudly.

A cat who likes to party, won't clean up after he does his business, expects to be fed, won't speak to me, and saws logs. I might as well be living with a man.

I go into my bedroom. Jocelyn is admiring my mother's wedding ring, the one that Justice gave me the night he proposed.

She raises her eyes to mine. "It was sitting on your nightstand," she says contritely.

"You can look. It's gorgeous, isn't it?"

"Do you think you and Justice will still get married?"

I crawl into the bed and lie down, facing her. "I want to. It's all I've ever wanted. But I messed up, and while I'm ready to move forward, Justice isn't."

She hands me the ring. I put it on my finger; the weight of it is foreign now. It stirs up all sorts of gross sadness in my gut. Is it possible for Justice to forgive and forget? Is it too much to ask of him?

Jocelyn tucks her hands under her head. "My mom cheated with Mr. Dexter, the algebra teacher at school. His wife had breast cancer and died last year. My mom took them meals and paid for a cleaning service when his wife was sick. After she died, Mr. Dexter started coming to our church. My mom talked on the phone with him all the time. I thought they were just friends. So did my dad.

"A few days after your engagement party, the school year ended. I realized that I'd forgotten a pair of my running shoes in my gym locker. I drove there in the middle of the afternoon the day after school got out. Mr. Dexter's room is close to the gym. I saw his light on, so I stopped to say hello, and my mom was with him. They were kissing. They didn't know I was there. Not then, anyway. I didn't know what to do. I ran out of the building. I thought I'd been seeing things, but then I spotted her van in the staff parking lot."

"Jocelyn, I'm so sorry." Justice shared the story with me, but he'd left out some of the finer details. I'm thankful that kissing was the only thing she saw.

"Everyone knows," she laments. "Everyone in town. Everyone at Schaeffer Dairy. Everyone at school."

Jenny's affair has been the front-page story around town, and it hasn't been easy for any of the Schaeffers. "I know it's hard."

"That's not the worst thing," she murmurs. "I did something awful. I think I might . . . I'm in big trouble."

She confides in me then, telling me a tale so despairingly horrible that it's a struggle to remain calm. When she finishes, she starts weeping so violently that the mattress wobbles beneath us.

How could she have done this? More importantly, why did she do it? For popularity? For love? For a power trip? To prove a point? For the pure pleasure of experimentation? Because she was so wounded by what her mother had done that she just didn't care how she behaved?

I want to strangle her for being so incredibly naive and stupid, and I want to hide her away and protect her from the world.

"When was this?" I inquire softly once she settles.

"Just this last weekend. On Saturday. They said they would keep their mouths shut, but I'm not so sure. People are starting to look at me funny, and Deanna—you know, the varsity cheerleading captain who hates me? Remember?"

I know who she is. How could I forget? Jocelyn has told me many stories about the pretty and polished girl who moved to town last year. Only a matter of days after arriving, she used her wiles and beauty to mercilessly and efficiently claw her way to the top of the high school food chain. She takes sick pleasure out of ridiculing and torturing others, even her closest friends. Last year, when she was crowned cheerleader captain, she made her squad strip down to their underwear and with a Sharpie marker circled their cellulite and fatty areas. When she wasn't satisfied with their weight-loss progress, she encouraged vomiting after meals. Jocelyn has heard some of the girls retching in the stalls after lunch.

If that conniving wench does anything to Jocelyn, I won't hesitate to put a stop to it. "Did she do something to you?"

"Not yet, but when she saw me in the hallway yesterday, she told me to watch out, because everyone was going to find out what I'd done. She has to know what happened—I bet she does. She was at the party. I'm sure she found out. I can't handle it. I skipped out after lunch yesterday because everything is such a mess."

"Jocelyn, you have to go to your parents."

Horrified, she tucks her chin into her neck and pulls the sheet up so that it covers her mouth. "No! I can't. And you can't tell them either. Please, Cane. Please. Don't say a word."

She's put me between a rock and a hard place, or more accurately, between a boulder and a concrete wall. If I move a millimeter, she's going to get hurt, and if I don't move, the outcome is the same. No one wins in a situation like this. "I won't say a word. But this isn't up for negotiation— you must tell them what happened."

"Can I stay with you for a few days, until I figure out what to do and how to tell them?"

She'd better figure out her game plan quickly, because most likely she won't have time to execute any plays. The Savage High School rumor mill is savage, and from the sounds of it, Deanna is manning the wheel, spinning it fast and taking perverse delight in doing so. "You can stay as long as you need to."

After Jocelyn falls asleep, I stare at the ceiling. She's in deep shit, and it doesn't matter how many shovels I use, I'm not going to be able to get her out of it. It's only a matter of time before she bumps her mother from the front-page news.

Jocelyn has come a long way in terms of confidence over the past few years; with my mentorship and help, she's lost a hundred pounds, gained confidence, and even joined the cross-country and track teams at school. Still, the predicament she's in, and the scandal that will surely follow? Even I couldn't withstand something like that.

Knowing I have to work in the morning and deal with Trina and Susie Homemaker, I attempt sleep, but it's impossible. I'm scarily awake. I'm convinced electrical wires are running through my body; it feels like I've been plugged into a socket. I jiggle my foot, chew on my lip, and nervously braid and unbraid the same strand of hair over and over. Unable to keep my eyes closed for more than a second, I wander into the kitchen and turn off the lights. I'm turning off the stereo when someone starts pounding on my door.

I jump an inch off the floor and suffer a minor heart attack. Lenny Kravitz wanders out into the living room and looks up at me with disdain.

"Hey, it's not me making the noise," I tell him, eyeing the door curiously. Who would be coming to my apartment this late? It's certainly not Justice making a booty call—I can't get him anywhere near my booty lately.

Lenny saunters over to the plaid couch, now freckled with drops of dried blood, and hops up onto the cushion.

The knocking starts again. "Cane! I know you're in there! Please open up."

I walk over and open the door. "What are you doing here?"

Doubled over with her hands on her knees and looking neon green around the gills, Mikayla looks up at me. Her beautiful cover-girl face, a perfect blend of Kate Moss and Niki Taylor, is covered in beads of sweat.

"Why are you here? Have you been drinking? Is Jeremy with you?" I peer down the hallway.

Geeky Neighbor Guy, who I haven't formally met, apparently keeps odd hours; he's walking down the hall, balancing a takeout pizza box on one hand and holding an electronic game device in the other. He spots me and smiles. I never noticed before how big his mouth is; it reminds me of Joker from *Batman*.

"Hey, Cane."

"Hi." I wave as he walks past. Wait. How does he know my name?

Mikayla, now swaying slightly, maintains her crouched position and moans.

"Are you going to stand there all night or what?" I ask.

She plows past me into the living room, grabs one of the leftover moving boxes, and hurls into it. When she's finished, she blindly reaches forward and grasps the arm cover on the edge of the couch. Plucking it off, she smashes it into her face and uses it like a towel.

When she's finished removing all the mucus and stringy drool, she deposits the cover on the floor and sits down next to Lenny, who must be accustomed to episodes like this: he's completely unfazed.

I plant my hands on my hips and stare down my former best friend, who I haven't spoken to since I crashed her wedding. "Thanks for ruining my couch."

She glances at it. "It was already a train wreck."

I can't disagree with her on that one. I kick the vomit-covered arm cover over to the vomit-filled box. "Take that out to the Dumpster on your way out the door."

"I can't leave."

"Oh, yes, you can." I point to the door. "Exit the same way you came in."

"Do you have any mouthwash or anything?"

"Are you drunk?"

Mikayla gathers her heavy, shiny blond hair in her hand and fixes her amazing navy eyes on me, the same eyes that have graced the cover of clothing catalogs throughout the United States. "I need a place to stay. Temporarily. Until I get things straightened out."

"I thought you hated me, you know, for not telling you about your mom sleeping with Nate while we were in high school. Which I was only doing to protect you. And then at my engagement party I find out you kissed Justice and were also hopelessly in love with him. And when I was away this summer, you tried to make me believe that you were going after him."

"I'm sorry. I really am. It was a seriously messed-up time for me."

I give her a dubious look.

"I know that's no excuse, but it's the only one I have. I was in a bad spot when the whole thing with Justice went down. If it makes you feel any better, I never loved him, and I never would have gone after him-not really."

"I bet you're here because now you've decided that you don't love Jeremy either. You're so messed up it's not even funny."

"I am messed up," she admits. "I've messed up everything around me." She sticks her mile-long legs out in front of her and leans back into the couch. Lenny looks her up and down like she's a piece of meat and then rests his paw on her hand. Even the cat isn't immune to her beauty.

Disgusted, I point at the box. "Dumpster."

Mikayla goes into the fetal position and looks up at me. "Can you keep a secret?"

Jocelyn was surprised this morning when she came out into the living room and spotted her sister-in-law passed out on the couch—though perhaps not as surprised as I had been last night. In a whisper, she asked what Mikayla was doing at my place and why she wasn't with Jeremy. I tiptoed around the issue, telling her that Mikayla is having problems and needed some time to work through some things. From the look on Jocelyn's face, it was obvious she didn't believe me. However, wrapped up as she was in her own drama, she let it be.

Samson picked her up twenty minutes ago, and I'm out biking on the country roads, watching the sun come up and trying to figure out what I'm going to do about Jocelyn's situation and whether I should allow Mikayla to runway-strut her way back into my life.

The timing is ridiculous. I haven't spoken to either of them in months, and on the same night they show up on my doorstep, unload their giant secrets, and ask me to keep my mouth shut. If that isn't enough, they both want to stay with me. I'm not going to refuse them refuge, but I'm not overly enthusiastic about the idea of running a halfway house. I just moved in, and I'm busy trying to solve my own dilemmas.

When I return from my fifteen-mile ride, I'm calmer but none the wiser and a whole lot more troubled. All that pedaling gave me ample time to think about things, and there are no solutions to either of these problems, only decisions. Whatever Jocelyn and Mikayla decide to do and say, there are going to be ramifications.

I wheel my bike into the building and open the door to my apartment. Caprice and Mikayla are in the living room, circling each other like boxers. I should have anticipated this. They've never liked each other.

They both look at me and ask in unison, "What's she doing here?"

Instead of answering, I prop my bike against the wall, remove my helmet, and take a deep breath.

"I thought she lived in Colorado," says Mikayla.

Caprice sneers. "I thought you lived in Chicago with your new husband. Don't you have a modeling job to go to?"

Mikayla serves it right back. "I'm sure you have a toilet or two to scrub."

"I could kick your ass right now."

"Because fighting solves everything, doesn't it?" Mikayla asks condescendingly.

"Sometimes a fist in someone's mouth is the only way to make them shut up."

Mikayla smiles coolly. "Says the tough Italian girl whose family probably has ties to the Mafia."

Mikayla is pirouetting on thin ice. Anyone who speaks of Caprice's

Italian family in a negative light risks his life.

"That's enough!" I yell.

Before round one has a chance to get started, I pull Caprice into the bathroom with me, and Lenny follows. Lenny hops up on the toilet lid, skids to a stop, and manages to make it up into the pedestal sink. He bats at the faucet. Poor thing is probably parched after last night's gin and tonic. I turn on the water, and he slurps happily.

Caprice glares at me accusingly. "Holy. Shitty. Balls. What's she doing here?"

"She showed up on my doorstep last night, around midnight."

I want to unload, but my word is solid twenty-four carat. I give Caprice the down-and-dirty explanation of what had happened, omitting the part about Mikayla's secret.

"What are you, insane? You're going to let her crash here?" Caprice raises her hand to smack me on the forehead but then spots my two black eyes and still tender nose and reluctantly withdraws. "Why? I don't get it! After what she did to you this summer?"

"We have a lot of history."

"What the crap has that got do with anything! I don't like her." Caprice scowls. "I never have."

"Sometimes I don't either, but I love her. She's practically family." Friends since we were two weeks old, Mikayla and I have been through thick and thin.

Caprice looks at me like I've lost my mind. Maybe I have. "You should call Jeremy and have him drag her ass back to their Chicago apartment."

"It's not that easy."

"Sure it is. Give me his number. I'll call him up and tell him to come get his skanky wife."

"Leave her be. Okay?"

"That's the problem. I have no choice but to leave her be, because I have to leave today." Caprice grabs her toothbrush and toothpaste.

While she's furiously brushing her teeth, I peel off my layers of sweaty clothes and turn on the shower.

Caprice spits, rinses, and bangs her toothbrush on the lip of the sink. "If you want, I can skip my cousin's bachelorette party and stay here another night to keep Mikayla in check and make sure she doesn't try to steal Justice from you again."

"I'm not sure he's mine to steal, and besides, she's not the thief at the moment. Susie Homemaker is."

After Caprice leaves, insisting that I call her and not Rhonda Riddle should I need to talk (halfway through my second gin and tonic, I'd told her all about my late-night psychic hotline call), I finish getting ready for work. I'm stuffing my lunch bag into my backpack when Mikayla comes out of my room, looking bleary-eyed and defeated.

Zombie-like, she staggers into the kitchen and clumsily sits on a barstool. "Don't tell anyone I'm here, okay?"

"I already told you I won't."

"I'm never going to work again. Everything is over. It's all ruined."

"Don't be so fatalistic." I throw my purse over my shoulder and slide my sunglasses on like a headband. "It's not the end of the world."

"It's the end of my world," she announces so dramatically that it sounds like she's seconds away from committing suicide.

Lenny, who has managed to climb to the top of the refrigerator, leaps off as soon as Mikayla says these words. It seems intentional, as if he's throwing himself to his death. Given his awkward angle, he might be, but at the last second he rights himself and lands on his feet.

Startled, he looks up at me with an expression that seems to say, That was close.

"What is wrong with that cat?" Mikayla asks. "He can barely walk straight."

"He's a recovering addict."

"Aren't we all," she remarks miserably.

CHAPTER FIVE

"Y ou were so late getting home yesterday! When are you going to be home from work today?" Mikayla asks petulantly.

"Is it just me, or is it beginning to sound like we're married?"

"We did snuggle on the couch during the movie last night," she reminds me.

"Very true, but only because you were blubbering." At Jocelyn's request, the three of us had a popcorn-and-movie night last evening. Blankets piled atop us, containers full of junk food in front of us, we watched the Disney flick *Beauty and the Beast*. By the time the happily-ever-after came around, I was the only one in the room not crying. Even Lenny Kravitz had watery eyes. Once I'd fetched tissues, I sat in the middle of my weepy friends and put my arms around them. Lenny took up residence in my lap, using his paws as earmuffs to try and drown out the sound of wailing.

I've been playing mama bear quite a bit these last few days, coddling, snuggling, and catering, and frankly I could use a break. I plan on taking my sweet old time getting home from work tonight.

"I'm in a precarious emotional state. Since Jeremy isn't here, you are by default my spousal equivalent."

"I'm so honored." I rinse out the dishes from last night's pig-out and shuffle them into the dishwasher. Lenny stands by, waiting for a scrap. I throw him a Dorito crumb, and he pounces, mauling it with his tongue.

"It's boring here. What am I supposed to do with myself?" she whines.

"Pack up and get out."

"That's direct. And rude."

I snap the dishtowel that I'm holding once and then again to release the wrinkles and hang it on the oven handle. "Once again, I suggest calling your husband and spilling your guts to him."

She shoots me a fat-chance look and goes back to waxing her eyebrows in the lighted cosmetic mirror that's propped up on my dining room table.

Lenny sits by her side, admiring her. I may be the one who feeds him and scoops his poop and pee out of the litter box, but being male, he's naturally more enamored of Mikayla.

For someone who claims her modeling life is over, Mikayla hasn't slacked on her grooming. Before Jocelyn arrived last night for another sleepover, Mikayla waxed her legs and underarms, applied full makeup, donned a skimpy outfit, and practiced her modeling poses while standing on my couch.

I adjust my backpack strap on my shoulder. "Later."

"Call me at lunch," she demands.

"If you're lucky." I close the door before she can say another word.

"Good morning, Cane." Geeky Neighbor Guy, who's standing outside his apartment door holding a large coffee, waves at me and walks my way.

Although we haven't yet had an official conversation, he knows my name and seems to coincidentally be in the hallway every time I am. He doesn't look like stalker material, but you never know. He has brown hair that swirls in strange, unpredictable patterns, a perfectly straight nose that's fat at the end, and a compact body that's neither muscular nor flabby. Below his strangely dark eyebrows, his deep-set eyes are a muddled greenish blue that remind me of the colors that erupt when you push a finger against a calculator screen. He's adorable in a nerdy kind of way.

"I just moved here a week before you. It's a small town, isn't it? My sister works in Clinton and told me about Savage. She said the rent was probably cheaper here. She was right."

"Oh, that's nice."

"You got some roommates, huh? Two girls?"

"Not roommates. Just friends."

"The tall one cries a lot. It's rather annoying. I heard her off and on all day yesterday. It got worse after she got off the phone. She was talking to some guy named Jeremy. She screamed his name a couple of times and told him to give her some space."

Does he have a peephole somewhere? A hidden video camera? "You can hear all that?" I inquire, my tone confrontational.

"Not all of it. Only some. The sound travels through the vents, but I bet you can hear the cartoons I watch at night. I have a tendency to turn up the volume."

"Oh." I'm not sure what to make of this nerdy motormouth. "You watch cartoons?"

"Occasionally. When I have a hard day at work, I like to watch something goofy to take my mind off of things. I've been wondering, what happened to your face?"

"I was moving a couch. I fell."

"I'm a klutz too. I run into walls. Objects. People." He waves his hand. "It's embarrassing. I used to get teased all the time when I was a kid. I still do, actually."

"I'm not normally a klutz."

"That's a good thing, because you're a runner and a cyclist, right? Klutziness isn't compatible with either of those activities."

Irritated because he's making me late with all this chatter, and even more because he seems to have been observing my routines, I employ an aggressive tone. "How do you know that?"

"It's merely a theory I have."

"No. I mean, how do you know that I bike and run?"

He looks at me like I'm slow on the uptake. "I see you leave every morning when I'm coming home with coffee. You're either rolling out on your bike or running out the building in your Nike shoes."

"Oh."

"Plus, I met your Grandma Betty earlier this week. She was very nice." He studies me for a minute and smiles. "Do you want to go out with me sometime?"

"I'm . . . I have a boyfriend. And . . . um, I'm engaged."

"You have a boyfriend *and* a fiancé?"

Good question. "No, actually . . . I'm not sure what I have at the moment."

"Do you like math?"

Talk about a topic U-turn. "Math?"

"Yes, math." He unzips his coat and points at his T-shirt. "I'm a fan."

"Math Is Delicious" is written across the middle of his shirt. Amused, I give a truncated laugh. "I've never seen a shirt like that before."

"Cool, isn't it?" he asks proudly. "I ordered it out of this catalog. I could get you one if you want."

"I'm not a big math fan. I was an English major. I love to read."

Disappointed by my answer, he frowns and lowers his head a bit. "I like to read, but I like to solve equations more. Do you like coffee?"

"Only with tons of cream."

"Hmm, right. Is that because you work at Schaeffer Dairy?"

Did Grandma Betty hand him my résumé? "No. I just like cream."

He strokes his chin. "Okay then. I'll see you around, Cane Kallevik."

Not until I'm pulling into the parking lot at work do I realize that he knows my full name, and I don't even know his first.

"And then Tom smacks Spike on the butt with a piece of the pier, and Spike is furious and retaliates, chasing Tom down. Jerry helps Spike. And by the end of the episode," she says, trying to control her laughter, "Jerry has Tom dangling from the end of the fishing pole, and—"

"Spike's at the other end, trying to jump up and eat him," I interrupt.

I was happily minding my own business in the boardroom, preparing for the weekly Friday planning session and jotting down notes, when Trina, who arrived to work inexplicably early for once, burst into the conference room and started yapping in my ear about the *Tom and Jerry* episode that she watched last night. For a woman who owns a spiked bra, a $400 replica of the one that Madonna wore, and hums "Like a Virgin" at least twenty times a day, this fascination with Tom and Jerry doesn't make sense. I would think she would appreciate a grittier, dirtier cartoon, like MTV's *Beavis and Butt-Head*.

Disappointed that I've rained on her cartoon parade, she gives me a tetchy look and doodles a mouse on the top of her legal pad. "You've seen that one, huh?"

"Didn't you have a television growing up?"

"Yes, but we were only allowed to watch the news."

"That's a crime."

She adjusts her shoulder pads, which are so large they could be used in an NFL football game, and regards me curiously. "What's with the new wardrobe? You've worn something new almost day this week."

"Nothing new—I just unpacked a suitcase of clothes that I finally got back from Colorado." I reach down and adjust my vintage wool pencil skirt, which makes me look like I have more curves than I do. Justice loves this skirt. He's told me more than once that it makes me look like a hot librarian.

Last spring, right before graduation, Justice took me out on a date, and I wore this skirt. When we returned to my apartment that night, I pinned him up against the wall and behaved deliciously naughty.

I thought of this when I spotted it in my closet this morning. Wanting nothing more than to make Justice drool, I slipped it on along with a lacy blouse and some sleek red pumps. To polish off the look, I had Mikayla take a break from her grooming and pin my long tresses into a messy bun.

"I love it. You look amazing."

I smile. "Thanks, Trina."

"You're welcome." She fluffs her permed hair. "What's this meeting about, anyway? I forgot my Day Runner at home, and my brain's been kind of scattered lately."

Her brain's constantly scattered, and I'm the one who's always on her to pick up the pieces. "We're focusing on the new ice cream flavor and the marketing and advertising campaign."

She gives me a blank look.

"You know, the strawberry cream with the salted pecans and walnuts in it. We were supposed to come up with a name and some ideas for promoting it."

"Oh, yeah! Isn't it scrumptious? I taste-tested it yesterday afternoon, and I couldn't stop. Divine!"

One of the perks of working at Schaeffer Dairy is that Samson encourages product sampling and also gives employees vouchers for free product. "It's delicious," I agree. "But what names did you come up with? More importantly, what about ideas?"

Trina gnaws on the tip of her pen cap. "Shoot! I kind of forgot about that."

Incredulous, I stare at this woman, who's eight years my senior but behaves like she's eight years my junior. Half the time I feel like I'm babysitting. The only reason Samson hasn't fired her is because she's been with the company for twelve years and has earned a college degree at night school and scratched her way up the ladder. He appreciates and rewards hard work and loyalty. Trina may be loyal and may have earned a degree, but she hardly works. "Trina, we've been talking about it all week. We talked about it yesterday before we left the office. How could you forget?"

"In my defense, I've been seeing this new guy, Blaze. He's totally amazing. He sings in a grunge band for a living."

"Of course he does," I remark caustically.

"Why do you say it like that?"

"Because I think you would be much happier if you would start dating real live grown-ups, as in men with real jobs and names. Guys with nicknames like Blaze, Biggie, or Stinky aren't marriage material." In the short time that I've been here, I've heard more than I needed or wanted to know about the men she dates and their strange names.

She dated Biggie for a year. A Wendy's employee for several years, he earned the nickname for his ability to eat several Biggie-size meals at one sitting. Stinky was her rebound, a garbageman with an aversion to paying for anything, Trina dated Stinky for two months, during which time she dished out over $2,000 to him. He always seemed to need money for rent, groceries, clothing, and his biggest vice, Pabst Blue Ribbon, which he drank by the case.

"I'm not sure I should be taking lessons from you when it comes to men," she retorts.

"Justice and I are working things out."

"Oh, please. The only thing he's working out is Susan." She raises her brow as Justice and Susie Homemaker waltz into the room, together as usual. "See what I mean?"

The second I see Susan, in a tulip-shaped skirt that accentuates her tiny waist and a tight blouse that flaunts her perfect C breasts, I go from feeling like a naughty librarian to a prepubescent library aide. Whereas I'm an athletic ruler, Susan's an exemplary hourglass—and not the kind that guys want to tell time by, but the kind they would like to hold and drink from.

"Morning! I baked three different kinds of cookies. Chocolate chip, oatmeal raisin, and snickerdoodle," Susan announces in her singsong voice, pulling the plastic wrap off a brightly colored tray. Smiling with her gigantic horsey mouth, she sets the tray in the middle of the table.

The cookies are all the same size and artfully arranged, with a chrysanthemum bud in the middle for decoration.

"I adore your skirt!" exclaims Trina, who half stands to get a better look. "Where did you get it?"

Susan does a twirl, making her skirt and wavy brown hair fly in the air. "I made it."

Of course she did. She's some sick hybrid of Mrs. Fields and Martha Stewart.

Trina gasps in wonderment. "You're so talented."

Susan tenders one of her I-don't-deserve-your-adoration-but-will-graciously-accept-it smiles. "Thank you, Trina. Now don't be shy, everyone. Eat as much as you can. I don't want to take any of these home!"

Susie Homemaker looks right at me. "Hi, Cane," she says sweetly. "Your eyes look much better today. How are you feeling?"

Life would be much easier if she was the kind of person I could easily and rightfully despise, but she's all sugar, spice, and everything nice. She even gave me a beautiful homemade card this Monday, wishing me a speedy recovery. However, I'm not going to get all chummy and start swapping cookie recipes and dress patterns with her. I mind my manners and plaster a generic smile on my face. "On the mend. Thank you for asking."

Justice squeezes my shoulder and leans down so that his lips hover near my ear. "You look great today." His eyes take in my outfit, which is snug in all the right places.

I can tell by his smile that he's remembering what happened against the wall in my college apartment.

Just like that, I'm back to feeling like naughty librarian. "That was my intention."

He lowers his eyes for a second. "I thought we could go to the Clinton Apple Festival tonight."

My heart does jumping jacks inside my chest. Maybe he's finally ready to move forward and throw those walking papers away. I would pay anything to see Susie Homemaker's face should I stride into the office on Monday with my engagement ring back in place. "That would be great."

"We could meet outside that coffee shop in downtown Clinton at six."

"Can't we drive together?"

"It will have to be separate. I'm leaving work early. I have some things to arrange today."

Susie Homemaker shoves the tray in my direction, and Justice glances up at her. They share this look. It's the kind of look that Justice and I share, or used to share, all the time when we have a secret or an inside joke. I look up at Justice, seeking out his eyes, and he slowly withdraws his hand from my shoulder. My heart goes from jumping jacks to flatline.

The rest of the employees trickle in. Samson arrives last. He looks exhausted—and he should be, with the run for his money his daughter and wife have been giving him.

He claps his large hands, his informal way of starting the meeting. He may be owner and CEO of a million-dollar business, but at heart he's a dairy farmer and always will be. No business suits for him, just flannel shirts, jeans, and work boots, even in the office.

After scanning the sheet in front of him, he looks up and smiles. "Let's get started. Since I want to get rolling on that new ice cream flavor, I would love to hear what Cane and Trina have come up with. Trina, what have you got?"

Trina gets all flustered and bats her eyes. Even though I've been running circles around her since I got here, Trina has seniority; she should have realized that he would start with her first. She glances down at her paper and spots the mouse. "I think we should call it Strawberry Spike and have this tough but lovable bulldog with a spiked collar sitting in a strawberry field, which would emphasize both the sweet and the salty in the ice cream. Our primary target market would be school-age children, and we could run with the cartoon theme and create Spike the Dog stickers, strawberry stickers, and, um . . . you know, little goodies?"

Strawberry Spike? Cute, but it's obvious that she's been watching too much Tom and Jerry.

Samson doesn't look thrilled with the idea, and neither does Justice, who has never been a fan of Trina. Even before I started working here, he complained to me numerous times about her inadequacy and poor performance.

Trina's shoulders, despite their big pads, start to sag. "We could test-market it at the local schools? And see what happens?"

Samson removes his Cubs hat, which is the equivalent of a sigh for him, pats his thinning hair, and raises his eyes to me.

"Cane? What about you?"

"I know that you like keeping true to the farm theme, so that's what I want to do. Typically we do cartoonish renderings of farm scenes, but I thought we should move into a more realistic direction with this. The flavor is sweet and salty, which suggests an 'opposites attract' theme. I thought about calling it Farmer and the Belle. We portray the farmer and the belle as real people. The farmer would be rugged and handsome, and the belle would be delicate and beautiful. We would enclose their portrait in a strawberry-shaped frame. We could even go so far as to make up a short three-sentence love story to put on the front.

"Marketing trends and current research data show that most grocery store purchases in Clinton and the surrounding rural areas are made by women between the ages of twenty and fifty. This concept would appeal to them, and even more so because this type of thing has never been done before when it comes to marketing dairy products. Women would be intrigued and curious—especially with two good-looking people on a carton of ice cream.

"We can launch it now, but when berry season hits in spring, we could do a more aggressive campaign at local stores. Get some media coverage. Have the actual models on hand to meet people. To keep things fresh, we could update the packages every so often. I would like to establish an ongoing romance between the farmer and his belle. Possibly, if it goes well, we could develop other flavors based on what happens between them. Merchandising is also a possibility."

When I'm finished, the room buzzes with excitement. Justice, who sits next to me, puts his hand on my knee. "Way to go," he whispers.

Samson looks thrilled. "I'd like to get started on developing this right away. We need to find models, a photographer, book a shoot, talk to the graphic designer about layout. Cane, why don't you spearhead this?"

Trina violently scribbles out her mouse sketches and sulkily puckers her lips.

"Now . . . about deadlines." Samson glances at his calendar.

While he's doing this, Trina writes "Blaze would be the perfect model" across the top of my legal pad and then waggles her eyebrows.

"Not going to happen," I mouth quietly.

"More cookies?" Susan leaps up and distributes baked goods to the group.

Justice nudges me in the ribs. "Where did you get this idea?" He pops one of Susan's oatmeal raisin cookies in his mouth.

"You came up with it." A few summers ago, when we were first dating, Justice and I'd gone to a strawberry farm together on a Saturday, picked berries for hours, and returned home to hull and wash our bounty. We then made numerous pies and crisps. With his fingertips and lips stained pink and an apron around his neck, he was domestically sexy. I remember thinking at the time that if they had advertisements for strawberries, Justice would be perfect.

The memory served me well in coming up with this ad campaign.

Justice drags a napkin across his lips. "I did?"

"Berry picking the summer before I went to college."

He smiles as he remembers. "Sticky fun."

"This is very ambitious, but could we try to pull this together by next Friday?" Samson asks. "If you need more time, that's fine, but we're ready for production. I want this on the market before the weather turns cold."

One week! I have a ton of things on my plate, and Trina isn't going to help me eat any of them. But because I want to impress Samson and make his life easier, I'm determined to meet the deadline. "That should work. And since I already have someone in mind for the farmer, we'll be able to get started rather quickly once I find a photographer."

Samson leans his Paul Bunyan–like frame back in his chair. "Who did you have in mind?"

"Justice."

The fifteen staff members turn and stare at Justice.

Justice looks at me in confusion and abject horror. "Me?"

"Yes, you. You're handsome, wholesome, and if you let your scruff grow in"—I give him a sexy smile and affectionately touch his face—"just the right amount of rugged." This kind of praise belongs in the bedroom, not the boardroom, but I'm trying to make a point. And besides, it's true. The women in the room nod in consensus.

Every female who works at Schaeffer Dairy has a crush on Justice, even the married ones. Ever since word leaked that we're no longer officially engaged, the single ladies have been circling like vultures.

Justice frowns in a self-deprecating way. "I'm not right for this."

Susan, who's sitting directly across from him, flashes a winsome smile. "You would make the perfect farmer."

Speaking of vultures, Susan's the biggest one of all. I want to take the tray of cookies and fling it at her.

Samson crosses his arms and shrugs. "I think you should give it a shot. To have one of the owners of the company on the front of a product? I think it's a great idea."

Justice glances at me and suppresses a groan.

Considering the matter settled, Samson moves forward with the meeting. Susan and Justice give updates on all location profits and losses as well as management problems and possible solutions.

I succumb to a semi-comatose state during their presentation, my mind wandering until Samson says, "I have some exciting news."

I tune back in, and out of the corner of my eye I see Justice staring intently at Susan. When I look at him, he lowers his eyes. What's going on? My eyes stray once again to the flat, heavy cookie tray, the shape of a Frisbee. If I threw it just right, I might be able to make Susan's face look just like mine. Two black eyes and a broken nose.

"We're launching our first store outside of Illinois," Samson announces. "We're opening a location in Iowa City near the university."

Everyone claps. I'm not going to applaud, because I know what's coming. Chronically short on management and because he knows the business inside and out, Justice has been in charge of opening many locations over the past three years. Lately Susan has been his right-hand woman. This doesn't bode well.

"Justice and Susan will be leaving in early October to help oversee the process."

Fears confirmed. They'll be in Iowa, conveniently holed up in a hotel together with lots of free time, and it won't be a short stay. Opening up a location can take well over a month. My fingers tap on the table and dance closer to the cookie tray. Should I pick it up and whip it through the air, the target won't be Susan. It will be thrown at the most eligible bachelor.

When the meeting ends, I gather up my things and bolt for the door.

"You forgot your cookies!" Susan calls after me.

Ignoring her, I stomp down the hall to my desk. Justice arrives seconds later, hands tucked into his front pockets.

"Samson asked to see you in his office," he says.

I toss my legal pad aside and flip on my computer monitor. "How long have you known about Iowa?"

"I didn't purposely keep this from you. We can talk tonight," Justice offers quietly.

Is this supposed to pacify me? Lest I say something I'll regret—and that surely everyone in the building will hear—I capture my tongue beneath my teeth and march down the hall.

I knock on Samson's door, and he tells me to come in.

"Have a seat." He gestures toward the chair in front of his desk.

"I'm not in trouble, am I?"

"Quite the opposite. I never doubted that you would be an asset to this company. Not once. That being said, the ideas you've been coming up with and your ability to execute them have surpassed all my expectations. I'm very pleased."

"That's good to hear."

He toys with the Cubs hat in his hand. His eyes wander to the window and then back to me. "Cane, I'm worried about Jocelyn. I'm wondering if you could shed some light, since she's been spending so much time with you."

Sworn to secrecy, I can't breach her trust—not yet. I offer something that makes sense. "She's upset about Jenny's affair. It's making school miserable for her."

"I figured. She won't talk to her mother. And she barely talks to me. I don't understand." His eyes land on a framed photo of the nine-year-old Jocelyn astride the blue bike I gave her. "I thought it would have gotten better, but it's gotten much worse."

He doesn't know how accurate this statement is—and he doesn't know how much worse it's going to get.

"My neighbor stopped me in the hallway this morning and asked me out. I think he loves me, but he might love math more."

Justice and I've been strolling through the festival, people-watching and eating. I want quality time with him where the tension isn't wrapped around our necks like a noose, so I've been pretending that everything is just peachy keen, even though the peach is rotten, and if Susie Homemaker were around, I would be the first to squeeze the foul juice all over her head.

Justice laughs. "How do you know he loves math?"

"He told me, and his shirt reads 'Math Is Delicious.' "

"Sounds like an interesting guy. What's his name?"

"No clue, but he knows everything about my life. I'm pretty sure Grandma Betty gave him a handbook."

Justice points to the Ferris wheel. "Want to ride?"

"Sure."

He buys tickets, and I save a spot in line.

"Do you like him, this math guy?" he asks.

"Are you trying to get rid of me so that you can make the Iowa trip more interesting?"

"Cane."

"Please." I step forward. "You knew it was going to come at some point."

"You're upset about it."

I give him an exaggerated smile. "I'm thrilled. What great bonding time for you and Susan."

The carnie, who has a cigarette hanging out of his mouth and a pair of jeans dangling off his butt, exposing a disturbing amount of crack, interrupts our conversation, commanding us to step forward and sit in the carriage.

"Keep the bar over your lap and your hands and arms inside the ride," he instructs.

"What happens if we stick them out? Will they be cut off?"

He plucks the cigarette from his mouth and taps the ash on the ground. He looks at me with dead, colorless eyes. "Why don't you try it and tell me how it turns out." He pushes a button, and we're propelled forward.

We're ten feet in the air when Justice smiles at me. "Remember when Mikayla dared you to climb up one of these things?"

A sucker for wagers and any phrase that begins with "I bet you can't," I'm never satisfied until I can prove that I can.

The summer after senior year of high school, when Justice and I were first dating, we'd walked through the Savage County Fairgrounds at two in the morning with a group of our friends. Mikayla was with us. When we passed by the Ferris wheel, which was decidedly smaller in scale than the one that Justice and I are currently riding, Mikayla jokingly said, "Wouldn't that thing be fun to climb?"

"I could do it," I said eagerly. A natural climber with monkey tendencies, I'd spent my childhood and even adolescence scaling trees, ropes, anything that went upward.

Mischievous smile in place, she said, "Prove it, then."

I took off in a dead run, heading for the structure. But just before I put my hand on it, Justice tackled me from behind. I never had the chance to prove it.

I stare up at the cages above us and then drop my gaze to the people below. "I remember that you stopped me. It would have been a piece of cake."

"It would have been suicide."

"I would have been perfectly fine," I assert.

I'm not so sure, though. I'm lucky that Justice has frequently stepped in to save me from disaster, like the time he pulled me into a boat when I was about to drown after a harebrained attempt to swim across Lake Geneva in Wisconsin.

He gives me an incredulous look. "You would have plummeted to your death if I hadn't stopped you."

"Do you have so little faith in me?"

"I couldn't risk losing you." His eyes slide away from me.

This phrase puts a stranglehold on my heart. He couldn't risk losing me then, but what about now? I can't take it any longer. "About Iowa," I say. "How long have you known about the trip?"

He grips the lap bar. "Two weeks."

"Why you didn't tell me?"

"Because I knew how you would react. I didn't want you stewing about it for that long. I didn't want you to be upset."

"It didn't occur to you that being blindsided would be more upsetting?"

"Poor judgment on my part. Susan and I are just friends."

"You do realize that when you keep things like that from me, it makes it look like you are more than"—I raise my hands and make air quotes—"just friends."

"I realize that now."

I want to say more about the "friend" tag Justice uses for Susan, but all these conversations are hopelessly circular. They exhaust and anger me.

The cart creaks along, higher and higher, until we come to a standstill at the top of the Ferris wheel. We have an incredible view of quaint downtown Clinton, the river that divides the town, and the fall foliage.

"Jeremy came into the office today," Justice says. "I guess Mikayla pulled a vanishing act on him, moved out without a word. She refuses to tell him what's wrong or where she is. He's devastated. The poor guy can't figure it out. She's a complete flake. He should have known better than to marry her. I should have talked him out of it."

I drum my fingers on the bar. I haven't informed Justice that Jocelyn isn't the only runaway staying with me. "She showed up at my place Tuesday night. She's been staying with me. She's going through some stuff right now."

He laughs disbelievingly and searches my face. "You're not serious?"

I bunch up my mouth and half nod.

"I thought for sure you two would never speak again."

"She apologized for everything. Besides, when you love Mikayla, you just have to accept the fact that she behaves like a complete idiot sometimes."

"You have to tell Jeremy where she is."

"No way. I'm staying out of it. I promised not to get involved."

"Like it or not, you're already involved. He's miserable. You need to tell him."

"I promised her I wouldn't, and I won't. They can figure it out on their own."

When the ride ends, Justice suggests we walk along the river path. He seems nervous about something.

"What's wrong?" I ask, taking his hand.

He fixes his eyes on me. "Nothing."

"You're a horrible liar."

We're quite some distance from the festival when he leads me over to a bench under a large maple tree that looks frosted in gold. We sit. Leaves rain down on us.

Justice folds his hands and leans forward. "We've always been completely honest and open with each other, and that's what I love about our relationship."

"I love that too."

He rubs his hand across his forehead. "It's been hard lately."

"I hadn't noticed," I quip facetiously.

"I wanted to talk to you this past weekend, but the timing wasn't right. Not with you hurting yourself, and Grandma Betty being here. Then Caprice was visiting."

My heart thumps painfully against my ribs. "Say what you need to say."

"I'm having a hard time getting over the things that happened this summer. You with that guy. I can't get it out of my head. I was ready to spend my whole life with you. I thought you were on the same page, and then when I offered you everything, you walked away. Now I wonder if love is enough, if our history is getting in the way of—"

"We've been over this time and time again. I only left because I panicked. I've told you that. All of a sudden I was done with college and you got down on one knee and there was our house that you were building and then you were talking about kids that night. And you gave me my mother's ring. I felt like we were on the same path as my parents, and they ended up dying before their lives even got started. They died before they even met me! I was spooked, and that's why I left. It had nothing to do with you."

He squeezes his eyes shut. "I don't want to do this to you."

He's going to drop the guillotine on our relationship. "Then don't."

"But I have to, for my sake and yours. This isn't the end."

"Don't patronize me, and don't lie to me. You've been stringing me along for weeks now."

"I haven't. I thought I could move on and get over things, but I'm kind of stuck right now. My wheels are spinning, but I'm not getting anywhere. I honestly love you, more than you know. I do, but what if you bolt again? What if you run on our wedding day? What if we've been married for a few years and have kids and all of a sudden you decide that you can't handle it?"

"You think I would do that?"

"You're very young. Sometimes you take things on without thinking it through. I'm ready to settle down, but I'm not sure you are. I think this past summer proves that point."

"Disregard this summer. I'm done with it. I ran away, but I came back.

I'm ready to settle down. I wouldn't leave you. Not ever. I'm loyal."

His eyes lock on mine. "Are you?"

His question feels like a kick in the gut. "That's not fair."

"None of this is."

"Don't do this."

"You got to leave for the summer, Cane. You were gone. You got your freedom. Now I need mine."

"For how long?"

"I can't put a time limit on it, because I don't know how long it's going to take me to get everything straightened out in my head. You said the other night that you can't do limbo, and I can't either. It's getting too hard and too confusing for both of us. We're stuck in the middle, going nowhere."

"Then let's move forward."

"I can't. Not yet."

"So you want to move backward? I can't believe you're doing this." I try for a contemptuous smirk, but the tears rolling out of my two black-and-blue eyes are probably ruining the effect. "You had this all planned out, didn't you? That's why you suggested we drive separately. I'm surprised you didn't do it when we were stuck at the top of the ride."

He reaches out and tries to touch my face. I block his hand, swatting it away from me. "Don't try to be nice about all of this."

"I don't want to hurt you."

"Too late."

The air has turned damp and heavy. The wind stirs, scattering the leaves on the ground. Justice and I sit inches apart, but there are galaxies between us. It would take serious rocket fuel and a few light-years to get back to where we once were.

"I can walk you to your car."

"Don't put yourself out," I respond flippantly.

"Cane, I'm trying to do what's right."

"Then why does it feel wrong?" I didn't know it was possible to cry so impassively, without even the subtlest change in expression, but that's what I'm doing. "I'm not going to wait around for you to make a decision. I might not be here when you're ready."

"I know."

I scoff. "You're okay with that?"

He wraps his hands around the back of his neck. His elbows jut out awkwardly to the side. "I'm not okay. With any of this."

"Neither am I," I say venomously.

"I love you."

I glare at him. "You're going to say that to me now? Under these circumstances? Leave already. Leave me alone. Get out of here. I don't want to be around you."

"I was hoping that—"

"You were hoping that what? I would be okay with all of this? Because I'm not."

I stand and walk down the river path. He tells me to come back, which seems ridiculous. He's the one who needs to come to his senses and come back to me.

When I'm a few hundred feet away, I sneak a look over my shoulder. He's gone.

A steady rain starts. I look up. The sky is falling, and Justice isn't here to shelter me.

CHAPTER SIX

"**A**re you okay?" Mikayla inquires as she hands me her plate, regarding me as if I'm fragile and might break into a million pieces. "I'm worried about you."

I haven't had time yet to dwell on whether or not I'm okay. I've been whipping up homemade pancakes, frying eggs, and slicing up fruit for my boarders. I dunk Mikayla's syrupy plate into the dishwater for a good soak. A stray bubble hits Lenny Kravitz in the nose, and he gives a disgruntled growl and skitters away from the sink.

"I'm perfect. Never been better." I've been keeping a stiff upper lip—so stiff, in fact, that it's hard to move my mouth.

Jocelyn ties up the garbage bag. "I can talk to him for you. He's being a jerk."

"No, don't say anything to him. He's not being a jerk."

Mikayla frantically waves her hands and feet in the air, attempting to speed up the drying of her newly applied blue polish. "Why are you defending him?"

"I'm not." I kick the dishwasher shut and start scrubbing the countertops with such vigor that my triceps ache.

Mikayla and Jocelyn study my frantic motion and exchange knowing looks.

Whenever I'm stressed, angry, or heartbroken (in this case all three), I keep myself in constant motion. If I sit still long enough to ponder what has happened between Justice and me, I'll start walking down a path of self-destruction, and I'm not sure I'll ever find my way back.

Since five this morning I've been on a cleaning bender. I've been bleaching, scouring, and vacuuming every surface in the apartment in an effort to calm myself, though it seems to be having the opposite effect on Lenny, who's been doddering around in a state of confusion. I don't think he's accustomed to such sanitary conditions.

Mikayla blows on her nails. "Good, because you shouldn't be defending him."

"I don't want to talk about this."

Jocelyn smiles perkily and tries to distract me. "How about we go for a bike ride and then a run?"

"Sure." I continue attacking the already sterile counter.

Mikayla eases off the barstool and walks on her heels, extending her arms like a mummy. She sits on the couch and props her legs up on the coffee table. "You guys have a serious problem. I don't know how you can be so into exercise. It isn't natural."

Her nails still wet, she gingerly pages through *Vogue*, critiquing the models. She holds it aloft. "Don't you think she needs braces? I mean, what is that about? You could park a car between her bottom teeth."

"Please tell me you aren't going to sit there and stare at *Vogue* and *Cosmo* all day. You told me you were going to call Jeremy and arrange to meet him for a talk."

Mikayla sniffs loudly, as if to say, Like that's going to happen.

"You can't stay here forever," I inform her.

"Seriously"—Mikayla squints as she peers more closely at the magazine—"all the models on this page need to visit an orthodontist."

Jocelyn, who has never held Mikayla in high esteem and has told me that she tried to talk her brother out of marrying her, gives her a nasty look. "You can't keep avoiding him! My mom and dad know that there's something going on between you two—he stopped by the house last night. I'm going to rat you out."

"I don't care what you do. Go ahead and tell him where I'm staying if you want. I'm not going back to Chicago with him."

"Why not?"

"Frankly, Jocelyn, it's none of your business."

"It is my business. He's my brother! He deserves better than a washed-up, uneducated model like you."

Mikayla flinches ever so subtly. "I'm far from washed up! I'm just getting started in my career. I'm going places."

"Maybe to the unemployment line to collect a check! Welfare is next! You just married my brother for money."

"How dare you accuse me of something—"

"Jocelyn, Mikayla, stop it!" I shake the feather duster at them to emphasize my point.

Lenny thinks I'm playing some kind of game, and he launches himself in the air, wraps his body around the duster, and promptly falls flat on this face. I pick him up and inspect him. His green eyes find me; he looks as miserable as I feel.

Mikayla resumes arguing. "Unemployment line! Please. I make more money than you ever will."

"I doubt that. Besides, I know you aren't working. Jeremy told my mom and dad that you aren't."

Mikayla grins imperiously. "You're being an absolute brat, which, given your age, I should expect."

"Why are you here? What are you hiding from?"

Mikayla throws these questions back in Jocelyn's face. "Why are *you* here? What are *you* hiding from?"

Since neither of them is willing to open the closet so their skeletons can roam free, this promptly ends their quarrel.

"Why don't you both go to your room!" I shout like the stressed-out mother hen that I've become.

Jocelyn's cell phone rings, and she answers. Her face goes ashen as she listens. A minute into the one-sided conversation, not having said a word, she hangs up.

"Who was it?" Mikayla asks.

Jocelyn flees to my room. I follow her and close the door. She's frantically pacing and holding her stomach.

"Who was that? What's wrong?" I ask.

She stops and looks at me. "Deanna."

"What did she want?"

Jocelyn's face crumples, and the tears start. I lead her over to the bed and sit her down. Reaching over, I grab the box of tissues that I've placed at a grab-and-go level, since everyone in this apartment is in the midst of an emotional breakdown.

"Deanna just told me exactly what happened. She knew all the details. She knew everything."

"They must have told her."

"No, no." Jocelyn shakes her head. "It was like she was there with us. Then she said that soon everyone was going to know what happened, that

86

people were going to figure it out for themselves. What does that mean? What's she planning?"

"She's bluffing."

"Deanna doesn't bluff."

"It's time to tell your mom and dad. They need to know. You should go to the doctor—"

"Absolutely not! I can't! I'm not going to."

My strict upbringing taught me a thing or two about parenting. Grandma Betty, consistently firm but loving, never backed down, not even when I pushed against her with all my might. "If you want, I'll go with you when you tell them. But you have to. It's time."

Jocelyn shakes her head. "Give me one week to figure this out. I'll talk to Deanna and work something out with her."

Wishful thinking. I know enough about Deanna to realize she won't be open to any kind of negotiating. "Jocelyn, you can't wait, this has to be addressed now. You've already waited too—"

Mikayla barges into the room, and Jocelyn cowers behind me. "Aristotle's at the door for you."

Is this her idea of a joke? "Have you lost your mind or something? I'm kind of busy at the moment."

She leans against the doorframe. "I can't use that excuse again. I used it last night when he stopped by and you were hiding in your room."

"I wasn't hiding," I say defensively.

"Sure you weren't. Anyway, you should go out there and talk to him."

"Are you talking about an actual person named Aristotle?"

"Are you having a hard time understanding me? Am I speaking in a foreign language? Yes, I'm talking about an actual person. Aristotle. Our neighbor, you know"—she lowers her voice—"the pocket protector geek?"

His name is Aristotle? Perfect.

"I'll be right back," I tell Jocelyn.

I find Aristotle standing awkwardly in the middle of my living room holding a gift bag. He thrusts it into my hands. "Cane Kallevik, I got you something."

"Oh. Okay. Thank you, Aristotle," I say, trying out his name.

"My friends call me Aris." He points at the gift. "Open it."

I take the tissue paper out of the bag and peer inside. There are two boxes of new Trivial Pursuit cards. Trivial Pursuit is my all-time favorite game. I've been obsessed with it since I was young, when I spent hours memorizing facts.

"Grandma Betty told me that you liked Trivial Pursuit, and I saw these in a store and knew that you would love them. I like trivia too."

I'm beginning to wonder if there's anything he doesn't know. Flattered and embarrassed by his thoughtfulness, I turn bright red. "Thank you, Aris."

"You're welcome. Do you like Chinese food?"

Mikayla takes a break from applying a layer of clear coat over her polish and glances up at Aris. "We love Chinese food!"

"I thought I could order some for us. We could eat and play Trivial Pursuit."

"I have to go for a run and a bike ride. I'm kind of busy today. I'm not sure I'll have time."

Mikayla waves her manicured hand, dismissing my excuse. "She'll be back in plenty of time. See you around six?"

"That works. See you then, Cane Kallevik." He walks himself to the door and leaves.

Mikayla screws the top back on the nail polish bottle and looks up at me. "He's weird, but kind of cute. You guys would make a good couple."

"You aren't seriously insinuating that we should be a couple."

"Think about how smart your children would be. We're talking Einstein-level intelligence."

"I'm not interested."

"I thought you could use him to make Justice jealous."

"That would be your kind of tactic, not mine." I slam the boxes of trivia cards on the kitchen table.

She grabs the *Vogue* and heads toward the bathroom, where she'll spend the rest of the day fashioning her hair into at least a dozen different styles.

Jocelyn comes out of the bedroom, dragging her duffel bag across the floor, and nearly bumps into Mikayla. They give each other dirty looks.

Mikayla slams the bathroom door and turns the lock.

"Sorry, but I don't feel like working out. I called my dad. He's coming to pick me up," Jocelyn says.

"You don't have to leave."

"I know, but I just want to hang out at home this weekend and think about what I should do," she mumbles.

We sit and talk until Samson arrives, and once she's gone, I go into my bedroom and quickly dress in my running clothes.

The urgency to run is getting stronger by the minute. If I don't start moving, and fast, the hunk of acidic grief that's been burning inside my stomach since last night is going to force itself up into my throat and out my mouth in the form of some kind of animalistic keening that has the potential of shattering eardrums and causing permanent deafness.

Foraging through my oversize nightstand drawer, I search for a hair tie and purposely avoid the box that holds my engagement ring. I find my favorite Harlequin romance novel, the *Jerry Maguire* movie ticket stub that I've had for two years, an old pile of Trivial Pursuit cards, a box of matches, random papers with miscellaneous notes, and a snapshot of Justice and me, taken at Frank and Grandma Betty's wedding. I examine the picture briefly, noting my naive face and the obvious adoration I had for Justice even then. It causes such agony, I flip it facedown.

I'm about to slam the drawer shut when it occurs to me that something vital is missing. It can't be. I rummage through the contents of the drawer again, and when that doesn't yield any results, I pull it out and dump out the contents on my bed.

Where could it have gone?

"Cane! Cane! You've got to see me!" Mikayla calls from the bathroom.

"Hold on a second." I ransack my room, but it's nowhere to be found. That scorching grief is no longer in my stomach; it's now pushing against my esophagus and poised at the back of my throat, ready to catapult out of my mouth. I need to get out of here. I'll have to resume the search later.

I pound on the bathroom door. "Mikayla, I need a rubber band for my hair!"

"Hang on, I'm almost done," she says gleefully.

"What are you doing in there?"

"Creating perfection."

She throws open the door, and I expect to be bombarded with a wave of sickly sweet hair spray, but instead a fart fog rolls over me. I pinch my nostrils and screw up my lips. "Did something die in there? Light a match!"

"Hey"—she points at me—"it's the food you served that's making me gassy."

I stagger backward and hold out my palm. "Toss me a hair tie, because I'm not going in there!"

"In a second, jeez. Be patient." She steps out of the bathroom, twirls, and pats her head. "What do you think?"

Her blond mane is curled into hundreds of perfect tendrils and piled artfully on top of her head. Subtle makeup makes her face look dewy and sun-kissed.

"Yes, you're gorgeous. How many times do you need to hear that?"

She smiles and farts at the same time; the sound stretches out for nearly ten seconds. She acts like nothing happened.

"You have a problem!"

"Not like I can help it or anything."

"It sounds like your butt has a dying duck stuck in it." Pushing past her, I snatch a rubber band off the shelf, conveniently hung at the right level for grab and go. I brush my hair and gather it up into a ponytail, breathing through my mouth.

Irritated, Mikayla stands beside me and moves her hands around her face in Madonna *Vogue* style. "You're missing the point of this whole look."

"There's a point? Right now I need a gas mask and an oxygen tank."

She peers into the mirror and for once studies my face and not her own. "I've never seen your eyes like this."

"I've had black-and-blue eyes for days now, and you've just noticed?"

"I'm not talking about the bruises, I'm talking about the color. Your eyes are amazingly green. The greenest I've ever seen them."

My almond-shaped eyes are hazel mood rings, going from gray to blue to coppery depending on my state of mind. Lately, I've noticed they've shifted into a sickly shade of green. "Compliments of Susie Homemaker, I've turned into a green-eyed monster."

"Huh. Whatever. It's working for you."

I turn to leave, and she grabs me by the ponytail. "Cane, look at me again."

"Quit it!" I slap her hand. "I have to get moving, or I'm going to lose it." The sadness mercilessly pecks away at my insides. If I don't start distracting myself with motion, I'm going to have a breakdown, and I can't afford to fall apart. I have to be strong for Jocelyn and Mikayla.

"Look at me again!" she demands and leaps out in front of me.

"Beautiful. Gorgeous. Stunning. Any other adjectives I should throw in there?"

She gives me a coy smile. "Do I look like the *farmer's belle?*"

I see where she's going with this. "You don't possibly want your picture on the front of a half gallon of—"

"I would make the perfect Belle. Isn't it obvious?" She gives one of her tendrils a slight tug, and it bounces back into place. "Justice can be the dark and handsome farmer, and I can be the blonde and innocent belle. I was born to be a belle."

"Innocent? Let's not go that far."

"I'm perfect for it, and I need the work. This is the last chance I'll have for a long time. Possibly the last chance ever. Please." She clasps her hands together and bats her ridiculously long lashes at me.

"I'm not male. That's not going to work on me."

"I can do this. I can rock this photo shoot. I know that you're stressing out about this project, and let's face it, Samson gave you a pretty tight deadline. I came up with the idea last night! I even wrote down a list of photographers who've worked with me. You can meet them this week and decide who to hire. By midweek, you could have everything booked."

I hadn't brought it up at the meeting, because it would have appeared self-serving and obvious, which it totally is, but I'd been planning on asking Samson if I could be the belle. Doing so would allow me to work closely with Justice, and quality time with him is more imperative now that he's dumped me and is leaving for Iowa with Susie Homemaker.

However, I realize the idea is half-cocked, if not downright ridiculous. I'm adorable, according to Grandma Betty and Frank, and sexy and gorgeous, according to Justice, but realistically, I'm a long way from a perfect ten. My Tinkerbelle-shaped face splashed with too many freckles is framed by long, wavy auburn hair that has a tendency to look like a lion's mane. My eyes can't even make up their mind about their color. Although fit and athletic, I have an obscene lack of curves. I have the cute-girl-next-door look, but Mikayla is the one who belongs on billboards. I envision Justice and her standing together; they would make a striking couple. Their picture and accompanying fictional love story would sell lots of ice cream, which, after all, is the goal.

Mikayla snaps her fingers in my face. "Earth to Cane! Come on, what do you think? I have ideas for the wardrobe, too. I can help you and do anything you need. That way you wouldn't have to rely on that Trina girl."

There's a knock at the front door. "If that's Aristotle again, we're canceling. I'm not in the mood."

"No, we're not!" Mikayla flies past me. "I want Chinese food, and he's nice. He brought you Trivial Pursuit cards. He's your ideal man!"

I chase her down, but I'm too late. She opens the door, and Jeremy, who looks so much like his older cousin, Justice, that it sometimes throws me for a loop, is standing there, holding two dozen red roses.

"Jeremy!" Mikayla's hands fly to her mouth, and she backs away from the door. "What are you doing here?" she snaps.

I give her a reproachful look. "Hi, Jeremy."

"Hey, Cane. Nice place." He smiles at me, but it doesn't reach his eyes. He looks positively miserable. I don't know what possessed him to hand over his heart over to someone as irresponsible as Mikayla, who would abuse it and then probably lose it.

"Jocelyn told me where you were."

Mikayla gapes at Jeremy and then looks at me. Her face drains of color. Beads of sweat form on her forehead. Her hands quake ever so slightly, as do the ringlets that drape around her face. I know what's coming, but before I can do anything about it Mikayla swivels sideways, leans over, and vomits all over Lenny Kravitz.

CHAPTER SEVEN

"Van Morrison is next on the list. Take a right here, onto Broadway," Trina says as she glances at the directions.

I wonder what kind of freak this photographer will be. Trina and I've spent our Wednesday driving around Chicago, meeting and interviewing five photographers that Mikayla recommended.

The first photographer we met with this morning was Peter Frawley, a gay man who apparently had a thing for women's clothing. Dressed in a tutu, fishnet stockings, high heels, and a black half shirt with the image of a fist and a middle finger extended, he looked like an off-Broadway burlesque actor. I explained the project to him in detail, but he didn't pay attention to a word I was saying. He was too busy fawning over Trina's outfit—a blazer with mile-high shoulder pads over a lacy hot pink polka-dot bustier, tight leather pants, and a Tom and Jerry necklace. They talked about their shared love of eighties fashion, Madonna, and even cartoons. I was beginning to wonder if I was the only person who wasn't watching cartoons on a regular basis. Peter was a huge fan of Woody Woodpecker. Given his sexual persuasion, I thought this apropos.

He loved Trina, but he didn't care for me. I didn't intuit this; he came out and told me.

"Honey, you're giving off this uptight, pathetic vibe. And those dark circles under your eyes add to the—"

"They're bruises," I inform him impatiently.

"Whatever they are, it doesn't matter. You look like a starved stray kitten, and I don't do well with cats. Period."

I stopped flipping through his portfolio, taking note that his photos had a sadomasochistic edge. Leather, whips, spikes, and chains seem to be his favorite props. "Excuse me?"

"Pathetic, that's how you look. You remind me of a homeless kitten. Cats are appalling creatures."

I stared him down. "I don't think this is going to work out."

"Honey, I could have told you that from the second you walked in. I don't do wholesome photo shoots—even if it's for Mikayla. It's not my thing." He turned to Trina. "Trina, honey, you're fabulous. Let's say you and me get together and storm the town. What are your digits?"

Five minutes later after exchanging cell phone numbers, email addresses, and briefly discussing the latest episode of *Melrose Place* (they were both in love with the dreamboat Andrew Shue and in awe of the character Amanda), Trina and Peter were best friends forever and would probably be ordering lockets to show the world how much they loved each other.

The second photographer, Janice Streit, was a bitter, beautiful intellectual who dressed in tight black Lycra head to toe, kept quoting Sylvia Plath, and seemed vaguely interested in the job. I didn't think I was vaguely interested in hiring her until I paged through her portfolio, which featured photographs that were lighthearted and frivolous in content. Puppies. Hot air balloons. Rainbows. Children cavorting in sprinklers. Not at all what I'd been expecting.

I told her about the absurdly tight timeline and what we were willing to pay her. "You would be a great fit. What do you think?"

She responded with a Sylvia Plath quote. " 'Perhaps when we find ourselves wanting everything, it is because we are dangerously close to wanting nothing.' "

Trina gave her a blank stare. "Is that a yes or no?"

Janet screamed "No!" in my face and then kicked us out of her studio as if we'd offended her.

The third photographer, whose studio was in a musty but well-lit basement apartment with blatant evidence of mice, was named Rico. He chain-smoked, knocked back a vodka on the rocks, and talked nonstop about Mikayla. He told me how fantastic she was, how much he loved her, how many times they'd slept together, and all the places they'd consummated their relationship.

When I tried to interrupt him to tell him about the job, he blew smoke in my face, stabbed out his cigarette in his ashtray, and then showed me pictures of Mikayla in some provocative poses.

Trina and I couldn't get a word in edgewise. When we thanked him and walked out the door, Rico was pouring himself another drink and still wrapped up in his monologue about Mikayla the goddess.

I hope we find a semi-normal photographer who's willing to do the photo shoot this Friday. As I battle midafternoon Chicago traffic, I finish eating my cucumber, spinach, avocado, and tomato sandwich and then take a giant bite of the apple I packed.

Trina regards my lunch with disgust and crumples up her McDonald's bag. "How can you eat that stuff all the time?"

I look at her empty supersize fry container. "I was wondering the same thing."

"What? You've never eaten a fry before, Miss Fitness Freak?"

"Yes, I've eaten a fry before, but I don't know how you can eat it without ketchup. Yuck."

"Ketchup isn't essential."

"Um, yes it is."

She points at the next intersection. "You have to turn left up here."

I take another bite of my apple, turn on my signal, and merge into the left lane. Some jerk driving a compact car with flashy hubcaps honks his horn at me, and I consider saluting with my middle finger. Then I remember Peter and his ridiculous shirt, so I keep my finger to myself.

Trina spies the inside of my shredded wrist. "What happened to you?" Her eyes widen in apprehension. "Oh, my God, you didn't try to kill yourself did you? You didn't cut yourself or something? Self-mutilation is so not cool. I should know, because I used to do that in high school. Cane, no man is worth that, not even Justice."

"I didn't do this to myself." I examine the tender, inflamed vertical lines, which are most likely infected, despite a liberal application of antibiotic ointment. "My cat wasn't too happy with me."

"Lenny did that?"

"I had to give him a bath."

"Why would you do a dumb thing like that?"

"I didn't have much of a choice. Mikayla hurled all over him."

"Gross!"

"You're telling me," I mumble.

I shudder at the memory of my taxing Saturday morning.

After Lenny recovered from the mild trauma of being doused with recycled food, he seemed to enjoy the fact that Mikayla had graciously shared her breakfast. He promptly started cleaning himself, gumming the tasty remnants of pancake and eggs splattered on his fur coat and the floor.

Astonished at what had happened, I backed away from the mess, gagging and looking around for something I could use to clean it up. Mikayla fled to the bathroom, and Jeremy, the concerned husband, shoved the roses into my hands, pushing a thorn right into the sensitive part of my palm, and chased his wife down. Wincing in pain, I tossed the roses onto the table.

"Honey, what's wrong? Do you have food poisoning or something? Are you hung over?" Jeremy peppered his wife with questions, but Mikayla was too busy spraying my beautiful, sparkling clean toilet with stomach juices to reply.

While she retched, Jeremy rubbed her back, murmuring kind words to her, telling her how much he loved her, telling her that whatever was going on, he would understand.

If only he knew what his wife of less than two months had done.

"Close the door, Jeremy," Mikayla whined as she scooted away from the toilet.

Jeremy and I made eye contact as he came to the bathroom door, and I said good luck with my eyes. He responded with an I'm-going-to-need-it look.

Lenny meowed and continued chomping on the puke.

Spectacular.

Holding my breath, I found a clothespin in the linen closet, yet another item conveniently located in a clear plastic bin at grab-and-go level, and clamped it on my nose. I put on my cleaning gloves, piled paper towels and clean rags on the countertop in the kitchen, and filled the sink with warm water. I didn't have cat shampoo, so I squirted a tiny bit of dish soap into the stream.

Lenny might not be able to walk in a straight line or land on his feet, but he's pretty insightful. He took one look at my gloved hands and the bubbles in the sink and took off at a dead run. I intercepted him and, before he knew what was happening, plopped him into the water.

Needless to say, it was a terrible, painful experience for both of us. Yowling, growling, and screaming—and Lenny made some pretty interesting sounds too. When I was done, I towel-dried him, pleasantly surprised to discover that Dawn not only cut grease but eliminated vomit residue and odor. The company could start a whole new ad campaign.

When I released Lenny, he bolted for the guest bedroom and cowered under the bed. I was cleaning up the pile by the door when Jeremy came out of the bathroom.

He bent down to grab the extra mop. "Let me help."

I looked up from my hands-and-knees position and sat back on my heels. "Don't worry about it. I got it."

"I can't get anything out of her." He glanced over his shoulder and leaned closer. "Cane, what's she not telling me?" he asked quietly.

There's so much she wasn't telling him. Besides her big secret that I wasn't to reveal under any circumstances, or she would cut my tongue out with a scissors, she admitted that she didn't love him as much as he loved her. She was contemplating an annulment or separation. However, her predicament and tenuous future in the modeling world, not to mention her affection toward Jeremy, were deterring her from dissolving her marriage.

I plucked the clothespin from my nose. "I can't say anything. It's not my place."

He nodded. "I understand. She said she just needed another week or two, and then she would sit down and talk to me. She's going to stay here, though, right? She's not going to run?"

I smiled reassuringly. "She's not going to, and if she's thinking about it, you'll be the first person I call."

"Thanks."

Jeremy left. I finished cleaning, and Lenny staggered into the bathroom to find Mikayla.

As I was getting ready to leave the apartment, I went to find her myself. She was sitting on the guest bed, stroking Lenny, who lowered his ears when he saw me.

"Feel better?"

"Kind of," she replied.

"What did you tell Jeremy?"

"That I loved him, but I couldn't talk to him yet."

"Do you? Love him?"

"Yes. I mean . . . I think I do."

"Then knock this off, go back to Chicago, and tell him everything that's going on in your head. You made your bed, and now you have to stay put. Marriage isn't a fast-food drive-through—you can't order something up, decide you don't like it, and throw it back through the window. For Jeremy's sake and your own, you need to try to fix your marriage and move forward!"

When I finished delivering my mini sermon, she went bat-shit crazy. She screamed about how unfair her life was and how she didn't know how marriage was supposed to work because she'd never had a good example. When she finished her five-minute rant (every word of which I'm positive Aris heard through the vents), she flung herself on the bed in starfish position and flailed her arms and legs, pure tantrum style.

I left her to cry a river of tears, and during my eight-mile run, twenty-mile bike ride, and marathon weight-lifting session at Fitness Bound Gym in Clinton, I cried a river of sweat.

It was a long Saturday.

Trina and I pull up in front of Van Morrison's photography studio.

"Those scratches are infected. You can die from stuff like that."

"I don't think I have to buy a headstone yet."

"Yeah, well, watch out for red lines going up your arm. It's like poison, and if it makes it to your heart, you die. You probably should have it looked at."

I grab my backpack from the backseat and take my phone out of the front pocket. There's a missed call from Justice. My heart reflexively squeezes, causing a searing ache under my breastbone.

I called Grandma Betty Sunday night to tell her what happened. I had every intention of being stoic, and I was for the first three seconds of the conversation, but then I nearly choked to death on my tears. The Heimlich maneuver wouldn't have done me any good. She soothed me as best she could over the phone. When I'd calmed down enough to have a normal conversation, she told me that the key to getting over something wasn't to look back on what had happened or to wallow in the misery of the present but to look into the future and find happiness there.

"Cane, you have to figure out what you want and move toward that without worrying about whether Justice will be there or not."

"I don't know how to do that. He's always been there, and I thought he always would be. Not to mention I have to see him every day! We work together. Am I supposed to twiddle my thumbs and pretend everything's spectacular when it's not?"

"Sugar Cane, I wish I could make this better for you. Maybe," she said softly, "if it's too hard seeing him every day, you should think about working somewhere else."

I look at my phone now, wondering why he called, what he wanted, why he didn't leave a voice message. He's been acting like my best buddy this week. It would be easier if he would just steer clear.

Trina angles her body toward me and peers at my phone. "What are you looking at?"

"Nothing." I shove it into my bag and look up at the squat brick building with the candy-striped awnings. "This better be worth it."

She tongues the straw of her supersize Coke and slurps the rest of it down. "Isn't Van Morrison a band?"

"A singer." I turn off the ignition.

"Oh, yeah. I knew that."

Doubtful. The only music she listens to, besides Madonna, is the latest and greatest pop music.

We're standing outside, knocking on Van Morrison's door, when Trina starts humming the Britney Spears song "Hit Me Baby One More Time."

If she doesn't stop, I *will* hit her.

Around five thirty that evening, Justice corners me in the conference room. I'm working alone (Trina had a hot date with Blaze), putting together the final touches for the photo shoot two days from now.

He closes the door and sits on the table next to me, all casual, like there's nothing wrong.

He smiles. I frown.

"Word around the office is that you booked a photographer for the shoot. Van Morrison? What's this guy like?" He tugs at the bottom of his navy button-down shirt and unbuttons the top three buttons.

He loathes dress clothes. Throughout the workday, he squirms, sighs, and groans. He always has a T-shirt and pair of jeans in his truck, and it isn't uncommon for him to be changed before he's even out of the parking lot.

However, given the way he's frantically scratching the top of his leg right now, he might not make it to the truck today. He's wearing gray wool trousers—the pair he hates because of how they make his skin crawl, and I love because of how they look on his long, muscular legs.

Why does he have to be so gorgeous? I want to tell him to go ahead and take off his pants, but I'm too angry with him to give him the satisfaction.

"It's not a guy. Her name is Vanna Morrison, but people call her Van. She was the only normal photographer I met today. The rest were a bunch of circus freaks. I called Mikayla and told her who we were working with. She's excited."

"I can't believe you're letting Mikayla be in the photo shoot with me. Actually, I can't believe you've just let her back into your life."

I can't help myself; I go right below the belt. "Unlike you, I know how to move on." Target hit. He winces. I should apologize for the nasty comment, but I'm not feeling particularly apologetic. "Anyway, what does it matter? It's not like I'm jealous of her or anything. She's married to Jeremy, and you're a free agent."

"Cane," he says, in a manner that indicates he isn't a free agent.

I mimic his tone. "Justice."

Susie Homemaker walks by the conference room, and I see her eyes settle on Justice and then on me. I've noticed that lately she's been stalking him; she seems to know where he is at all times.

He's mine! I want to yell, and if she lingered for a second longer, I would have. But, she walks off, her lips arranged in an obscene smile.

"I called you earlier today."

"I saw that."

"I wanted to talk to you about something."

"After Friday night, I assumed we were all talked out," I say slowly. Argument bait, but he doesn't take it.

He gives me a tolerant smile. "We are ahead of schedule in Iowa, which means I'm needed out there sooner than anticipated. Provided everything goes well at the shoot on Friday, I may be leaving as early as Monday. I wanted to let you know."

"Thanks for sharing," I say in my best singsong Susie Homemaker voice.

"I know this isn't easy to—"

"Do you?"

To avoid the issue, he rolls the conversational dice and lands on something else. "Are you going to the homecoming game Friday night?"

"Probably. Jocelyn wants me to go with her." Jocelyn has been calling every day with updates. She assures me that she has it under control. Supposedly Deanna is being friendly and promises not to tell anyone what she knows. I've been trying to convince Jocelyn that when an enemy makes grand gestures of friendship, it's usually because she's setting booby traps.

"Jeremy and I are going," he says. "You could bring Mikayla."

"We can meet up and have a double date! Perfect!" The sarcasm leaves a nasty taste in my mouth. I cover my face with my hands. This isn't who I want to be. "I'm sorry. This is so hard."

He looks in my eyes. "I didn't expect it would be easy."

"Remember last year? Dancing in the field?" I ask him.

Last year at homecoming, we'd spent the afternoon tailgating with Jeremy and some of our friends. After watching the parade and football game, we'd returned to Schaeffer Farm for the annual hayride and bonfire. When the party ended, Justice and I were too riled up for sleep. Feeling antsy, we filled a backpack with beer and an old transistor radio, climbed onto one of Samson's tractors, and drove out to the forest preserve off County N, where we parked in a grove of trees and trekked through the woods to a twenty-foot clearing. Under a sky weighed down with a million stars, we turned on the oldies station and slow-danced to "Brown-Eyed

Girl," "Under the Boardwalk," and "I Want to Hold Your Hand." Feeling young and free, we kissed until we were dizzy and talked until the only sound in the world was our two voices. Justice drank most of the beer, and when the time came to leave, I drove the tractor back to his small apartment and tucked him into bed. When he woke the next morning, I served him breakfast and Advil in bed.

He smiles at me now. "A great night."

"I want one of those nights again."

He leans purposefully toward me, his hand reaching out to touch my face. I see desire in his eyes, and I can feel my own. It's so strong that if he doesn't kiss me, I'm going to pounce on him. I could knock him backward so that he's sprawled defenselessly on the table. I'll push the papers aside and take advantage of him right here and—

"Knock knock!" Susan says brightly as she throws open the door.

She grins. I hate her gigantic mouth.

"I have chocolate chip pumpkin bread, and I thought you two would like to take some home."

Embarrassed, Justice runs a hand through his short hair and pulls away from me. I deliberately stay where I am. I'm even considering planting a lewd kiss on him right now, and not just for Susie Homemaker's benefit, though I'd love to see her reaction when I put my tongue in Justice's mouth. It's because I honestly want to kiss him. He knows what I'm considering, and he stands quickly. That just goes to show you the key difference between us. Whereas I throw caution to the wind and hope it doesn't get blown back in my face, Justice charts the velocity and direction of the wind and only does things when he knows he won't get blown off course. Personally, I think getting blown off course is when the best stuff happens.

Susie Homemaker keeps on smiling. "I'm sorry to interrupt."

I've never been blatantly rude to her, but I'm not in the mood to be Miss Manners. "I bet you're not."

"Excuse me?"

"I said, I bet you're not."

"I—did I?" Flustered, she looks at Justice and then back at me. "Were you two discussing something important? Because I can come back."

She has the innocent charade down to a science! She knew exactly was she was doing when she barged in holding her tisket, her tasket, her chocolate-chip-pumpkin-bread-filled basket.

"Yes, why don't you come back," I suggest acerbically.

Susan must not have bitch radar, because she thinks I'm joking. She laughs.

On the other hand, Justice does have bitch radar, and he knows that I'm serious. He nervously clears his throat. "No, no, we weren't discussing anything important. We were just . . . talking."

Since when is almost making out considered talking? He reaches into Susie Homemaker's basket, which is lined with gingham cloth, and takes a piece of pumpkin bread. Traitor.

He moans with pleasure as he chews. Disbelieving, I give him a dirty look, but he's too lost in the rapture of her homemade treat to notice.

I'm supposed to make him moan with pleasure! That's my job, and if Susie hadn't interrupted, I would have done just that.

He holds up the piece in front of him like he's eating manna from heaven. "This is excellent."

"Thank you so much! It's a new recipe. Cane, I know you want one," Susan says as she dangles the basket in front of my face.

CHAPTER EIGHT

I shove the last bit of pumpkin bread in my mouth as I walk down the hallway toward my apartment door.

Yes, I took three pieces of the damn pumpkin bread. I wanted to prove to Susie Homemaker that she wasn't a threat, or maybe I wanted to prove it to Justice as well. It's not like I planned on actually eating it. I wanted to place it under my car tire and back over it, but since Samson followed me out to the parking lot to chat about the photo shoot and congratulate me on getting things arranged so quickly, I couldn't very well do that.

I got in my car and placed the bread on the seat next to me, intending to launch it out the window into a cow pasture, but I was starving. If Justice wasn't going to make me moan with pleasure, I figured something might as well.

As I enter my apartment building, Aris is dawdling in the hallway, where I'm sure he's been waiting for me to arrive home from work.

"Hey, Aris."

He turns, and I give a lackluster wave.

"Cane Kallevik, I'm glad I caught you!"

He has this strange habit of using my full name when he's nervous. The other night when he brought over Chinese takeout, he spent the first hour calling me Cane Kallevik every time he said something. Mikayla found it hilarious, and she's been referring to me as Cane Kallevik ever since.

I screw up my face into a look of disappointment. "I'm afraid I don't have much time to chat." I have to tell him this up front, or I'll be stuck out in the hallway for at least forty-five minutes. A computer programmer who works from home, Aris doesn't get out much. His social interaction is pretty much limited to me and his sister, who he says he calls every day. I wonder if she's as weird as he is.

"Real quick, name the hurricane that devastated Louisiana in the early eighteen hundreds."

Ever since I trounced him and Mikayla in the Trivial Pursuit game last Saturday evening, he's been trying to stump me.

"The Great Louisiana Hurricane of 1812. It passed just west of New Orleans and devastated the area."

"What president frequently used the phrase 'There you go again'?"

"President Reagan." I unzip my coat and drop my cell phone in my pocket. I might be here awhile.

Impressed and making lovey eyes at me, he whistles. "You're a genius."

"Memorization of facts does not a genius make."

"I beg to differ. How about I buy us some coffee and doughnuts Saturday morning, and we watch CNN together?"

"How about you come running with me?" Aris has an aversion to all things physical, and I've found I can deflect his invitations with my own.

He shifts his feet and crosses his arms. "There's a high probability that won't happen. Do you like trains?"

Having a conversation with him is like pulling unrelated topics out of a hat. "I've never thought much about trains."

"They fascinate me. I collect train sets. I just set one up in the spare bedroom today."

"Um, that's nice."

"Cane Kallevik, would you like to take the train with me this Friday night? We could ride all the way to Chicago and go to Navy Pier. We could have dinner there and go on rides, if you like, but I have to warn you, I get motion sick and have been known to throw up. I once threw up on the Ferris wheel, but if you wanted to go, I would go with you."

"Thank you for the invite, but I'm going to the Savage High homecoming game this Friday."

"What time does the game start? What time should I pick you up? We can go out to Savage Suds before, or if you would prefer, we could order from the concession stand. I should warn you, I can't eat chili or chili dogs. It gives me horrible heartburn and gas. So maybe it would be safer to eat at Savage Suds."

Mikayla opens the door and pokes her head out. "Hi, Aris." She waves at him and then looks at me. "Van Morrison! She rocks. She just called me and told me that you booked her. Thank God! Because I was actually kind of worried that Rico might make a play for the shoot. Hey, I'm starving! What's for dinner?"

Before I can give her the stink eye, she ducks back into the apartment.

"It's your choice in terms of where you want to eat. What do you think?"

"Aris, you are very sweet, but I'm going to the game alone."

Looking immensely pleased, he grins. "Sounds like a plan! Maybe you'll be up for a trivia game afterward."

He turns and heads down the hallway toward his open door.

I'm not sure what plan he's talking about, but I'm not about to ask. I walk into the apartment, kick off my ballet flats, and grip the area rug with my bare toes. Lenny saunters over, rubs up against my legs, and meows a greeting, kneading the carpet with his front paws.

"Feels good, doesn't it?" I ask him.

He gives me a look that says, I wouldn't be doing it if it didn't feel good.

"We've got nothing in here," Mikayla announces with disgust. She's standing in front of the open refrigerator, taking inventory.

"Why did you even put Rico on the list?"

"He's a great photographer. We had a thing, but I figured he would be over me by now."

"He's not, and from what I can tell, he won't be any time soon. He was listing all the places you had sex. On the eighteenth hole of a golf course. In the bleachers at Soldier Field. The Comfort Inn pool in Amarillo. The—"

"Stop! Ugh! It's been two and half years since we broke up. He needs to move on." She kicks the refrigerator shut with her bare foot. "Let's order pizza. My treat."

I push the phone book her way. "I want all the toppings, but no sausage and onions."

An hour later, after we've plowed our way through a large pizza, and Mikayla, whose digestive system is in a precarious state, has belched and farted at least a dozen times, she says, "I told Jeremy I would hang out with him at homecoming."

"That's a step in the right direction." I pick a piece of leftover cheese out of the box and give it to Lenny.

"I don't know if I can tell him everything."

"You have to, and you know it."

Mikayla eases herself off the couch and arranges herself on the floor in a supine position, her arms stuck out to the side and her feet up on the coffee table. Lenny takes advantage of her position and crawls onto her stomach.

"I called another agency today," she says. "The Stiletto Agency out of New York. They offered me a contract a year or so ago."

Mikayla didn't take a break from modeling, which is what she told everyone this past June. Prime Figures, the modeling agency that signed her right after high school, fired her.

Over the past few years, she'd gotten herself in some serious credit card debt, and she tried to solve her money woes by stealing from the petty cash account and turning in bogus expense sheets. That didn't quite cover the $40,000 hole she'd dug for herself, so she set her sights on digging for the real pot of gold. She put the moves on the president's son, Angelo, and had great success with Angelo and the thievery until the accounting department discovered her crime.

Angelo went from adoring her to pitying her, for which she should thank her lucky stars, because it kept her out of jail. Angelo, his father, Sutton Beckworth, and Mikayla worked out a deal. To repay the more than $20,000 she'd stolen thus far, she would work for them without pay for three months, at the end of which she would be fired. What Mikayla didn't anticipate was that she would be blacklisted in the industry because of what she'd done. Sutton made sure of it. Unfortunately, Sutton wasn't the only one who screwed her over-his son did as well.

"What did Stiletto say?"

"They said they'll get back to me, which is the same thing as a big fat no-way-are-we-going-to-work-with-you." She indulges in another of her self-pity moans. "I've destroyed my life."

"Not completely. You did something right. You married Jeremy."

She raises her brow and laughs mirthlessly. "Yeah, and now I've destroyed his life as well, only he doesn't know it yet. The Corvette is getting repossessed on Monday, and I can't even imagine how many bills are back at the apartment just waiting to be opened and unpaid."

"You have debt, and I have someone after Justice. Just found out that he's leaving for Iowa on Monday," I announce miserably. "It's only a matter of time before he and Susie Homemaker shack up."

Mikayla rolls onto her side, reaches up onto the coffee table, and scrounges for leftovers in the pizza box. "You know what I think about Justice?"

"No, but I bet you're going to tell me even if I don't want to hear it."

"Be done with him and move on."

Whenever I try to visualize the end of my relationship with him, I start seeing the beginning of it. A random slideshow of our six years together plays in my head.

My nineteenth birthday, he baked me a nineteen-layer chocolate cake that was as tall as me, and inedible, since it was held together with not only frosting but also superglue.

A month after his father's funeral, when Justice was still emotionally shut down and barely saying a word to me or anyone else, I packed us both a suitcase, stuffed a cooler with food, and forced him to get in the car.

"Why?" he asked.

"Because I'm going to take you to the place that your father promised to take you but never did."

"I don't want to go there," he said, sounding like an angry six-year-old boy, which was the age he'd been when his father promised to take him to the Grand Canyon.

"We're doing this. Get in the car."

When we arrived, we camped and hiked for an entire week. The incredible beauty of the canyon healed Justice in a way that nothing else could have—not even me.

February, last year, I had a horrible cold that turned into pneumonia. Justice was in Florida, visiting a friend, so he couldn't come to nurse me back to health, but he sent a care package that included an industrial-size bottle of NyQuil, tissues laced with soothing aloe, microwave popcorn, some trashy romance novels, and four of my favorite movies: *Jerry Maguire*, *Man in the Moon*, *Good Will Hunting*, and *Sleepless in Seattle*.

The Justice and Cane slide show continues playing, but I can't stand to watch any longer.

What does the end of something this meaningful look like? Surely it's not a teary good-bye scene, because Justice and I've been there, done that, more than once. What I picture instead is a kind of relationship murder scene. Me standing there holding a dagger, with Justice's body nowhere to be found. Or, equally traumatic, I'm standing there with a dagger stuck through my heart. The end of a relationship is like enduring the death of a loved one. You're left without the person, and stuck with all the bittersweet memories.

Mikayla pops a mushroom in her mouth and chews thoughtfully. "Ditch him and see what happens."

"Taking relationship advice from you is not a good idea, considering your past"—I pause and look her in the eye—"and your present predicament."

"I'm really trying to straighten my life out. I am. I don't claim to know what I'm doing, but I'm trying to make sense of it all. I don't want to make any more mistakes. I want to do things right. That's why I came here—that's why I came to you."

I give her a skeptical look. "You're not insinuating that I can help you, because I've made plenty of mistakes. I'm not doing anything right."

"Oh, please. You didn't steal money or sleep with too many men. You didn't marry some guy after dating him for three weeks only because you were scared out of your mind. You've dated the same guy for six years, gone to college, worked hard and earned a degree, started a respectable career, and you have your own place. And you've never racked up any debt. You probably have half a million in the bank, for all I know.

"But the coolest thing? You've been taking care of Jocelyn and me. Feeding us, playing counselor. Mopping up puke. I've known you for twenty-two years. You're the most responsible, driven person on the face of the planet."

I'm taken aback by her praise. Mikayla typically behaves like she's God's gift to mankind. Just when I think she might be a lost cause, she says or does something incredibly sweet. "Thank you."

She waves her hand in the air like it's no big deal, stands, and walks over to the stereo. She flips through the stack of CDs and selects a classic Aerosmith album.

"Want to dance?" she asks, putting the CD into the player and turning up the volume.

Lenny, who doesn't tolerate Steven Tyler's screeching, bolts for my bedroom.

"No, I promised Grandma I would check in with her this week."

Leaving Mikayla to her singing and dancing, I take my phone into the bedroom.

Frank answers on the first ring. "Hi, Frank."

"Sugar Cane! Good to hear your voice."

"Yours, too."

"I assume you're looking for Grandma, but she's out with some gardening friends."

"Oh." I sit on the edge of my bed and open my nightstand drawer, rifling through the contents for the sixth time this week. I still haven't been able to find it.

Taking note of my distracted silence, he asks, "You okay?"

"Did Grandma mention anything about seeing my silver compass when she was here? I've misplaced it. I've been looking everywhere, but I can't find it."

"She hasn't said a thing about it. Want me to ask her?"

I push the drawer shut and aimlessly work my way around my room, hunting for it in the oddest of places while I talk on the phone. "Would you?"

"Absolutely. Hey, I hear you're coming to visit in a few weeks! We can't wait. We miss you dearly."

"I've missed you guys more."

He chuckles. "Not possible."

"What have you been up to?"

"I captured a storm on video the other night. It was a doozy! Funnel clouds like you wouldn't believe, right over the ocean. Had the potential to be a waterspout, but sad to say it never made it to that point. I was watching this documentary on hurricanes the other day and—"

Frank adores meteorological events and watches the Weather Channel twenty-four/seven; his goal in life is to capture the perfect storm on film. Should the occasion arise, he's more than prepared. He has all the high-tech gadgets, including radar equipment, video cameras, and computers. Knowing he'll go on about this documentary for a good half hour, filling me in on sustainable winds, property damage, and flooding, I tune out. Sitting on the floor of my closet, I pull out a rubber container labeled "Keepsakes" and pry off the lid. Could I have put the compass in there?

Frank cuts himself off after ten minutes and asks, "Have you seen any good storms lately?"

"Only the kind between Justice and me."

"Aw, kiddo," he says sympathetically. "I heard things aren't so hot right now."

"More like ice cold, as in frozen solid." I fish around in the keepsake container and happen to pull out a birthday card Justice gave me on my twentieth birthday. "I wish I knew if there was going to be a thaw. I could use one."

Frank sticks with the analogy. "That's the thing about a weather front—sometimes you can't predict when it's going to come through, or what it will bring."

After I hang up the phone, I open the birthday card. A huge fan of David Letterman, Justice has made me many top-ten lists over the years. In this particular card he'd inserted a typed list.

It reads:

The Ten Things I Hope You'll Still Do Even Though You're No Longer a Teenager

10. Stretch like a cat in the morning, because there's nothing better than the sight of your cute butt in the air

9. Leave your hair long, because the way it tickles my face when you're kissing me drives me crazy

8. Insist that we splash in the puddles after a summer rainstorm

7. Sit on a tree branch to watch the sunset

6. Hop up on the coffee table and dance when Guns N' Roses' "Sweet Child O' Mine" comes on the radio

5. Skinny dip whenever possible

4. Get up at the crack of dawn on Christmas day to run outside and make snow angels

3. Smile every time I come into a room

2. Hug me until I can barely breathe

1. Love me forever

Mikayla barges into my room right as I'm finishing, waves a stack of envelopes in the air, and then flings it at my feet. "Mail delivery."

On the verge of blubbering, I take a deep breath and surreptitiously tuck Justice's top-ten list under the bed.

"What have you been doing in here?"

"Reminiscing."

"Don't do it. It's bad for your health." She flips her hand palm up and wiggles her fingers at me. "Whatever you just stashed under there, let me see it."

"You're going to make fun of it."

"Probably."

"I appreciate the honesty." I retrieve it for her.

While she reads, I put fifteen small braids in my hair and inhale deeply and carefully, hoping to dry up the tears and snot that are ready to roll. I've learned a hard cry isn't good for my freshly broken nose. If I don't watch it, I'll have blood shooting out my still tender nostrils, which is what happened the night Justice broke up with me. When it wouldn't stop, I did what Dr. Gettinger had told me to do should I get a gusher at home. I took a tampon, cut it vertically, and pushed the pieces up each nostril. I don't relish the idea of having to do it again, not to mention that Lenny had a blast with it the other night. He thought it was great fun batting at the dangling strings.

When Mikayla finishes, she screws up her nose and makes a raspberry sound. "That makes me want to vomit."

"Everything makes you want to vomit lately."

She holds her stomach. "Only because I'm in a precarious emotional state."

"Just don't do it in my room or on the cat." I hold up my arms and show off Lenny's claw tracks. "I don't feel like being attacked by Freddy Krueger again."

Mikayla does a runway walk over to my mirror and stares at her perfectly perfect reflection. "You know what he should have added to that list: 'I hope that when I'm being a ridiculous jerk, you'll walk away and forget about me.' "

"Hey, you haven't by chance spotted that silver compass yet, have you? It's still MIA."

Suppressing a less-than-tolerant sigh, she rolls her eyes. "No, and why are you obsessing about it? Didn't you say it was broken? What good is a compass if it can't tell you which way to go?"

Good point. Shrugging, I sort through a week's worth of mail. Junk. Junk. More junk.

Mikayla primps in the mirror, arranging and rearranging her hair. "I can't wait for the photo shoot! Van Morrison rocks. She totally gets me, and I know this is so going to be a home run. I could transition into doing more local modeling. I'll be a free agent. Screw all those modeling agencies and Sutton Beckworth. And screw Angelo most of all. I should have known better than to think he would help me."

As worldly-wise as Mikayla is, she should have known that helping was the last thing on Angelo's mind.

In the stack of mail, I find my MasterCard bill. Ripping it open, I glance at the total and nearly pee my pants.

"Two hundred dollars! That stupid psychic!"

Squealing with delight, Mikayla turns toward me. "I love those hotlines. Which one did you call?"

A cheapskate to the core, I can't get over it. "Two hundred dollars," I lament. "I'm going to wring Rhonda Riddle's neck."

"No way! Rhonda Riddle? I've talked to her before. Isn't she fabulous! She told me that I was destined for greatness."

"That isn't general at all."

"You have no right to mock me. You called her too." Mikayla does an about-face and walks toward the door. "I'm going to go get a snack. Want anything?"

"We just ate a large pizza."

"Yeah, well, I'm hungry again."

"I'm going to give that Rhonda Riddle a piece of my mind."

"Have fun with that," Mikayla says and closes my bedroom door.

I dig Rhonda's phone number out of my dresser drawer and call.

"Hello."

A television blares in the background. "Rhonda?"

"Yes?"

"This is Cane, Cane Kallevik, you know, the girl who's—"

"Oh, my gosh! I've been dying to find out what's happened to you!"

Immediately, the television mutes.

"I'll tell you what's happened. I just opened my MasterCard bill. Two hundred dollars for a ten-minute conversation!"

"Oh, sorry. I don't set the rates, honey, they do. You'll have to take it up with them. Highway robbery, isn't it? You can try to fight it, but they get you with the fine print. Too bad I don't see hardly a penny of that. Minimum wage, can you believe it? But I'm retired and doing it for kicks. You wouldn't believe all the neat people I get to talk to. Something to supplement my pension and social security." She pauses and chews on something crunchy. "Hold on a second. I got some boxed wine waiting for me in the fridge, and I've been dying to have a glass all day. Be just a minute, and when I get back on the line, I want you to tell me everything that's been going on since the last time we talked." She sounds as if we're the best of friends.

I stuff my bill back into the envelope, embarrassed that I called. "I'm sure you don't want to hear about my life."

"I certainly do! Your story is better than all the stupid shows they have on television. Now hold on a second. I'll be right back."

Should I wait until she gets back on and then tell her that something came up, and I can't talk? I could go the passive-aggressive route and hang up. But who am I kidding? I've never gotten the hang of passive, only aggressive. I'm still analyzing what I should do when Rhonda gets back on the line.

"Got my white zinfandel," she announces. "I'm ready to go. Now spill."

Oh, why not. I give Rhonda all the latest and greatest, telling her about my broken nose, my broken relationship, Susie Homemaker, or as I'm referring to her now, Susie Home Wrecker, the photo shoot, Jocelyn and Mikayla's dramas, and Justice and Susie Home Wrecker's temporary relocation to Iowa.

"Honey, I didn't get a buzz off my wine, but I'm buzzed off that story! If that isn't something! But what I want to know is, what makes this Justice guy worth it? I mean, what's the big deal? From what I can tell, you're a catch! Make him catch you. Make him jealous. Or make him work for it. For that matter, leave him in the dust. Start over completely. You're young. You have your whole life ahead of you!"

What Rhonda doesn't know is that Justice *is* worth it. All the things he's done for me over the years, all the memories we've created together, do I want to leave that behind and start over? Evidence of Justice's love for me is everywhere in my life. I glance at the top-ten list on the bed. Lenny seems to have taken an interest in destroying said evidence, or at least tampering with it; he's pouncing on the list and batting at the edges. When I try to take it away, he rolls onto his back on top of it, his four legs pointing up into the air. Just try to get it now, I dare you, his green eyes say.

"Moving on doesn't feel like a viable option right now," I tell her.

"I totally understand and respect that! This is love, after all, right? You can't turn it on and off. I want you to call me again in a week or so, give me the updates."

"It feels like I'm using you as a therapist."

"Use me all you want, honey! You are fascinating! And best of all, I don't have to worry about predicting your future. I get to watch it unfold."

While I'm saying good-bye to my new wannabe psychic friend and promising that, yes, I will call her again to let her know how it turns out, the other line beeps. I rush Rhonda off and take the other call.

"Holy. Shitty. Balls. How come you didn't call me sooner, as in when it happened!"

She must have gotten my voice mail. I called Caprice yesterday and left three long-winded messages (I had to keep calling back because I'd exceeded the time limit) explaining what's happened since last week. "I've kind of been busy dealing with the drama of it all."

"You okay?" she inquires gently. "I know how you get. You're probably running yourself into the ground, aren't you?"

Caprice knows that my appetite for motion increases exponentially when I'm stressed and broken-hearted. "I think I've run a total of three hundred miles since last Saturday."

She exhales a giant puff of air. "Do you want to talk about it?"

"I'm all talked out. Just got off the phone with Rhonda Riddle."

"Who?"

"My not-so-psychic friend."

Displeased, Caprice yowls. "You're calling her and not me!"

"Don't be jealous. It's not attractive. I did call you, remember? You were indisposed."

"Well, I'm available now. Though I'm not just returning your call . . . ," she says with an air of mystery.

"What's going on?"

"I have an interesting, attractive proposition for you."

CHAPTER NINE

October 1998

"How about in the pasture, next to the cows," suggests Trina, glancing at our clipboard and then over to the split-rail fence and the field beyond, where Holsteins are grazing peacefully on this unseasonably warm October day. "That's the only location we haven't done yet."

"That's on purpose. It has to be last, because chances are, they're going to step in a cow pie or two."

She taps the pen against her lips, which are frosted in a milky shade of pink. Confused, she scrunches up her face and looks at me. "There are pies out there?"

"Cow pie means cow shit," I translate.

"No way!"

How this little tidbit of knowledge has escaped Trina, as long as she's worked at Schaeffer Dairy, I'm not sure.

"Let's take five, people!" yells the bubbly, dreadlocked Van Morrison.

For the past two hours she's been snapping pictures of Justice and Mikayla at the beautiful Schaeffer homestead, an ideal location.

Farmer Justice, wearing crisp blue jeans and a gray, blue, and white plaid flannel, and belle Mikayla, wearing a clingy denim dress that displays her generous "cow udders"—her words, not mine—have had their photo taken in various locations: in front of Samson and Jenny's three-story restored farmhouse, which was once featured in a country magazine spread, next to the pristine cherry-red barn, sitting together on top of stacked hay bales, and in front of the split-rail fence. Mikayla's in her heyday, and Justice looks like he's been dragged through the hay.

Shoulders sagging and a frown on his face, he walks over and grabs a water bottle off the refreshment table. "I'm trying to be a good sport about all of this." He twists off the top and guzzles. "But are we done yet?"

"Only another hour or so," Van Morrison responds, adjusting the settings on her camera.

He gives me a despairing look. "This is humiliating. I had to hold a pitchfork."

"Come on, you love a good Kodak moment," I tease. "Besides, as memory serves, you're good with a pitchfork."

His lips curl into a sly smile. "I do have a history with them, don't I?"

He's referring to a homecoming night three years ago. While everyone was in front of the bonfire, Justice and I slunk off to the barn. In the middle of our up-against-the-barn-wall make-out session, I accidentally kicked over a tall pitchfork next to us. Having some uncanny sense that it was about to fall, Justice stuck his arm out to the side and caught it while we were still lip-locked, our eyes closed. When I heard the handle hit his palm, I opened my eyes, laughed disbelievingly, and told him it must be his barn-cat reflexes kicking in.

Trina looks from Justice back to me. "Come on, a pitchfork story? What happened?"

Justice grins at me. "I never kiss and tell."

I laugh. Things have been fresh and light between us today, all because Susie Homemaker is missing in action. It's much better when I have him to myself, and tonight at the homecoming football game, I plan on making it a homecoming for Justice and me as well. Or at least I'm going to try. It's my last shot before he leaves for Iowa City.

"Justice, we need you over here!" yells Mikayla. Totally in her element, she's sitting at the makeshift makeup station on the other side of the barn, conferring with Van about the next series of shots.

Jeremy, proud husband, stands off to the side, watching every move his wife makes. Mikayla has been extra sweet to him. I hope she doesn't run out of sugar, because poor Jeremy doesn't know how sour things might get.

"I never thought I would be forced to wear lipstick for my job," Justice laments.

"It's a business casual look," I joke.

"Justice!" Mikayla beckons him impatiently again.

"Duty calls," he says.

"Or lipstick calls."

When he walks away, Trina sidles up to me. "What happened between you two? What's going on?"

"What do you mean? Nothing's going on."

"Come on! He's acting like you never even broke up."

"It helps when Susie Homemaker isn't around."

"Oh, yeah." Trina glances over at the refreshment table. "But it was super nice of her to make those pumpkin bars, wasn't it?"

"Super-duper nice," I respond sarcastically.

Van Morrison claps her hands. "Okay, people, let's head out to the field and pray we don't step in cow shit."

Mikayla bends over to put on rubber galoshes, and Jeremy rushes to her side, takes her hand, and helps her step into them.

Trina grabs one of Susan's pumpkin bars and stuffs it in her mouth. She's chewing and moaning with pleasure. Must everyone do that when they're eating Susan's baked goods? Spectacular. Now my mouth is watering. I pluck a celery stalk from the vegetable tray and stick it in my mouth to try and staunch my drooling. Trina grabs another pumpkin bar.

Are they that irresistible? I think back to her chocolate chip pumpkin bread and grimace. Yes, they probably are that good.

Taking three giant bites of celery, I chomp away until I forget all about Susan and her stupid pumpkin bars and her stupid, chipper comment at the morning meeting today.

When Samson announced that Justice and Susan would be leaving for Iowa City on Monday, Susan said, "Justice and I will make you proud, Samson. We make great partners."

To add insult to my injury, she winked at Justice. I wanted to take her cellophane-wrapped pumpkin bars and smash them in her face.

Trina and I are halfway to the field when she says, "Blaze broke up with me; he said I wasn't edgy enough."

"I'm sorry."

She sweeps her hands along her torso, showing herself off to me. "Can you believe he said that? I'm the edgiest person I know."

I take in her white shirt. Straight from 1985, it's draped with small decorative gold chains. Her clingy red pants highlight her ample bottom, making the lower portion of her body look like an upside-down exclamation point.

"You're better off without him."

She pushes air out her nostrils and wipes crumbs off her frosty lips with the back of her hand. "I wish I could find a good man for once. Someone with half a brain. Someone who would shower me with gifts and take an interest in me." Reaching into her pocket, she pulls out the frosty pink lipstick and smears on a thick layer.

Shower her with gifts? She needs Aris. Every time I open my door in the morning, he's left me something. A calculator with a rainbow-colored case—my rainbow-colored bike helmet tipped him off to my love of colorful things. A book titled *10,000 Jeopardy Questions*. A large coffee thermos. This morning, while I was in the shower, he delivered a dozen chocolate cake doughnuts with chocolate frosting, my favorite. Perhaps another bit of information gleaned from Grandma Betty? By the time I emerged from my bedroom and discovered the doughnuts, Mikayla had already eaten three of them. Two of them reappeared on the way to the shoot.

Trina and I lean on the fence and watch Van's two-man crew adjust the portable lighting.

"I might have just the guy for you," I say to her.

Intrigued, she inches closer. "Who? Who?"

"What you are you, an owl?" I deadpan.

"Hilarious."

"You left yourself wide open with that one."

Resting the clipboard on the fence, she frowns. "You don't have anyone in mind."

"I do, actually."

"Then introduce me to him."

"I'll work on it. I'm not sure he's the blind-date kind of guy."

She considers this and then smiles smugly. "I might not need an introduction. Remember Peter Frawley, the photographer? We're going out tonight."

"You are aware that he's gay."

Pursing her lips, she shakes her head. "You are aware that you aren't funny, right? I called Peter last night after Blaze dumped me, and he said that he's going to take me to an eighties dance club. He said he'll find me a man."

"Will this man be straight?"

"Of course! I mean . . . probably. In case he isn't, maybe you could set me up with the guy you have in mind."

Van Morrison stands in the field pointing to a cow that looks due for a milking. "Guys, you're going to need to get a little closer to that big girl. I want her in the background and to the side." She lowers her camera. "Justice, would it kill you to look like you're in love with Mikayla?"

"Actually, it just might," he responds.

Mikayla sneers at him. "That's not very nice."

"Think about someone you love," Van encourages.

When she says this, his eyes automatically seek me out. Victory!

We share a private Justice and Cane kind of smile. My heart skips out of my chest and across the field.

"That's more like it!" Van exclaims and snaps away.

Trina nudges me. "You guys are back together or something, aren't you?"

"Or something." I smile.

The photo shoot wraps up two hours later. Trina, who's meeting Peter for drinks, leaves. Justice, Jeremy, Mikayla, and I huddle next to the refreshment table, where Justice eats two pumpkin bars. At least he doesn't moan. I should have made some chocolate chip cookies for him. Side by side, would he choose the pumpkin bar or the cookie?

Jeremy zips up his sweatshirt. "Since we all plan on going to the game tonight, what's the use in taking more than one car? I'll drive everyone.

Justice and I can swing by and get you girls, maybe around six? Sound good?"

Mikayla smiles. "Sure."

"I don't think that's going to work." Justice looks at Jeremy. "I'll drive separately."

Separately? I've heard this song and dance before, and nothing good can come of it. Last time he pulled this, he dumped me. My heart, which has been busy skipping across the fields, comes to a screeching halt. "Why?"

"I'm bringing a friend."

Before I have a chance to ask who, Jenny Ryanne Schaeffer crashes our small gathering, gives her son a hug, and kisses her daughter-in-law on the cheek.

"My boy married the most gorgeous woman, and I can't wait to see how the photos turn out," she says.

Jeremy beams at his wife. "I think we'll have a hard time picking just one."

"I bet, I bet." Looking distracted and not at all like her usual focused self, Jenny's eyes land on me. "Cane, I need to talk to you right now."

"Sure."

Jenny spins on her heels and walks toward Samson's office at the back of the barn, and Mikayla gives me a what's-that-about? look.

I shrug and follow her down the hall. When I step into the office, she closes the door and takes a shaky breath. She tugs on the bottom of her long-sleeve shirt, which displays a giant, bejeweled pumpkin in the middle. "I know that you and I have never been the best of friends, and I still don't necessarily approve of you. Not after how you handled things with my nephew. Not after how you handled things with Jocelyn this past summer. Certainly not now, after you've been allowing Mikayla to hide out at your apartment and not telling Jeremy where she's been all this time. You make everything harder for people. What's most disturbing is that you seem to love it."

"Did you call me in here for a lecture?" I place my hand on the doorknob. "Because if that' the case, I'm not going to stick around. I think you've made it abundantly clear how you feel about me and—"

"Jocelyn is sexually active," she interrupts. She looks stricken. "I know it. You know it."

My hand drops from the doorknob. So that's what this is about. Jocelyn finally spilled the beans, and Jelly Roll's angry at me for not telling. She probably thinks I enjoyed withholding this information. "I told Jocelyn that she had to tell you and Samson, and if she didn't, I was going to speak with you both and tell you what happened."

Shock flashes across her face. "What? What's going on? What are you talking about? What happened?"

She'd been bluffing? Spectacular. Now I've betrayed myself and Jocelyn and ticked off her mother, who's so mad she's foaming at the mouth.

"She hasn't talked to you yet?" I ask meekly, trying to ascertain what she does or doesn't know.

Jenny might be standing still, but her body jiggles with fury. Her triple chin flushes, and the vein that runs near her temple looks close to bursting. "I swear to God, Cane, if you don't tell me this minute what's going on with my daughter, I will snap your neck like a twig!"

"Jocelyn came to me in confidence. She asked me to give her time, and I love her, so I'm respecting her wishes. She will talk to you. I know she will. If she doesn't, then I'll come forward."

"Do you think this is some kind of game? This is my child! I have a right to know, especially if she's in danger."

Whatever I say or do can and will be used against me; that's how Jenny operates. "Talk to your daughter."

"You think I haven't tried? It's all I've been doing!" Narrowing her eyes, Jenny advances on me and pushes her pointed orange fingernail into my chest. "I was right. You love making things harder for people. Tell me this instant what's going on with my daughter."

I take a giant step back, freeing myself from her fingernail blade. "I don't enjoy this at all."

"Why did she tell you what's going on with her, and not me?" Enraged and confused, Jenny throws her arms out to the side. "Why?"

Because you would have reacted like this, or worse. Because she still hates you for what you did to this family. I could say any one of a hundred malicious things, but dishing out hate would be cruel and unusual punishment for a woman who's clearly devastated. I may love Jocelyn, but it doesn't even come close to how much Jenny loves her. "Jocelyn loves you more than me, Jenny—that's why she came to me first. She's afraid of hurting you. She's ashamed."

Jenny's anger fades, and I see it for what is was, nothing but a mask for her fear. "I want to help her." Her eyes find mine. "I want her to let me help her."

CHAPTER TEN

While Jeremy drives around looking for a parking space, Mikayla and I pay for tickets and walk through the entrance. Once we're in, my eyes scan the throngs of Savage High students and parents, hoping to spot Jocelyn, who called to tell me she would be waiting somewhere behind the bleachers.

"Cane Kallevik!" Aris waves his girly arms in the air. "I'm over here!" he announces with such enthusiasm every person within a fifty-foot radius turns to look at him and then me.

What's he doing here?

He's stationed in front of the concession stand, but now that he's spotted me he's on the move, doing this weird shuffling, jogging thing. His head goes side to side like one of those bobbleheads. No wonder he doesn't want to run—he looks ridiculous. He's staring me down with an intense look on his face, as if he's trying to figure out if I'm real or merely an apparition.

133

Mikayla, who's been fighting the urge to puke yet again, thanks to downing three more of my chocolate doughnuts in the car on the way here, burps and then whispers disbelievingly out of the side of her mouth. "You invited him?"

"Absolutely—I'm totally hot for him. Move over, Justice, I'm in love with Aristotle. No, I did not invite him," I say under my breath. "I very explicitly told him I was busy Friday night and that I was going to the homecoming game. Alone."

"Well"—Mikayla's eyebrows shoot skyward—"it's a good thing he's here."

"Why?"

"Because you're going to need him," she says, her eyes traveling to the entrance. "Look what Justice dragged to the game."

Turning, I spot her. Susie Homemaker is the friend he was referring to earlier? This night keeps getting better and better. "So that's why he had to drive separately—so he could pick up his date."

"God." Mikayla squints her eyes as she assesses my nemesis. "She does look like a perky Disney—"

Before she can finish, graceless Aris trips and nose-plants right in front of us. He's sprawled out at my feet.

"Aris, are you okay?" Mikayla and I reach down at the same time and offer him our hands.

When he removes his face from the gravel, it's clear that he isn't okay. His top lip is split open, and blood trickles from his nostrils. Bloody noses are all the rage lately.

Embarrassed, he waves away our hands and scrambles to his feet. Pressing his hand against his mouth, he blushes. "That's why I don't go running."

"Do you have any tissues?" I ask Mikayla.

She digs in her pockets. "Nada. Maybe Jeremy has some in the car, I could go see."

"No, no, no. I'm perfectly fine." Aris pulls his hand away from his swollen, bloody lip and smiles, which only causes it to bleed more.

"You're not. We should get you to a first aid tent." I unwind the red scarf from around my neck, the one that Grandma knitted for me back when I was in high school. "Here, use this." I hand it to him.

"Cane Kallevik, I'm not going to ruin your scarf."

"I insist." Before he can protest again, I gently press the scarf against his mouth and nose. "It will help stop the bleeding, and it's red, so it's a win-win."

"I told you I was a klutz." He removes the scarf long enough to smile self-deprecatingly. "Every time I try to run, something like this happens."

"I don't think it would be a bad idea if the paramedics had a look," I suggest. "Just to be sure it's not broken."

Mikayla, who doesn't do well with blood, turns away from us and takes short, shallow breaths through her mouth. "I'm going to puke."

"I didn't break it. I don't need paramedics," Aris says, his voice muffled.

Mikayla grabs hold of my shoulder and clutches her stomach. "Oh, those doughnuts," she moans.

"Keep breathing through your nose."

By this time Jeremy walks over with an armful of blankets. Mikayla releases her talon-like grip on my shoulder and leans against Jeremy. He kisses the top of her head. "What's wrong?"

She puts a fist against her mouth and merely shakes her head.

"She ate too many doughnuts," I explain.

"Let's go sit down," Jeremy says. "I can get you some water or something."

135

"I'm Aris." Aris, scarf pressed awkwardly to his face, sticks his hand toward Jeremy, and Jeremy shakes it.

"Oh, sorry," I say. "I should have introduced you. Aris, Jeremy, Jeremy, Aris."

"Nice to meet you, man," says Jeremy.

Justice and Susan have spotted us and made their way over. Hooray. One big happy gathering. I give Justice the stink eye, but he's too busy dodging my stare to notice.

"Aris! I didn't expect to see you here!" calls out Susan in her singsong way.

"Cane Kallevik invited me," he says proudly.

So not true; I merely mentioned that I couldn't take the train with him because I was going to the homecoming game alone. How he interpreted this as an invite, I don't know. The more pressing issue at hand: How does he know Susie Homemaker? I look from Aris to Susan and back again.

Wait a minute. They have the same Joker smile. The same wavy brown hair. There's something similar in the shape of their eyes. What a small, tragic, humorless world.

"Is this. . . are you related to her?" I ask Aris, pointing at Susan, not caring that I sound rude and accusatory, like he's committed a crime by sharing DNA with her.

"Yes." Aris smiles. "She's my sister. I mentioned that she worked for Schaeffer Dairy, didn't I?"

"No, actually. I would have remembered."

Aris scratches his head. "Huh. I thought I did."

"Yes, I'm his older sister," chirps Susan, giving her brother an adoring look. "Oh, my gosh! Wait a minute. Cane isn't your new neighbor, is she? The one you you've been talking about nonstop!"

"She is," confirms Aris bashfully.

"Isn't this a wonderful coincidence," I remark with a dollop of cynicism.

Mikayla seems suddenly cured of her stomachache. She scowls at Justice and then looks Susan up and down disapprovingly. "Who are you, exactly?"

"My manners!" Susan says, appearing contrite. "I'm Susan. I work at Schaeffer Dairy, and you must be Mikayla, right? I've seen your pictures in magazines. You are very beautiful! It's simply wonderful that you're helping us with this new ad campaign. I'm sure the pictures you took with Justice today will be marvelous."

"Uh-huh." Mikayla nods. "Why did Justice give you a ride tonight? You couldn't drive yourself? Broken leg?"

I adore my best friend right now, but Justice doesn't seem to share my sentiment.

He gives her a stern look. "Mikayla, enough."

"What?" I fix my eyes on Justice. "She only wants an explanation, and so do I, as a matter of fact."

Susan, who is immune to all things negative, or at least pretends to be, smiles amiably. "Justice mentioned the game, and I rather rudely invited myself. My car is getting serviced before we leave for Iowa. He offered to give me a ride."

"How sweet of him," I remark sarcastically.

Mikayla gives Susan her infamous razor smile, the one that can make men and women beg for mercy. "Susan, you know that Justice worships Cane. He's head over heels in love with her. Lots of history there. Lots of future, too."

Have I mentioned how much I love Mikayla right now? I forgive her for kissing Justice last spring, for thinking she was in love with him, and for making me think she was in love with him, and for puking all over my apartment and Lenny. I also forgive her for eating my doughnuts.

Susan laughs much too zealously. Her eyelids flutter, working overtime like a hummingbird's wings, and she says, "That's great-it really is. Justice and I are just good friends."

Methinks she doth blink too much. Not for a minute does she think it's great that Justice and I have history and future. She may claim to be good friends with him, but obviously she wants more.

Mikayla's eyes find mine. Yeah, right, she says, without saying a word.

Jeremy, who's very much like his father, Samson, uncomfortable with confrontation of any sort, takes a step back, tugging on his wife's hand. "Why don't we go find a place to sit?"

"When things are just starting to get interesting?" Mikayla stands up straighter. "I don't think so."

Susan inspects my bloodied scarf, which is secured around her brother's face. "Aris, are you okay?" she asks, taking a closer look. "What happened?"

He shrugs. "I tried to run. It didn't work out well."

"It never does. You should know better," she chides gently.

Everyone stands still for a minute looking at each other, unsure of the next move, and then Justice, the polite peacemaker, says, "I never introduced myself. I'm Justice." He shakes hands with Aris. "It's nice to meet you."

Aris nods. "Likewise."

"The parade is starting soon," suggests Justice. "I'm sure the bleachers are filling up. We should all sit together."

"That would be wonderful! And"—Susan ramps up her voice like she's trying to entice a group of toddlers—"I brought snacks with."

Mikayla catches my eye and pokes her tongue out of the corner of her mouth like she wants to die. "Goody," she mumbles with zero enthusiasm.

Aris, however, is obviously thrilled. "Did you make lemon bars?"

"As a matter of fact, I did."

Aris looks at me. "Her lemon bars are out of this world! You have to try one."

If Aris eats one and moans with pleasure, I will consider that incest.

"I also made chocolate chip cookies without nuts," Susan tweets in her bird voice, smiling up at Justice. "They're right in here!" She holds up her oversize, authentic Coach bag, decorated with at least a thousand Cs.

I can only think of one C-word right now, and it certainly isn't Coach. "You made chocolate chip cookies without nuts?" I ask.

She shrugs. "I know that Justice doesn't like nuts."

I give her a pointed look. "You're right, he doesn't. You might want to keep that in mind."

My clever insult earns me a frown from Justice. Aris and Susan, cut from the same cheerful cloth, remain clueless, Mikayla guffaws, and poor Jeremy doesn't know what to make of this whole mess.

Justice clears his throat and stuffs his hands in his faded, worn red-and-white Savage High sweatshirt, the same one I've worn on many cool, autumn nights. "Jeremy, Aris, and I will go buy some drinks. Why don't you girls go find us a seat, and we'll meet you in there."

You girls? Like Mikayla, Susan, and I are best friends?

"What do you want, Cane Kallevik? My treat. Hot chocolate? Pepsi? Water?" Aris places his hand solicitously on my arm.

This is the direction my life has taken. I'm in the middle of the ultimate sibling swap. Aris is hot for me; Susan is hot for Justice.

"That's a fantastic idea." Susan hoists her Coach bag up on her shoulder over her fashionable cashmere wrap.

I've had enough of Justice's and Susan's chummy let's-all-be friends attitude. Mikayla isn't the only one who feels nauseous. I'm about to hurl all over Susan's impractical high-heeled leather boots, which look even more expensive than the Coach bag.

I imitate Susan's sunny smile. "Drinks? Lemon bars? Chocolate chip cookies sans nuts? Sitting together in the bleachers? Wow! Sounds like great fun, but I'm going to pass. I made plans to meet up with Jocelyn."

"Jeremy and I are going to find seats. Cane"—Mikayla pauses and gives Justice a nasty look—"you and Jocelyn can join us if you want."

"Sure. Maybe in a bit."

"Cane Kallevik, I'll come with you," Aris volunteers.

"Thanks, but I kind of want to hang out with Jocelyn alone."

His smile shrinks at the speed of light. "Um, okay."

Susan, seeing her brother's crestfallen expression, cheers him up by pulling the lemon bars out of her C bag and handing him one.

Before Aris chomps down and starts moaning, a sound I don't think I can tolerate right now, I turn on my heels and walk away as fast as possible. Not fast enough, though: out of the corner of my eye, I see Susie Home Wrecker smiling like a fiend as she loops her arm through her good friend's arm and leans into his bicep.

Justice wants space, time to think, time to make sure I won't run away. What a crock. He broke up with me so that he could pursue what he wanted without feeling guilty.

I'm sick and tired of my life being all about him. I've been orbiting around him, the center of my universe, for six years. It worked so well for so long, but it's not working anymore. It hasn't been for months.

Peter "Fishnet Stockings" Frawley might have been onto something; maybe I *am* giving off a starved-kitten vibe. Pathetic is something I definitely don't want to be, but I'm fearful that's what I've become.

If I stick around, will it get worse? I don't have to stay. I have a clearly defined and lucrative escape route. When Caprice called the other night, she made me a sweet offer, one that I'm not sure I want to refuse.

"We're expanding," Caprice informed me. "Maid Hot isn't only hiring beautiful women; we're also hiring hot men. I figure, why not exploit both sexes? Equal opportunity. There are plenty of young professional women, stay-at-home moms, and even old gals eager for beautiful males to clean their houses. Great things are happening businesswise, but the problem is, Nikeo's jumping ship."

"Why? I thought everything was going great."

"It was, but all of a sudden he has a music career. Some industry guy heard him sing this past July at Briar Days, and was very impressed. Impressed enough to offer him a contract with his label, Star Records. Nikeo signed on the dotted line. Got an advance. A manager. A bunch of gigs lined up across the country. It kind of came out of nowhere."

Having seen Nikeo perform several times, I know what an exceptional talent he is. He has star quality. When he plays to a crowd, he owns it. "I can totally see him in the role of rock star, but talk about happening fast."

"That's how it is in this industry—at least, that's what Nikeo says. Things happen quickly or not at all. He's actually in Chicago right now—he's going to be playing at a bunch of places. He hasn't by chance stopped by, has he?"

"Is he planning to?" My heart, the truest barometer for emotion, knocked against my ribs, surprising me. Do I still have feelings for him, or is it that we never had proper closure?

"I gave him your address—he mentioned that he might. Be prepared."

At this news, I started clumsily braiding my hair with one hand. Nikeo and I have a kind of combustible chemistry that works for us and against us—one minute we want to rip each other's clothes off, the next minute we want to beat each other senseless. In my current state of mind, if he shows up on my doorstep, I don't think I'll feel much like throwing punches.

"What am I going to do if he comes over?"

"You'll figure it out if it happens. But this phone call isn't about Nikeo, it's about how I need to replace him. Frankly, I can't keep the company thriving with him gone, especially now that I've decided to hire man candy. I need you on board. You're a genius when it comes to marketing. Whatever you're making at Schaeffer Dairy, I'll double it, and not only that, but you'll get bonuses every quarter depending on revenue."

"I can't," I responded immediately. "With all the things going on with Justice—"

"Holy. Balls. Are you listening to yourself right now? Stop making your life about Justice. Make it about yourself. I'm giving you one month to think it over. I don't want an answer until then, unless it's yes."

Now, stewing about my current predicament and my pathetic state, I mull over Caprice's offer yet again. New job. New state. New life. No confusion. No drama. No Justice.

No Justice.

That's the part that gets me every time. If I went through with it and left, though, I wouldn't be pathetic anymore. I'd be independent. Courageous. Bold. Fearless. Those adjectives are infinitely more appealing.

Weaving my way through throngs of students, I spy Jocelyn standing next to the fence that surrounds the track and football field. She's alone, nibbling on her lip and furtively watching the group of varsity cheerleaders, who are dancing around their float.

"Jocelyn!" I call.

Turning, she waves and smiles halfheartedly.

"I thought you wouldn't come," she says as I walk over.

"Why would you think that? You asked me to be here, I'm here. So are Mikayla, Jeremy, and Justice." I incline my head toward the bleachers. "They're somewhere in the stands. Want to go over and find them?" I'm hoping she doesn't want to sit next to her older cousin, because that would require me to beat my pride into oblivion, tuck my tail between my legs, and possibly go suck on a lemon bar. But I would do it. That's how much I love her.

"I don't want to be around anyone." She pulls a Savage High stocking hat out of her pocket and yanks it down over her beautiful spiral-curled hair. "I'm staying right here." She continues chewing on her bottom lip, which is raw and chapped.

She appears so troubled and anxious that I fear that Jenny may have confronted her or said something. "What's wrong?" I ask tentatively.

Her eyes dart to the cheerleaders. "There's Deanna," she says, pointing to a petite, bronzed brunette with her hair in pigtails and sparkly red and white dots on her cheeks.

"Is she still being nice to you?"

Jocelyn shrugs as she studies the rows of floats, many of which have the phrase "Maul the Hawks" splashed across the front. "She said to make sure that I sat in the front row of the bleachers, because she wanted to wave to me and so did all her friends."

"But you're out here."

Jocelyn's blue eyes tear up as she looks at me. "I don't trust her."

That makes two of us. I glance over at Deanna and her followers, who are laughing too loudly and practicing their backflips and cheers. Every so often one of them looks over here, smiles, and waves.

"You think she's going to do something?"

Jocelyn tucks her head into her neck. Taking a deep breath, she drags one of her Adidas sneakers through the gravel. "Yes, and I think it's going to be bad." A shadow of despair flashes across her face. Her eyes squish together at the edges.

"How do you know? Did someone say something?"

"Cane"—she says my name like it's the heaviest thing in the world—"I just know, okay?"

A high yelp sounds from the direction of the cheerleader float. Jocelyn and I glance over at the same time and catch Deanna midair, her legs split and her arms raised. If she does anything to hurt Jocelyn, I'll make sure those legs stay permanently split.

Mr. Pete Peterson, the retired athletic director who's been announcing football games for what seems like the past hundred years, comes over the speakers. "Welcome to the Savage High homecoming game, where the Savage Lions take on the South Clinton Hawks in what's sure to be an incredible matchup. We're about forty minutes to game time, and until then, we have a fantastic pregame parade planned. Let's kick it off!"

Savage High used to have the parade downtown, but given that downtown is more than eight miles from the high school, it didn't make sense. A decade ago the school decided the parade should be at the school, before the game. All the floats, decorated cars, school teams, clubs, and groups march proudly around the high school track, making for a convenient and very brief procession that ends right where it began and gives everyone ample time to get back to the stands to enjoy the game.

The large gate at the back of the football field swings open. The high school band, playing loudly and slightly off rhythm, marches in, numerous floats behind them.

"I don't see the dairy float," I say, craning my neck to see if I can spot it at the end of the lineup. Because Samson donates an exorbitant amount of money to Savage High each year, he and Jenny are always in the parade, riding atop a magnificent Schaeffer Dairy float that's constructed by the Schaeffer family and takes nearly a month to complete. Two years ago Justice and I spent hours finishing a float that featured a very realistic cone, at the top of which were two oversize bean bags that resembled heaps of ice cream, on which Samson and Jenny sat.

"Dad said he didn't feel like it this year. He said it was too much work." She pushes her weight against the fence and briefly looks at me. "But you know that's not the real reason."

Samson likes to keep his private life private, but that's been impossible as of late. With his wife's affair the tabloid sensation of Savage, he's been avoiding all things social.

"Is he here?" I ask.

"I'm not sure. I think so. Mom stayed home with my brothers. They wanted to help get ready for the bonfire."

The band passes us by, and the varsity cheerleader float, pulled by one of the football player's pickup trucks, is next in line. Deanna and her sparkly-cheeked crew are tumbling, clapping, and shouting cheers at an earsplitting volume, thanks to their megaphones.

At regular intervals they point to the middle of their float, which features a very tall poster board shrouded in a velvety red blanket.

As the float rolls by, Deanna shouts a greeting at Jocelyn and winks, but there's nothing friendly about the gesture. She smiles menacingly, followed by an I'm-going-to-get-you sneer that makes the hairs on my neck prickle. Her fellow cheerleaders, though busy whooping it up with the crowd, are sneaking looks at both Deanna and Jocelyn.

I don't know what Deanna has up those tight cheerleading sleeves of hers, but I'm positive I'm not going to like it.

Jocelyn is about to raise her hand to wave at Deanna, but I grab her wrist and keep it anchored to the top of the fence. "She's toying with you."

Jocelyn swings her eyes to mine, and we both watch as the cheerleader float passes, tracking the procession not just with our eyes but also with our feet. Automatically, as if we instinctively know something is about to go very wrong and we need to prevent it, we walk briskly along the fence line, keeping up with the float and making our way toward the arched side entrance to the bleachers.

"There you are!" Justice grins like all is right in his world as he walks over to us. "I've been looking all over for you both. Susan drove Aris home—his nose started bleeding again and wouldn't stop. Where are you two headed?"

With building dread, I note the way that the first few rows of bleachers, all seniors, are dividing their attention between the cheerleader float and Jocelyn. They know right where she is, and their eyes bounce from her to the float. As suddenly as we began advancing toward the bleachers, we stop, our weight poised on the tips of our toes.

"Would you look at that, folks! The varsity cheerleaders always outdo themselves. The streamers and artwork are something else," Pete Peterson remarks. "Flying the red and white school colors. It looks like they're about to unveil something right now. Want to place any bets on what it might be?"

Justice takes note of our strained faces. "What's wrong? Did something happen?"

As soon as he says this, Deanna and one of her friends remove the red velvet blanket with dramatic flair.

A confused, rippling wave of silence sweeps over the crowd, starting at one end and making its way down to the other.

Pete Peterson guffaws, splitting the quiet right in half. "Well—that's the way to do it girls—distract the other team with a glossy poster of a beautiful girl, and we'll be sure to win."

The crowd, most notably the students, cheer and holler and clamor to their feet, standing on the metal bleachers, while the parents filling the other half of the bleachers cross their arms and frown, not looking too pleased.

Many of those students are looking boldly at Jocelyn now, laughing, pointing, and jeering. We're close enough to hear what they're saying.

"It's her, Jocelyn Schaeffer! I told you that she really did it. It's true!"

Alarmed, I reach out and take Jocelyn by the elbow, ready to pull her away from all of this. She stares blankly at the poster; I'm not sure it's sunk in for her yet.

It has, however, sunk in for Justice, who stares in horror at the poster. It features a color photograph of a girl shown from the neck down, standing provocatively, football tucked under her arm, wearing nothing but a lacy red bra and matching red underwear. The words "Let's Maul" run across the top of the overtly sexual poster. Though the girl's face and eyes aren't visible, it's obvious that it's Jocelyn; the pale pear-shaped body and long brown hair curled in signature tendrils betray her identity.

The wave of silence that overtook the crowd has become a riptide of chatter. In a matter of seconds, everyone will know who the Let's Maul poster girl is.

Jocelyn opens her mouth, and a strangled gasp comes out. Stumbling sideways, she falls into her cousin's chest. Justice wraps his arms protectively around her, already retreating.

"I'm getting her out of here now." He backs away and turns, sheltering her with his arms.

Holding my position a moment longer, my weight still balanced on my tiptoes, I mentally tick through my options. I could jump the fence, knock down the poster, and kick Deanna's cheerleader butt. Appealing in its own right, but it wouldn't work out in Jocelyn's favor, since it would only confirm that she is the poster girl.

No, I've got something better in mind. I look up at the skybox where Pete Peterson sits and hastily formulate a plan.

Spinning around, I follow Justice and Jocelyn back behind the

147

bleachers. We're practically running toward the exit. Jocelyn, tucked under Justice's arm, is crying violently but not making a sound.

"Take her home! I'll catch up with you in a minute!" I yell, stopping and staring up at the back of the bleacher structure, a monstrosity of metal that crisscrosses all the way up to the rear of the skybox. Ideally I would go around front, walk up the bleacher steps, and enter through the skybox door, but the crowd is too large. Besides, if I did it that way, the parade would already be over. Time is of the essence.

Out of the corner of my eye, I glimpse Samson, Jeremy, and Mikayla rounding the corner at the far end of the bleachers.

"Justice!" Samson cries, stopping short and then immediately running toward his daughter.

Jocelyn releases her hold on Justice and enters the fold of her father's arms.

"It's going to be okay. Let's go home," Samson murmurs.

Jocelyn staggers alongside her father and out toward the parking lot.

Justice sees me eyeing the bleachers. "Don't do it! You'll hurt yourself!"

Smiling determinedly, I shake my head. "It's not me I'm going to hurt."

Justice, who doesn't like me taking chances, advances. He's about to reach out and grab me when Mikayla surges forward and snares him around his waist.

"Oh, no you don't! This isn't a Ferris wheel. She'll be fine." She winks at me. "Go for it!"

I'm already two rungs up when she says this.

"Cane! Don't!" Justice shouts.

No one can ever stop me once I've made up my mind. Putting my incomparable monkey skills to the test, I effortlessly scale the back of the bleachers, keeping my eyes trained on the back of the skybox, where the large sliding window happens to be open wide.

CHAPTER ELEVEN

We're sitting at the table in the Schaeffers' expansive dining room. Samson plunks a bottle of whiskey down in the center of the table; a man's man, Samson only drinks beer or expensive whiskey, no exceptions. Justice distributes shot glasses like he's dealing a hand of cards. Jeremy pours generously.

Justice, Samson, Jeremy, and I raise the small glasses in a toast of sorts and drain the amber liquid. I've never had the pleasure, or should I say the displeasure, of slamming a shot of whiskey.

Justice squeezes my shoulder. "You okay?"

I wipe my watering eyes and suppress another cough. "Not particularly."

"Round two," Samson states, already pouring.

I hold up my hands. "I'll pass."

"You should have another," encourages Jeremy. "You took a lot of heat tonight."

"Cane, I appreciate what you did." Samson throws back another shot. His tired eyes meet mine. "How you were treated by the security guard? It wasn't right."

I gingerly touch the inside of my wrists, which I'm sure will be as black and blue as my eyes were last week. "The guy thought I was a student."

Justice snorts and indulges in another shot himself. "I doubt he would have reacted much differently had he known you were an adult."

"He would have if he would have known you were a Schaeffer." Samson palms the whiskey bottle.

I'm not a Schaeffer—I'm not even sure I ever will be—but that doesn't matter to Samson. He's always considered me one of his own, and for this I'm grateful.

"Your wrists hurt, don't they?" Justice asks.

"Yes."

"I'll go get you something."

I'm about to tell him not to bother, that I should be getting back to the apartment, but he's already on his feet and headed toward the kitchen, where Jenny keeps one of the cabinets stocked with medication.

As it turns out, scaling the bleachers was the easy part—it's what came after that was tricky.

I climbed up without incident and pushed myself in through the open skybox. Pete Peterson, the principal of the school, the cross-country coach, and a few others were more than surprised by the intrusion—rendered speechless, in fact. It's not like I was a stranger; I'd been valedictorian of my high school class and over-involved in every sport and club. All of these men knew me, respected me, and even liked me. Most of them had presented me with an award at one time or another.

Mr. Wessels, the principal, tilted his head. "Cane? What are you doing here?"

He regarded me as if I had superpowers, as did the others. From their expressions, you'd think I'd not crawled through the window but just appeared out of thin air.

Using their astonishment to my advantage, I plucked the microphone from Pete's hand before their brains caught up with their vision.

Smiling innocently, I said, "This will take just a minute, promise."

Holding the microphone up to my mouth and ignoring my hammering heart and dry mouth, I leaned forward so that my upper body was just out the front window, my tiny butt positioned near Pete Peterson's face. In a booming, overconfident voice, I said, "Ladies and gentleman, I'd like to focus our attention back on the varsity cheerleader float. Why don't we give Deanna a round of applause for her bravery in displaying that poster of her nearly naked body!"

From my perch above the chaos, I witnessed Deanna whipping her head around in my direction, her eyes traveling upward, as she tried to figure out who was saying these things. The rest of the student body was confused as well, many of them turning and peering up at the skybox, trying to figure out who Pete's understudy was. I gave them a princess-type wave and then pointed at Deanna.

"That's right, ladies and gentlemen—that poster on display, the rather crude photo of the girl in the bra and panties, that's Deanna, captain of the cheerleading squad, the girl with the sparkly dots on her cheeks, the one who is putting her hands on her hips and glaring at me. It takes a lot of bravery and stupidity to do what she did. But after sending in a bunch of photos to *Playboy* and getting rejected, she did have extra photos on hand, so why not make a poster!"

"What do you think you're doing?" Mr. Wessels boomed, his voice amplified slightly by the microphone.

My time was almost up. Time to hammer the nails into Deanna's coffin. "She decided to put one of those photos to good use for homecoming! Wow, Deanna, how creative, how spectacular that you would be willing to display everything you have—and I do mean everything—to your community! If you get the chance, why don't all of you write Deanna's parents a short note, thanking her for her generosity in sharing her most private parts—"

Before I could finish, Mr. Wessels tore the microphone from my hand. I kind of jumped back, only to see glassy-eyed Pete Peterson still staring right at the spot where my butt had been. Good thing he was a horny old man. It had bought me some time on the microphone. He'd been too busy enjoying the view to try and stop me.

A morbidly obese security guard with limp, greasy hair and two missing bottom teeth took hold of my wrists. Too absorbed in making sure Deanna and the rest of her clan and the crowd had heard me loud and clear, I hadn't seen him coming through the door—he definitely hadn't come through the window. His slimy hands yanked on me. Since he outweighed me by at least a couple hundred pounds, he had a distinct advantage.

"Why did you do that?" my former track coach asked. "Bullying a high school student like that! That's not like you at all."

"Wait a minute! She's the bully, not—"

"Get her out of here!" yelled Pete Peterson, who had finally snapped out of his ogling-my-ass daze.

I wasn't going without a fight. I hooked my legs around the corner of the desk.

"Come on, now! Let go, or you're going to get suspended!" shouted the sweaty security guard.

His hands were like a pair of Chinese handcuffs. The harder I struggled, the tighter his grip became. My wrists were going to snap. I gave

152

him a dirty look. "I'm not a student."

He shrugged and pulled harder, becoming a huffy, puffy, sweaty mess. "Mr. Wessels"—I struggled to break free—"that poster is not Deanna. I was only trying to take attention away from what she's done. It's a picture of Jocelyn Schaeffer. Deanna didn't have permission to use it. She did it to bully Jocelyn. She needs to be held accountable."

Wessels told the security guard to release me, and when he did, I fell hard on my tailbone.

Narrowing his eyes, Wessels toyed with the end of his waxed mustache and glanced out the window, undoubtedly trying to see the float, which by now was out of sight. He looked back at me. "You're sure about this?"

"I'm positive. Ask any one of the students what's happened, and they'll tell you. Jocelyn doesn't deserve this. Deanna should be suspended."

Wessels held out his hand and helped me up off the floor. "You could have just talked to me about this matter in private. Instead you had to make a spectacle."

Valid point, but Deanna wouldn't care about a slap on the wrist by administration. She needed something louder and clearer, and my style is all about being loud and clear.

Justice returns from the kitchen and hands me water and two Advil. "This should help."

"Thanks."

He rubs my shoulders and kisses the top of my head. Too exhausted for relationship analysis, I let it go.

Jenny storms into the dining room, takes one look at the Maker's Mark bottle, and makes a sound of disgust. "You're all drinking?"

"You should have one, Mom," Jeremy says. "Have a seat."

"Whiskey won't fix this," she states, her eyes meeting mine, her gaze accusatory.

She hates me for not coming to her and Samson straightaway—she's made that more than clear. After we got home and Jocelyn told her parents what had happened, Jenny pulled me outside and verbally abused me for five minutes. I gave her free rein to do so because I knew that she was shattered, not only by what Jocelyn had done but also by what had happened this evening. I knew that the days, weeks, and months ahead were going to be one trial after another. I managed to keep my muzzle in place until Jenny told me that it was all my fault, that Jocelyn had done this because of my influence, at which point I unhooked the muzzle and attacked.

It's obvious from the way she's looking at me now that she hasn't gotten over what I said. I don't expect her to; you can't get over the truth. You have to accept it—but Jenny isn't good at accepting much of anything from me.

Samson rests his chin in his left palm and pours himself another shot. In a lazy, disinterested way, he raises his eyes to his wife and gives her a woeful look. "Nothing will fix this, Jenny. Not one thing."

In an instant, Jenny goes from enraged to forlorn. She turns her head toward the wall. Her mouth goes into a squiggly line as she struggles not to cry. Tugging on the bottom of her shirt, she looks at me. "Jocelyn wants to talk to you."

Samson nods, whether at me or the whiskey bottle, I'm not sure. I stand and leave the dining room. I'm almost at the top of the stairs when I hear Jenny say resentfully, "Mikayla's asleep on the couch? I can't believe she could sleep through something like this!"

Knocking once, I enter Jocelyn's room, a pink paradise replete with a white canopy bed. It belongs to someone younger and more innocent. Jocelyn has forfeited her innocence in the most tragic of ways.

Tucked under a sheet and lying on her side, she turns her head toward me. "It would be easier if I could just die."

"Don't say that." I close the door.

"If you did what I did, wouldn't you want to die?"

"Jocelyn, you're going to have to give it time."

"Time? I don't have time! I'm a senior." Angry now, she sits up. "I'll never live this down, not ever. I'll forever be known as the drunk girl who took ecstasy at the quarterback's party, stripped for him and his running-back friend, and then had sex with one of them while the other one took pictures. I can't live that down, especially not after tonight, when I was on an eight-foot poster board. I hate myself."

"Don't hate yourself—please don't."

"Too late."

I sit on the bed and take her hand in mine. "You're going to have to forgive yourself. You've been beating yourself up ever since this happened. What you did doesn't make you an outcast, and it doesn't make you worse than anyone else. Anyone could have gone down the path you did. I'm sure some of your classmates have been in a similar position—you just don't know about it. It happens all the time to people."

Pale and frantic, Jocelyn scoots up until her back is pressed against the headboard. She winds the sheet tightly in her hand. "Dad didn't even say a word to me. He could barely look me in the eye."

"Because he's shocked, that's all. He loves you. He hugged you after you told him."

At Jocelyn's request, I'd been in the room when she told her parents, and afterward, Samson hugged her and wouldn't let go. I think he'd been at a loss as to what else to do. He wasn't much for words when the waters were calm, and when the waters got choppy, or in this case unnavigable, he lost his ability to speak completely.

His wife, on the other hand, wouldn't shut up. Typical Jelly Roll, she was all business. The shell of the story that we'd heard from Jocelyn—how she'd been invited to popular quarterback Taryn's party, how she'd had one too many drinks, taken a hit of ecstasy, ended up in a room with Taryn and Colin, and had sex with Taryn—hadn't been enough to satisfy Jenny. She wanted the whole story. Like a one-woman firing squad, she shot questions point-blank at Jocelyn, who was too despondent to even form responses.

Stomping back and forth across the room, exuding rage with every step, Jenny asked, "How many drinks did you have? Where did you get the ecstasy? Who gave it to you? Have you ever had drugs before? Were both boys in the room the entire time? Are you sure it was consensual? Did he rape you? Who took the pictures? How did Deanna get a hold of them? Why? How could you have let this happen? Were you raised to behave like this? How could you have disgraced this family? How—"

"Enough!" Samson gave Jenny a look that could mortally wound, if not kill.

I'm glad he stopped his wife when he did, because I was about to punch her lights out after those last few questions. Don't throw stones when you live in a glass house—and Jenny was living in the gigantic, fragile glass house that she'd moved into as soon as she made the decision to fornicate with Mr. Dexter.

"Mom's taking me to the doctor tomorrow," Jocelyn mumbles. "If I'm . . . you know, mom says that I'm having an abortion."

"He used protection, right? You aren't. Don't worry about that."

She closes her eyes, and her head falls forward onto the crest of her knees. "I think he did, but I'm really not sure," she admits in the smallest of voices. "I can't remember a lot of it."

Startled by this admission, I get queasy. "Does your mom know about this detail?"

"She'll find out soon enough, won't she?" Jocelyn looks at me. "Justice told me what you did at the game. Thank you."

"I just hope it makes a difference."

"I don't know if it will. She already did what she wanted to do." Jocelyn pulls her frilly pink-and-white duvet up to her chin. "When I think back, it seems like it happened to me, not like I actually did it. It's like I was outside my body, watching it happen. I don't know how to live with what I did, and how to live with the fact that everyone knows."

"You aren't the only one who messed up here. Those boys are to blame as well, and they should be feeling just as much shame as, if not more, than you."

"But that's not how it works." She looks up at me. "Is it?"

After I kiss Jocelyn good night and tell her to get some rest, I go downstairs and find Mikayla waiting for me on the landing.

"We have to get out of here now," she hisses in my ear. "Jenny's on the warpath. She's been lecturing me on what an incompetent wife I am and how I'm making her son miserable by not staying with him. Then she brings up the fact that I haven't worked in months and wants to know why."

"You're surprised by this? She isn't in the best of moods."

"Jeremy's waiting in the car." She thrusts my coat into my arms. "Come on."

"Are you staying at the apartment, or are you going back to Chicago with him?"

"Don't you start! That's the same question Jenny asked me. It's late, and I'm exhausted. I invited Jeremy to spend the night at your place."

We're near the bottom step when Justice rounds the corner.

"How's Jocelyn?" he asks.

"Destroyed," I respond.

"I'm sure."

But he can't be sure. Not yet. He's only seen the poster; he hasn't heard the story that goes with it.

Behind us, the kitchen light turns on. Jenny throws open the dishwasher and turns on the faucet. Glowering, she looks over at us. "Why are you dallying? Jeremy has been out in the car for five minutes. It's rude to keep someone waiting. Besides"—pausing, she anxiously peers up the stairs past us—"I don't want you waking any of the younger kids. The last thing I need is for them to figure out what's going on tonight."

As if on cue, the youngest Schaeffer, Jade, who hasn't outgrown his obtrusive nose-picking habit, opens his bedroom door. "Hi, guys," he says, removing his finger from his nostril. "Can we have the bonfire now? Please?"

All of Jocelyn's younger siblings were devastated when Samson returned from the football game and banished them to their room, canceling the homecoming festivities.

"No bonfire, sorry, honey," Jenny tells her young son and then levels us with a nasty stare. "Everyone is leaving."

Mikayla looks at me one last time. "Hurry up." She bolts for the door.

"Let me drive you home," offers Justice.

"I'll ride with them," I say, already making my way to the door. He follows me outside.

"I want to take you home, Cane. I want to talk. I need to debrief after tonight, don't you? We could go grab an ice cream cone or maybe take the tractor out to the field and listen to some music. Have a drink? I'm leaving on Monday, and I don't know . . ." He shrugs. "I want to spend time with you."

Mikayla, who's sitting in the front seat of Jeremy's truck, wipes the fogged window with her hand and mouths "Hurry up" at me.

"You're the king of mixed messages, and frankly, I don't have the energy to translate. Susan might be up for the job, though."

He sighs. "I only brought her to the game because she's having a hard time lately—she just got out of a relationship. She asked about the game yesterday, and when I told her I was going, she invited herself."

That makes me feel fractionally better, but still. He could have told her that he was coming to the game with me. "She just got out of a relationship? You have so much in common. I bet you have lots to talk about."

"It's not like that," he insists sincerely.

Because there's not a dishonest bone in his body, I believe him. Or at least I want to believe him. "Why do you have to be her friend? She has her brother."

"Who's obviously very in love with you." He grins like it's some kind of joke.

"Exactly, and his sister is in love with you. Let's trade, shall we?"

"It's not like that."

"Not for you, maybe, but for Susan, it is like that. Trust me, she pictures herself with you."

Mikayla honks the horn, which prompts Jenny to open the door and glare at her. At the sight of her mother-in-law, Mikayla slinks down into her seat and turns toward Jeremy.

"If she honks that horn again, tell her she's not welcome back here!" Jenny yells and slams the door.

Through the window, I see Samson standing next to the kitchen island, holding a glass tumbler filled with Maker's Mark. When his wife walks in, he glances at her and walks out of the room.

Justice pulls his keys out of his pocket. "How about it?"

I nod toward the house. "I'm riding with Jeremy and Mikayla. I'm not making tonight about our little drama, because that would be incredibly stupid and selfish. Tonight is about Jocelyn and what happened to her. Stay here with your uncle. Keep his glass full of whiskey and see if you can get him to talk."

Chastened by this, he deposits his keys back in his pocket. "You're right. Can I see you tomorrow? We could spend the day together at our house."

Our house? That reference puts my already precarious emotions into a tailspin, and it's only a matter of seconds before I crash-land on my face and break my nose again. I don't know what Justice wants, or what he's trying to do. For that matter, I don't think he knows either. "You can't break up with me one week and ask me to come to *our house* the next." I look up into his aquamarine eyes. "I'll see you later."

"You're right," he mutters dejectedly and takes a step backward. "I'll go talk to Samson."

Before I change my mind and accept his invitation for a ride, I walk over to Jeremy's car. When I buckle myself in, I pull extra tight. Frankly, I don't trust myself to stay put.

Mikayla raises her butt off the seat and checks her reflection in the rearview mirror. She pops an Altoid in her mouth. "About time."

Jeremy pulls out onto the highway and flips on his high beams. "How's my sister?" he asks.

"Not good."

His jaw muscles tense. "What happened?" Jeremy asks.

"You honestly want me to tell you?"

"Not really. But I feel like I should know what she's up against so I can prepare myself."

I provide Jeremy and Mikayla with a rough outline of the events and omit the horrid details that only I know, details that Jocelyn hasn't even told her parents.

Jocelyn set herself up for disaster; the whole thing was her idea. Thoroughly drunk and high off the ecstasy that Taryn had given her, Jocelyn, feeling unnaturally invincible and bold, dragged Taryn and Colin into a room and locked the door. She did a strip tease for them, and when she finished, she took Taryn's football off his dresser and held it under her arm. She climbed up on the bed and danced for them, which I figure is when one of them took the pictures.

One of the boys, she couldn't remember which, dared her to sleep with one of them. Feeling euphoric and without inhibition, she pointed at Taryn and said, "You."

Colin may or may not have left the room—she couldn't remember. Days later, after her mind and body had recovered, as much as anyone can recover from something like that, she recalled that at one point Taryn had laughed cruelly, tossed the football up in the air, and said, "I had to go for the easy touchdown, even with a chunk like her."

The little I do share with Jeremy is enough to infuriate him. "I want to kill them," he growls.

Stunned, Mikayla exhales slowly. "Wow. I didn't think it was anything that bad. I never thought—" She shakes her head. "I mean, it's Jocelyn."

"I know," says Jeremy. "I can't believe it."

Obviously, I'm shocked by what's happened, but I was privy to Jocelyn's behavior this summer, so I'm not down for the count like everyone else. While staying with me in Colorado, Jocelyn escaped my watch one night and went to a party. After hitting the vodka hard, she put herself in a compromising position with Kevin, a slimy guy in his early twenties who wanted nothing more than to take advantage of her. Thank God I found her before anything serious happened.

But when I think back, I realize that something serious *did* happen. She started down a path of destruction that night, and instead of recognizing that and doing something proactive like calling her parents and getting them to pull her off that path and redirect her, I confidently handled it on my own. Looking at the situation Jocelyn is in now, I realize I made a huge mistake.

A couple hours ago, when Jenny and I were alone in the driveway, she accused me of being responsible for what had happened. "She idolizes you. It's because of you that she did this. You have no morals, no sense of right and wrong, and Jocelyn has followed your path!"

"My fault? Are you kidding me? This has nothing to do with me. It's all on you! She saw you pressed up against a chalkboard with Mr. Dexter at her school. How could you have let that happen? How could you have disgraced your family like that?" I said, intentionally asking the same questions she had asked her daughter. "I didn't ruin her. You did. And we both know it."

Looking miserable and ill, Jenny retreated to the house.

I felt victorious and justified at the time. Now? Not so much. Having picked apart the situation, I recognize my culpability. It's not about me being a poor moral example—it's about me keeping secrets that I shouldn't have kept.

We're nearly back to the apartment when Mikayla announces that she's starving and needs a shake from McDonald's, or she'll die.

Jeremy's jaw goes slack with disbelief. "A shake?"

In her former life Mikayla never touched sugar, fat, or anything with more than a few calories. Her lettuce-eating, binge-drinking days are long gone, and Jeremy doesn't know how long gone they are.

"Yes, a shake. A large vanilla shake with a cherry on top. Maybe chocolate. No, definitely vanilla."

Indecisiveness, another one of her adorable new qualities.

"Is that too much to ask?" she whines.

Most likely believing this is some kind of booby trap set by his model wife, he seeks my input. "She really wants a shake?" he asks me.

"Yes, she's being serious. Why don't you drop me back at the apartment, and you two go to the McDonald's in Clinton and get your shake with a cherry. Then maybe you could head back into the city and spend the night at your apartment."

Mikayla, who's obsessively adjusting the vents because she's cold one minute and hot the next, shoots me an impatient look. "No, we're staying at your place. I'm exhausted."

"Sleep in the car."

Jeremy pulls up to the curb in front of my apartment building.

Mikayla catches my eye as I'm exiting. "Leave the door open for us."

There's nothing I can do short of locking her and Jeremy out. I'm tempted, but I don't have it in me to be that cruel, at least not to Jeremy.

I'm digging in my coat pocket for my keys, listening to Lenny meow like crazy from inside the apartment, when Aris's door creaks open.

"Cane Kallevik! Hi there! Sorry I had to leave the game in such a hurry!"

"That's okay. You didn't miss much." Only Jocelyn being humiliated, and me over the loudspeaker seeking vindication, and then being escorted off the premises.

"Want to hang out for a bit?" He shuts his door and gives me the world's biggest grin. "Susan left me some of her lemon bars!" he exclaims with such fervor that you'd think he'd won the lottery.

Not only do Susan and Aris share the same extra-large mouth, but they also inherited the same annoyingly cheerful attitude. I smile at him with only an eighth of my face. "No, thanks. It's been a long night. How's your nose?"

Head bobbing, he moves down the hallway toward me so speedily that

I'm afraid it may end disastrously.

"Better, see?" He moves his head to the right and then the left so I can inspect. "Susan took your scarf home to wash it. She can get stains out of anything."

A whiz in the kitchen. A miracle worker in the laundry room. Big surprise. Before I can help it, my eighth of a smile transforms into a sarcastic grin. "Spectacular, but tell her that I don't want it back. She can throw it away." Or better yet, she can tie it around her neck. Really, really tightly.

"It's only ten," he announces, glancing at his watch. "Would you like to watch a movie? Or maybe you would be interested in helping me set up my train set. I've been working on it since I got home, and the tracks are giving me a bit of trouble. I could use an extra pair of hands."

"Aris, I would like to set you up with someone. A blind date. Would that be okay?"

This throws him far off his train tracks. He bobs his head as if I've smacked him with something. "But . . . what about us?"

"We're friends."

He reddens so fiercely that his blue-green calculator eyes tear up from the heat. "I thought we were more than that. We've been on dates together! We're an item. You asked me to the game. We've eaten takeout together and played games. I've brought you doughnuts. Coffee. You even introduced me to your ex-boyfriend ex-fiancé tonight! I don't understand!"

He may be great at math, but he's not so hot when it comes to the simple equations of relationship and life. With Aris, I can't beat around the bush; I'm going to have to burn it down. "It's not going to work out, Aris. I'm in love with Justice."

"But you aren't together anymore! That's what Susan says, and she loves him."

A low growl starts in the very back of my throat. I try to keep it in check, but it comes out anyway.

Confused by the sound, Aris sets his mouth into a concerned line. "What's wrong?"

Where do I begin? "I'm setting you up with my friend Trina. She's great."

"I don't know about that. I like you. A lot. What's Trina like? Does she like math? Does she like coffee?"

"She likes fries without ketchup, and she likes cartoons."

He frowns thoughtfully. "Interesting. I like both of those things as well."

"We'll talk about this later—got to go. Lenny needs to be fed."

Before Aris has a chance to get another word in edgewise, I unlock my door and step inside my apartment. I don't even have to close the door behind me because Lenny, green eyes narrowed accusingly, raises his paw to bat my leg, misses, and whacks the door with impressive strength. It shuts right in Aris's face.

I flip on the lights, noticing how my apartment no longer smells like Windex and bleach but rather cat poop. Sighing, I look at the litter box. I'm tired of cleaning up everyone else's messes. "You would think I have four cats, not one," I say to Lenny.

Meowing viciously, he trots to his food bowl. Lenny won't pardon me or interact with me until his belly's full. I dump some vittles into his bowl.

Shrugging off my coat and stepping out of my worn tennis shoes, I drop my keys onto the counter and head to the refrigerator. Samson relies on his Maker's Mark, but I'm going to make a mark of my own with a gin and tonic. Tonight calls for a cocktail. I open the fridge and set about mixing the ingredients and squeezing the lime. I'm stirring the ice with a butter knife when I hear a knock at the door.

Aris is back. I should have known that our parting had been too sorrowful and a bit too abrupt for him.

I pull the butter knife out and lick it. Delicious. "Be there in a second." Wanting to give the impression that I'm headed off to bed, I stash my drink in the fridge.

Lenny, now satiated and willing to acknowledge my existence, follows me to the door. I open it. My heart falls right out of my chest and lands on top of my feet.

He's more beautiful and predatory than I remember. Darker. Sexier. As delicious as that stupid cocktail I've just hidden.

Lenny, sensing that he's been outdone, runs from the room.

"When you left this summer, I told you that I don't give second chances."

Adept at x-ray vision, his light green eyes don't look at me but into me. His smile comes out of nowhere and cuts me to the quick.

Though he hasn't received an invitation, he doesn't wait for one. Stepping into my apartment, he deftly kicks the door shut with his foot.

Reaching for me, he puts his hand on the side of my neck, a possessive gesture that excites me as much as it angers me. I inhale slowly. He smells the same, like heat and smoke.

"I changed my mind."

Before I know what's happening, his lips are on mine.

CHAPTER TWELVE

"Put your tongue back where it belongs!" snaps Nikeo. He gives Lenny a shove off the couch. Lenny has been making a meal out of Nikeo's bare arm, which I can't help but notice is tanned and muscular from all the road cycling he does. It looks very appetizing in his formfitting white T-shirt.

If I were a cat, I might be inclined to do the same thing as Lenny. Honestly, though, I wouldn't even have to be of the feline persuasion. The thought of licking Nikeo has crossed my mind more than once since he arrived. This summer I learned that it's possible to be in love with one person and in lust with another. When that happens, lines get blurred, crossed, and jumped.

"I said nearly the same thing to you a few minutes ago," I remark, offering my alcoholic cat a bowl of tonic water with lime. Purring, he laps up his virgin cocktail, not yet realizing he'll never get that buzz that he wants.

Tamara Lyon

"You wanted me to keep going. Don't pretend otherwise." He flashes one of his overly confident, provocative smiles.

Nikeo and I—we aren't so much a match made in heaven as a match made in hell. Dancing with the devil may be exciting, even desirable, but when the tango ends, those flames would cremate me, body and soul.

"I understand that Caprice offered you the job. You should take it."

"I'm busy making a life of my own around here." I strategically place myself on the floor in front of the coffee table—I have to have at least one piece of furniture between us.

"What's this life like?" He reaches into his pocket and pulls out car keys, three guitar picks, and some folded-up dollar bills, unceremoniously tossing them on the table as if he's planning on being here awhile. I should have kicked him out immediately, but nope. I had to offer him a cocktail.

He has to appear when my relationship with Justice is swirling around in the toilet and Susie Home Wrecker is dying to flush me away. I'm in much too vulnerable a place right now to have Nikeo lounging around in my apartment. Past behavior predicts future behavior, and my past behavior with him isn't all that innocent. Being around Nikeo in my starved-kitten state—a state that has me thinking about licking his salty skin—is not a good idea.

Not wanting to discuss what kind of life I've been making for myself, because I'm not sure it's much of one, I pick up Nikeo's demo disc, which he brought along as a gift. "Should we listen to it?"

"Why not."

I insert his disc into the stereo. "Time of My Life" by Green Day is the first song. It takes me right back to this summer, to the night when Nikeo and I stood beneath a sky mottled with fireworks and kissed each other for the first time.

My heart jumps around like Pop Rocks. I try to keep my voice steady.

"I've missed hearing you play."

His translucent green eyes lock on mine and stay there. It feels like he's reading my thoughts. Turns out he is. "Unquestionably, the best kiss of my life. How about for you?"

Instant blush. To think I was sure I was completely over him. Nope. He's still able to evoke a visceral response in me. As for it being the best kiss of my life? Second best. First place goes to Justice.

Avoiding his question, I glance at the clock hanging in the kitchen. "Mikayla will be home soon."

Smirking, he takes a long drink of his gin and tonic. "Your friend who stole Justice?"

"I'm surprised you remember the details of that drama."

He leans forward, elbows resting on knees. "I remember everything."

He's putting out a strong sexual current, and it's a struggle not to drown in it. I've taken precautions. I've done all I can to make the environment as unromantic as possible. After I rejected Nikeo's much-too-familiar greeting at the door, which I'm ashamed to admit was not until at least five seconds into the kiss, maybe six (I'm weak when it comes to him), I nervously flitted around the living area and flipped on every single overhead light and also the three table lamps that Grandma Betty strategically placed around the living area for adequate ambience lighting.

I also turned down the thermostat, because whenever Nikeo's around, things simmer. Despite the room temperature hovering somewhere around sixty-five degrees, I'm flushed and fevered. If I move closer to him, which I'm not doing because I have a feeling he might try to kiss me again and it might be thirty seconds before I remember to keep my lips to myself, every part of my body will boil.

Proximity is obviously a problem, but to make matters worse, his voice is serenading me through the speakers. I can see, hear, and smell him.

Tasting and touching could be arranged. Nikeo sensory overload.

Clearing my throat and dodging his smoldering glare, I focus on the conversation at hand. "Turns out Mikayla didn't steal him. She's married to someone else. We've moved past all that. She's living here—temporarily."

"She's married and living with you. How does that work?"

"She's, um—well—she's going through some stuff with her husband. So she's staying with me for a while."

"From what I hear, things aren't going so well for you in the relationship department either."

Sighing, I scoot over to the plaid armchair that matches the hideous couch and sit in front of it, getting fractionally closer to Nikeo. A risky move. Let's hope he doesn't try to take advantage of the location change. Lenny gracelessly leaps onto my bent knees and falls off before trying again. This time he's successful. He sits formally, like a sentinel, acting as a guard against Nikeo. "It's nice to know that Caprice is being so open about my relationship status."

He finds this hilarious. His laugh, a rough-and-tumble sound, makes the insides of my ears itch in a good and bad way.

"What's so funny?"

"She didn't tell me anything. I figured it out myself. No ring on. Your own apartment. A roommate, a married one at that. Almost eleven on a Friday night. No Justice. Things aren't working out the way you hoped. Not that I'm surprised. When you left Briar this summer like a bat out of hell, I could have told you it was doomed. Let me guess, he found someone else? Someone the opposite of you?"

Nikeo is annoyingly insightful and effortlessly lands on the right conclusions. "I've forgotten how disgustingly irritating you can be."

"I've forgotten how sexy and irresistible you are."

"You aren't going to win me over."

"Who said anything about winning? Although scoring would be nice."

I narrow my eyes. "What a high-school-boy comment. I would expect more from you."

"The key is never to expect anything." He stands and holds out his hand. "Give me your glass. I'm refilling our drinks."

I pull my almost empty drink against my chest, and Lenny sniffs the air as it passes and eyes me suspiciously. I think he's figured out that I slighted him earlier. "No thanks, and you're having another? What, now that you're a musician you've become an alcoholic, too? And apparently you haven't stopped smoking," I say, noting the pack of cigarettes he's left on my table.

"Still uptight. Still judging. You haven't changed a bit." He rises from the couch and saunters into the kitchen.

"And neither have you," I reply in a singsong voice. "Don't you realize that it was a huge mistake to drop by? We're all wrong for each other."

He pours himself another drink and curiously eyes the glittery pink journal that Jocelyn left behind last week. "Being wrong for each other is infinitely more interesting than being right for each other. Besides, we're young. We're supposed to be exploring all the wrong things."

"I'm focused on finding the right one and then marrying him."

"Your fascination with marriage is ridiculous. You know my position on that institution. Antiquated. Absurd—"

"Stop. I don't want to hear it."

He picks up the journal, holding it in the air for me to see. "Please tell me that you're not writing down all your thoughts and feelings, because if you are"—he shrugs—"I might have to read it. Only to see if my name pops up every now and then. I'm sure it does. You fantasize about me. Try and deny it."

Scoffing, I finish my drink. "Has anyone told you that you're an absolute narcissist? That journal isn't mine, it's Jocelyn's."

He drops it. "How is she?"

Humiliated. Ashamed. Possibly pregnant. Hopefully not disease riddled. "She's gotten herself into serious trouble."

He waits patiently, and when I don't say anything, he inclines his head toward me. "Be more specific."

Nikeo rarely asks questions. He issues orders. "No. I'm sparing what little dignity she has left."

He considers this as he raises his glass to his lips. "Show me around your apartment."

"Actually, um—" I pause and set my drink down. Lenny catapults off my knees and hurries over to my glass. He dunks his paw in and raises it to his mouth. When that gin hits his sandpaper tongue, he closes his eyes in ecstasy.

I snatch it away, and he growls at me. "Sorry, buddy, you're not falling off the wagon."

Nikeo regards Lenny with pity. "You ruined his night."

"I'm about to ruin yours too."

"Don't you dare."

"It's been kind of a long night for me. I mean, the thing with Jocelyn, everything kind of hit the fan tonight. I'm exhausted, and you—"

I intend to keep talking. The words are right there. You need to leave. Go back to your hotel or motel. Go sleep in your car if you have to. Get out of my life, because if you don't, I'm going to start picturing you in it again. I can't let that happen, because this time, I probably would jump down that relationship rabbit hole and never find my way out. So see you later. Don't let the door hit your butt on the way out.

Grinning as if he knows something I don't, he rakes his eyes over my body, starting at my feet and working up until he seems to be staring at my lips. "Did you have something you wanted to say?"

"Yes. No." I heave a gigantic sigh. I don't know if it's chemistry, stupidity, or that our wills and personalities are too similar, but Nikeo is the only man who has ever thrown me off my game. When I'm around him, I spend half the time feeling like an idiot and the other half behaving like one. "Can you leave now?"

"Absolutely not. I'm spending the night."

"Who invited you?"

He takes affront. "I don't have to be invited."

"You do. That's how it works, Nikeo, and I didn't extend an invitation. Verbal or otherwise."

He walks over to where I'm positioned, which happens to be right next to the front door. Have I subconsciously wandered over here, knowing that at some point I'll need to escape? I think I knew when I let him in that he wouldn't be leaving, so now I was preparing to flee. My hand is less than six inches from the doorknob. All I have to do is reach out, turn it, and run for my life. Aris would be happy to accommodate me. I could sleep on his train tracks.

Nikeo puts his hands on either side of my face. My cheeks catch fire under his fingertips. I look up into his green eyes.

"What happened here?" he asks, dragging the pads of his thumb under my eyes, which are still plagued with bruises and over my chin, rough and red from where the stitches were removed just yesterday. "Get in a fight?"

"Broken nose, two black eyes, some stitches."

"Did you win?"

"No, but it wasn't a fair fight." My lungs aren't working. I try to inhale but can't. All the air is trapped in the back of my throat. There's all this pressure building. I could scream or just as easily moan—it all depends on where this goes.

If it goes where I think it's going, odds are it's going to be a moan, but

173

moaning is the least of my concerns. It's just a sound. What frightens me most is that if he kisses me again, I won't be able to keep my lips, tongue, or anything else to myself.

He tilts his head, and I think he's going to move in for the kill when he says softly, seductively, "I drove from Chicago to see you, and you're glad that I'm here. I'm not going anywhere. You don't want me to go anywhere. I intend to stay the night."

He's so close to my lips that he's not speaking as much as he's pouring the words into my mouth. I should spit those words back out, but instead I swallow them one at a time.

"Has anyone ever told you that you're incorrigible?"

He leers at me and then flaunts his devil grin. "You have. Now show me around."

As quickly as he pounced on me, he releases me. "You're not going to leave no matter what I say, are you?"

"Nope."

"You've already seen most of the apartment." Stepping diagonally, deliberately keeping my distance, I walk past him. "Twenty-second tour, follow me."

Once I've shown him the bathroom and bedrooms, I'm anxious to get him out. He has other ideas. He makes himself comfortable on my bed, lounging there as if he doesn't have a care in the world.

I station myself at the doorway, and Nikeo and I engage in a staring contest. I'm telepathically telling him to get lost, and it's pretty obvious he's telling me to come find him.

Lenny amuses himself by winding through my legs in a figure-eight pattern. He does this at least ten times, and then gets so dizzy he falls over and rolls onto his back, legs and paws relaxed at his side—exactly the way Nikeo is positioned on my bed.

"I'm going to be in Chicago for a month, doing gigs here and there," Nikeo informs me. "Some pretty big venues."

This past summer, Nikeo mentioned that he wanted a music career, but he hadn't elaborated much on the subject. "I didn't know you were really that serious about being a rock star."

"Who doesn't want to be a rock star?" He reaches behind his head and plumps my pillow.

"I don't," I respond wryly.

"I've always wanted to be a professional musician, but I didn't think I could make a living doing it. Hence the stint in law school. When that didn't work out, I jumped into the business world with Caprice. I was planning on making a career of it."

He looks over at me. "I was rather enjoying myself, too, especially when you were around. But then you left, and an opportunity came along. Some music producer named Texas was at Briar Days this summer when I performed. He liked what he saw. Called me a month later. Signed me with his company. Hooked me up with a manager."

"Are you excited?"

"I'm being realistic. I intend to enjoy the ride. It could go nowhere fast."

I think he should be more focused on it going somewhere quickly. I've seen him perform several times, and the crowd adored him. He makes women and men swoon. With his passion, desire, and talent, not to mention his undeniable sexuality, I've no doubt that he'll find success in the industry. "You know how good you are. You'll be successful."

"Time will tell," he says, accepting my vote of confidence with equanimity. "I'll be in Chicago quite a bit."

"You've already mentioned that."

He finally gets off the bed, and due to severe lack of square footage in my bedroom, he's standing in front of me in a fraction of a second. "There would be an opportunity for us to be together. I could stay here during the week when I'm not playing. We could see where things go."

I'm shocked by his suggestion—it sounds much too domesticated for his taste. Nikeo told me that he loved me this summer, but I chalked up his proclamation to toxic levels of sexual chemistry. I didn't think for a second he was serious about pursuing a relationship. "You honestly want that?"

"I wouldn't drive here to see you if that's what I didn't want. I'm giving you a second chance. It's yours to take." He smiles as if he's doing me a favor.

For dramatic flair, I pretend to grow faint. Leaning against the wall, I press the back of my hand to my forehead. "I've been pining for you. I never thought this moment would come."

"You can't deny that we have something," he says, angry now. "I told you I loved you this summer. That hasn't changed. I don't want a fling. That's not what this is."

I immediately regret my flippant response. "I'm sorry."

"You should be."

There's a loud knock at the front door. Lenny dashes from the room to investigate. I've never been more grateful for Mikayla's return, though she wouldn't bother with knocking, which can only mean that her polite husband is doing it.

"It's open!" I yell.

The door opens and then closes.

"Tell me what you think about my proposition," Nikeo demands, taking a step closer, pinning me against my dresser.

"You're being serious?"

"Isn't it obvious that—"

Before Nikeo can complete his sentence, I hear a familiar voice. It isn't

Mikayla. Or Jeremy. My eyes go all egg yolk style, and for the second time tonight, my heart falls out of my chest—only this time it splats on the ground.

Panicked, I push Nikeo away from me and duck out of the room like a trapped rodent, but it's too late. He's already rounded the corner.

"I saw the pack of cigarettes," Justice says. "Please tell me you haven't picked up—" He stops abruptly when he sees that there's someone in my bedroom.

"Hey, um, I didn't know you were stopping by." My voice, all weak and quivery, isn't doing me any favors.

Nikeo steps out into view, and he and Justice are facing each other in the crowded hallway, having a nonverbal showdown with me stuck in the middle. We're a century past the Wild, Wild West, but if either of these men had a gun, I have no doubt they would be seeing who had the faster draw and trigger finger. I've never seen them together, and now that they are, their differences in appearance and in personality astound me. Bossy and brooding green-eyed Nikeo squares off against calm and truthful blue-eyed Justice. A true bad-guy-versus-good-guy scenario unfolding in front of me.

Which is why I'm completely thrown for a loop by what happens next.

Inching forward on my bed, I sneak a look at myself in the mirror above my dresser. A hundred braids or more. I'm on a roll. In no time at all I'm going to resemble an island girl. Tucking the phone between my ear and my shoulder, I sink back into my pile of pillows, and as I wait for her to answer, I anxiously braid some more.

It rings six times in a row. Seven. Eight. This is downright rude, needy, and admittedly crazy. I'm in the process of hanging up when I hear a groggy voice on the other end of the line.

"Hello?"

I push the phone back against my ear and cease my braiding marathon. "Hi, it's Cane Kallevik. I shouldn't be calling. It's very late, or should I say early."

"Cane! I've been dying to hear from you! Just a second."

I can't believe I've sunk this low. I should be relying on friends and family, and instead, I'm calling Rhonda Riddle at three in the morning.

On the other end of the line there's shuffling feet, followed by the sound of water running. I hear two distinct smacking sounds, immediately followed by a yelp. Is someone beating her? I can't handle any more violence tonight.

"I'm back, what's the scoop?"

"Did someone hit you?"

"I hit myself, honey. Ran some water, splashed it on my face, and then slapped myself silly. It's a trick I discovered when my babies were little and I had to get up every two or three hours to feed them and change their diapers. Gets me wide awake."

"I'm embarrassed that I called." Picking at the ends of my braids, I start unraveling them one at a time.

"It's four in the morning here, and I have to get up at five thirty anyway, so it's not that big of a deal."

Confused, I glance at the clock, thinking it's wrong, and then realize I've never actually asked Rhonda where she lives. "Where do you live?"

"On the coast, right by the beautiful Atlantic ocean in Florida."

I don't have supernatural powers, but I'm suddenly struck by a strange feeling that Rhonda Riddle lives near Grandma Betty. "Where?"

"St. Petersburg. I have myself a lovely condo a few blocks away from the beach."

"My grandma just moved down to St. Pete with her husband, Frank. They live right on the beach."

"No kidding! If you ever come down here to visit your grandma, you should stop on over at my place. Wouldn't it be a hoot to meet in person!"

"Um, sure. That would be fun."

"What's going on with you? I'm dying to know!"

I can't have Rhonda dying on me, so I give her the latest. Chattering for fifteen minutes with barely a breath in between sentences, I cover Mikayla's vomiting on the cat, Susie Homemaker's relentless pursuit of Justice, Aris's infatuation with me, the annoying fact that Aris and Susan are siblings, and Justice's mixed and hopeless messages. I finish my rant with the Jocelyn drama and what went down at the football game.

Rhonda gasps when I'm finished. "You've had quite a rocky go of it, haven't you?"

"But that's not all."

"Knock me over with a feather! What else could there be?"

"Remember Nikeo, the guy I had an almost-affair with this summer? He happened to drop by my apartment. Turns out he's still interested."

"And are you interested in him?"

I'd be a liar, liar pants on fire if I tried to deny our chemistry (and often when I'm around him, my pants do feel like they're on fire), but in terms of his personality? I'm over the bad-guy, bossy thing. I couldn't put up with it long-term. It would drive me insane. "He's not right for me—so no, not interested, just attracted."

"Attraction can be dangerous, but you know where you stand, and that's half the battle, right?"

"It's not about where I stood when Nikeo showed up, it's about the fact that Justice decided to stop over unannounced right after Nikeo did."

"Oh, dear." Rhonda makes a *tsk* noise with her tongue. "I take it that didn't go over so well."

"It was a disaster."

I still can't believe what happened, how Justice responded.

His aquamarine eyes flinty and angry, he stared me down and then shifted his eyes to Nikeo. "Who's this?"

Not being polite under any circumstances, Nikeo offered up a cocky grin. "I think you already know who I am, and it's pretty obvious who you are."

A stillness fell like a brick, and chipping away at the silence was Nikeo's melodic, sexy voice crooning through the speakers in the living room.

He sang about walking up high and stepping to the edge to see the world below. I had no idea that Justice planned on shoving Nikeo off the ledge.

Justice took a giant step past me and delivered a right hook to Nikeo's cheek, sending him flying into the plaster wall—nearly a complete knockout. Nikeo slid to the floor, but it took only a second for him to regain his balance, dignity, and sneer.

Nikeo doesn't subscribe to the turn-the-other-cheek rule that Justice lives by—or used to live by. Nikeo is more of an eye-for-an-entire-body kind of guy. I saw him beat Kevin, the man who tried to take advantage of Jocelyn, senseless this summer, and if not for my intervention, he would have ended up cuffed in the back of a police car.

So imagine how stunned I was when Nikeo crossed his arms and acted as if he didn't have a care in the world. In a rather bored voice, he said, "I could go for a smoke right about now."

"Don't touch her. Ever again," Justice warned him, with such malevolence that I didn't recognize his voice.

I searched the face of the man I loved, and he looked at me as if I'd done something unforgivable. Although I hadn't, I felt compelled to defend myself. "I didn't do anything."

A pot-stirrer to the core, Nikeo laughed audaciously and pegged Justice with an arrogant stare. "No worries, buddy. She hasn't done anything yet, but I intend to work on that. After all, from what I hear, she's a free agent."

From the way Justice curled the fingers of his left hand, I could tell he was about to hook Nikeo's face on the other side, and if he did that, I was positive that this time Nikeo wouldn't be so blasé.

Reaching out, I gripped Justice's tightly balled fist. "Leave before you do anything else you'll regret."

He glanced down at my hand on his and then dragged his eyes up my arm to my face. Pain was etched across his face. His brow was dangerously elevated, and his lips fell sharply at the edges. Nikeo had sustained the injury, but Justice was more wounded than I'd ever seen him.

"You still there, honey?" Rhonda asks in a soothing voice.

"I'm still here," I reply wearily. I've been so wired from adrenaline that the need to sleep hasn't hit me until now. My head feels like it's packed full of wet sand.

Lenny meows beside my bed and attempts to jump up but falls short and ends up on his back. Staring forlornly at me, he waves his paw. Help me, help me, he sends out a distress signal. Helping is all I've been doing lately. I scoop him off the floor and settle him on the blanket next to me.

He licks my forearm, his tongue working overtime, making my skin raw.

"If you don't want to talk about what happened—"

"No," I interrupt. "I need to tell you."

When I finish recounting the tale of the one-sided fight and what was said and done by all involved, Rhonda whistles, an impressive, earsplitting sound. Even Lenny hears, and it's making him uncomfortable. His ears stand at attention, and so does his tail.

Only it turns out it's not her.

"Sorry about the racket. I've got a kettle on the stove. I start the day

181

with tea and finish it off with wine. After hearing that story, I would actually like to reverse my habit and start with the wine."

"Have you ever tried a gin and tonic?"

"Never," she says.

"You should."

"Why don't we drink one together when you come to Florida?"

I picture Rhonda and me sitting on the beach together, wearing large sun hats, toes stuck in the sand, and drinking cocktails. "I'd like that."

A long, steady rush of air fills the phone line—I assume Rhonda is holding that cup of tea up to her mouth and blowing on it, trying to cool things down. Earlier, when Justice slammed the door as he left, I did something similar, pushing a long ribbon of air through my lips as I tried to cool the emotions within and around me.

"What do you think I should do about all of this? About Justice? Nikeo? Jocelyn? The job offer? What do you think is going to happen?" I ask Rhonda.

"I don't know, but I can tell you what you should do right this second. Go to sleep."

"I can't, not with all of this going on."

"You can and will."

Turns out Rhonda Riddle's prediction came true.

CHAPTER THIRTEEN

I'm in a dead sleep when Mikayla dumps Lenny on my chest.

"It's almost ten!" she announces in a dramatic whisper.

Lenny kneads my neck and makes a suckling noise. I push him to the side and sit up on my elbows. The abrupt change in position causes my head to tighten and pound accordingly. I could use a gallon of water and 800 milligrams of Advil right about now.

After Justice left and before I dialed Rhonda Riddle, I enjoyed three too many gin and tonics, compliments of bartender Nikeo, who makes his drinks strong and large.

As soon as I'd finish one, he'd make me another. When he handed me the last, he said he needed a smoke break.

Cocktail in hand, I followed him outside.

He lit his cigarette and nodded at his vehicle. "My new wheels." He propped his foot up on the fancy bike rack on the back. "And my new road bike. Decided to take that advance check from the record company and put it to good use."

I eyed up his carbon-fiber Scott road bike, which I knew retailed for at least $7,000. The Jeep? I wasn't sure, but it had to be close to $30,000. "You should have saved the money," I told him critically.

The cigarette dangled from his fingertips. "No thank you."

"Don't you think this is extravagant?" I waved my hand at his shiny new purchases.

"I know how to handle finances." He raised his cigarette to his mouth.

While I took a drink, he sucked on his cancer stick like it was the best thing in the world. The end of the cigarette glowed orange and warm, and I shivered uncontrollably. Drunk and intrigued by the stupid glow, thinking that somehow it might give me a buzz of warmth, I stole it from him and took a drag, prompting a hunched-over coughing fit.

He took it out of my hands. "Hadn't seen that coming," he said, laughing at me.

Once I recovered, I pilfered the cigarette again, dropped it to the ground, and smeared it across the pavement. "There's nothing about this night that I saw coming."

I hadn't seen what was coming last night, but I should have known what was coming for me this morning: physical pain.

Lenny crawls over my stomach and then legs, the force of him making my hangover and body aches more painful. I force my crusty, dry eyes to open and glare at Mikayla. "I don't appreciate having you as my alarm clock. When did you get here, anyway?"

"About twenty minutes ago. We wanted to have breakfast with you."

I press my pillow over my face and push down in a self-suffocating maneuver. "I'm so lucky."

"You never sleep this late, so I'm assuming," she says, sitting on the edge of my bed, "that you got busy with that hot man who's on the couch. Who is that by the way? Friend? Stranger? Male escort?"

I toss the pillow across the room. "Do I look like I got busy?"

She regards me, tilting her head one way then another. "You look hungover."

"Bingo."

"I can't believe I slept so late," I grouse, sitting all the way up and pushing my hair off my forehead. "I need to get to the gym. Or go for a bike ride or something."

Throwing off the covers, I swing my legs over the side of the bed. Mikayla plants her hands on my shoulders. "Stay," she commands. "I'm not letting you out of my sight until you tell me where you found that hot guy out there. And please, don't tell me you're the one who screwed up his beautiful face. It's all bruised and swollen."

"I didn't find him anywhere. He found me. That's Nikeo."

"That's Colorado Nikeo?"

"One and the same," I answer and start dressing.

"Good move. Justice would never be jealous of Aris, but Nikeo? Nice tactics."

"You think I planned this? He just showed up unannounced. And so did Justice. They dropped in, like two atomic bombs." I report the encounter.

"Justice hit him?" she asks in utter disbelief.

"Unbelievable, right?"

She shrugs. When it comes to Mikayla, events aren't as important as looks. "He's hot."

"He's trouble."

Smiling a Lenny-type smile, she raises her perfectly waxed eyebrow. "Now that's a fun combination."

"For about five minutes," I respond, pulling on my thermal tights.

"You're not running out of here."

"Watch me."

My cell phone rings, and before I can see who it is, Mikayla snatches it off my nightstand.

"Hello, Justice," Mikayla says, winking at me. "No, she can't talk. She's indisposed at the moment."

She pauses. "I'm sure that you do."

"What is he saying? Give me the phone," I demand. I'm in no mood for Mikayla games.

She dances out of my room and down the hall, and at the same time Nikeo rounds the corner.

Perfect timing as usual. I'm standing in front of him in tights and a sports bra. I guess I should be glad he didn't catch me topless.

Leaning against my doorframe, one hand in his pocket, his eyes skim the surface of my body. I wait for the heat to rise within me, but nothing happens. Am I unable to respond to stimuli because of my hangover? Am I distracted by the fact that Mikayla is talking to Justice? Or could it be that I no longer have the desire to dirty-dance with the devil?

His usual self, he skips the good morning, how did you sleep, and barks out orders. "Get dressed—we're going biking."

"It's probably best if you leave," I tell him, pulling on my thermal shirt. My long hair flies up at the ends, making me look like an unfortunate victim of electrocution, and I'm positive my crispy eyes, pale skin, and parched, cracked lips only enhance the effect.

"I'm going to change." He picks up a duffel bag that he deposited in the hallway late last night or early this morning or whenever it was.

"We're not going."

"Yes. We are."

I look him in the eye. "You're not making this easy." I lean against my dresser.

We both know that I'm not referring to the bike ride. Last night, after I'd smeared his cigarette, he told me that he was determined to be with me.

"Justice gave up on you, but I won't. You're worth it. You and me? We're going to be together," he said, not possessively but confidently.

I didn't know how to respond last night, and I still don't. I couldn't tell him no; he wouldn't accept it. A bulldozer to the core, Nikeo pushes until he gets what he wants. Kind of like me. Takes one to know one.

"I never make things easy," he adds, ducking into the bathroom.

One door closes, another opens. Mikayla comes out of the guest room, smiling victoriously, and hands me the phone. "Victory. He's absolutely miserable."

"Why didn't you let me talk to him?"

"Cane, don't you know anything about handling male-female relationships? In this situation, it's best if you act like you're so angry you can't even stomach talking to him."

"Again, I find it ironic that you're giving me advice, the woman who hasn't told her husband—"

"Shut up!" She clamps her hand over my mouth. "Jeremy is going to be back here any second! He's bringing bagels."

"More carbohydrates? He has to be getting suspicious. It's not like you can hide it forever. It's not like you can escape either. As of Monday you won't even have a car; he's going to notice your lack of transportation, and it's only a matter of time before he starts opening up your mail—"

She cuts me off. "No comments on my diet and debt. And that's the last time I do you a favor."

"What favor would that be?"

"Making Justice think you're mad at him."

"I am mad at him! So how is that a favor exactly?"

"The problem with you is that you're always too willing to talk. When it comes to Justice, you're incapable of holding a grudge, and sometimes you need to hold a grudge! It makes the man work harder and appreciate you more. Which is why, when he invited you for dinner, I made him sweat it out a bit. I made sure he knew just how upset you were about the whole thing before I told him that you would in fact be there."

"I'm going over there for dinner?"

She peers into my eyes. "Are you not keeping up with the conversation? Just how much did you have to drink?"

Nikeo opens the bathroom door, dressed in his tight biking clothes.

Mikayla eats him up with her eyes, and Nikeo does the same to her.

I look back and forth between them. "I guess that takes care of breakfast for you two."

Mikayla flashes him one of her model smiles, the ones that she saves for photo shoots. "I'm Mikayla."

"I figured."

"And you are?" she inquires coyly.

Nikeo doesn't play games. "You already know."

He's out the front door before Mikayla realizes that she's been dissed. "What an arrogant prick."

"Can't disagree there." I open the hall closet, jump up, and attempt to snag my bike helmet from the top shelf. I miss once, and then again. I should have had Grandma Betty mount a hook near the door.

"You're going to end up with another black eye if you're not careful." Mikayla, whose arm is probably the same length as my leg, reaches up and easily pulls it down for me. She plunks it on my head.

"I'm proud of you," I tell her. "You must be over the bad-boy thing. I thought for sure you would like Nikeo."

The front door opens and then closes. Jeremy waves the bag in the air. "Hi Cane, hi honey."

Mikayla grants him a silky smile, and from the look on her face and his, it's pretty obvious that they didn't just sleep in Chicago last night.

"I've got cinnamon sugar, blueberry, apple strudel, and plain. I figure we can eat and then pack."

"You're moving out?" I ask her.

"She didn't tell you?" Jeremy grins. "We had a great talk last night. Yes, she's moving back to Chicago."

"That's right! I am!" Mikayla flashes an adoring smile at her husband and then yanks me to her side, whispering urgently in my ear. "I might be married to a good boy, but that doesn't mean I no longer appreciate the bad ones. I like Nikeo, and I think you do too. Think about using him. It could be effective."

She releases me, walks into the kitchen, and slides her arms around Jeremy's waist. Resting her chin on his shoulder, she peers down at the bagels and inhales deeply. "I'll take a cinnamon sugar and an apple strudel."

Jeremy tears open the bag and looks up. "Both?"

"Yes, both!"

"If I were you, Jeremy, I would get used to this. It's only going to get worse."

Puzzled, he studies his wife, but she's too busy glaring at me to notice.

I don't know when she's going to confess her sins, but I no longer care. For the moment, I have my apartment back to myself—though I obviously don't have the day to myself. I still have to deal with Nikeo.

Nikeo and I are twenty miles into the ride when we stop at a gas station in the middle of nowhere to replenish our water supply and get something to eat. We shed several layers of clothes, as the weather has warmed to an unseasonable seventy-four degrees. When we're finished slamming a couple

Gatorades and eating a few granola bars, I suggest that we turn around.

"No."

"You have a gig tonight, don't you?"

"At ten tonight." He clips back into his pedals. "I have more than enough time."

"Chicago traffic is going to be a nightmare."

"You can't get rid of me."

"I've been trying."

"I've noticed." He glances at me as we ride. "That proves you're afraid of what will happen and what you'll do if I stick around. Justice punched me last night because he feels threatened. And for good reason."

I drop my gaze to my handlebars and shift into a harder gear, making my quadriceps burn. "Don't bring him into this."

"You liked what he did," remarks Nikeo. He shifts into a harder gear once, and then again, and soon we're in a competition, pushing each to the limits. It's a familiar pattern between us, always trying to drop the other.

"Yes," I admit. Unlike me, a fighter who battles with myself, my volatile emotions, and others, Justice is a peacekeeper. Always the pacifist, he never initiates fights; he only concerns himself with stopping them. When he punched Nikeo last night, starting the fight because of me, I fell head over heels in love with him again.

"Why didn't you hit him back?" I ask.

"He threw that punch"—Nikeo pauses, his breathing ragged— "because I took something from him. I had it coming."

"You didn't want to hit him back?"

"I did." He meets my eyes. "But it would have cost me the one thing I want."

Although I still react physically to his presence, my body tingling in all the right places, my mouth going dry, my heart rate accelerating so rapidly it feels like I've been injected with adrenaline, I'm emotionally divorced from him. I'm no longer intrigued in the same way. Like can attract like, but bring them close together, force them to stay there, and eventually they repel.

Instead of returning his eye contact, I fix my gaze on the horizon. Much of the corn has been harvested; the fields are naked and broken. The damp earth smells used up and worn out, and the decay is visible for miles. I can't escape it; there's no visual relief in this part of the country. Thousands of flat miles.

I find myself thinking about the vastly different Colorado landscape. The jagged, snow-capped mountains. Pockets of pines. Hidden rocky trails. Cascading water. Thin, fragile, oxygen starved air, infused with the scent of aspen and resin. Not for the first time, I ponder returning. I miss it.

"If anything, we're going to be friends." I make this declaration after fifteen minutes of strained silence between us.

He pushes air through his nostrils, a pure sound of disgust. Grabbing his water bottle, he takes a long drink and then slides it back into the cage on his frame. "We aren't equipped for friendship. It would be like drawing a line in the sand. Tell me you know that."

I try to picture what our friendship would look like. All I can see is a cycle of sexual tension that would either make us murderous toward each other or adulterous. I look over at him, acknowledging that yes, I know.

"All or nothing." His eyes drift out over a field sprinkled with desiccated cornstalks that have escaped the wrath of machinery. A flock of wild turkeys startles as we ride past. Gobbling in terror, they fly into the air, dispersing into a grove of trees. They cluck loudly and angrily.

"Nothing," I respond quietly.

"I figured. How about a fling? You never know what could happen; what you would feel if we—"

"I can't do that." I meet his gaze. "I would never do that."

191

We finish the ride in silence. When we return to the apartment, Mikayla and Jeremy are gone. I find a note from Mikayla on the counter, telling me that they went to check on Jocelyn, and she'll call me later.

Lenny stands on the counter, walking circles around the bottle of gin that Nikeo left out overnight.

"He's hard-core." Nikeo puts the gin back in the refrigerator. Lenny meows forlornly and leaps off the counter, barely landing on his feet.

Hungry from our long ride, Nikeo and I raid the bagels that Jeremy left behind and then make scrambled eggs.

Nikeo is dishing a serving of eggs onto plates when he glances up at me. "Isn't this conjugal? You couldn't get used to this?"

I grin with my mouth closed. "To us being friends? Sure."

Nikeo pushes the pan to the side. "Not going to happen."

"Enemies, then? That might be fun."

"We would make great adversaries," he agrees.

When we're finished, Nikeo showers, and I call Samson to check on Jocelyn. In a strained voice, he tells me that they're leaving for the doctor.

"Can I come over later?"

"I don't know. We're trying to sort things out."

"I understand."

He takes a shaky breath. "I don't. I don't understand any of it. I don't know what to do."

In the background, I hear Jenny calling for him. "I have to go," he says and hangs up.

Nikeo emerges from the bathroom, dressed in dark blue jeans and a fitted white button-down shirt. With his face covered in light stubble, coal black hair damp and purposely mussed with gel, and bruised cheek and eye, he looks every bit the rock star.

"I'm not going to stay away from you," he announces as he stands next to the door, bag in one hand.

"I don't doubt it, and the way you're spending money, I'm sure you'll be back looking for a handout sooner than later."

Amused, he smiles drolly. Placing his hand possessively against the side of my neck, he leans toward me and kisses me on the corner of the mouth. My lips part automatically, betraying my desire.

He shifts his mouth from my lips to my ear and whispers, "I left a pack of cigarettes in your room. Figured you might like them."

And with this announcement, he's gone. Lenny stands at the door and looks up at me as if I've committed some unspeakable sin.

"What? Did you think we were getting another roommate?"

Tail twitching, he emits a long meow and heads toward the kitchen, eyeing up the pan of scrambled eggs on the counter.

There's a knock at the door.

"Back so soon? I'd be happy to return those cigarettes. I'm not going to need them," I say loudly, opening the door.

It isn't Nikeo. Quite the opposite.

Susie Homemaker stands in front of me, sporting a pulled-together weekend look. Full makeup. Hair wavy and gleaming. Tight designer jeans. Plum cardigan over a cream shirt. Understated brown flats made of the softest leather. This is in sharp contrast to my windblown hair and sweaty biking outfit, which reeks of body odor.

"Oh! Hi, Cane." She glances nervously down the hall toward her brother's apartment. "I could have sworn this was Aris's apartment. I've only been here once—guess I mixed them up." She looks back at me. "No matter. I was going to give this to Aris to give to you."

She opens her oversize Coach handbag, a deep plum color (Grandma Betty would approve of her matching accessories), and removes my knit scarf. "But this works out better. No middleman. Got all the stains out.

Washed it a few times. It's clean as a whistle."

I inspect the scarf and try to smile gratefully. "Thank you. You didn't have to do that."

"Nonsense! It was my pleasure. Getting out stains is kind of a specialty of mine, a hobby actually. It thrills me to no end. Besides, you were kind enough to help my brother. It's not uncommon for him to get bloodied up. Poor guy has two left feet. That's why he works from home, you know, because he's so accident-prone. He's a terrible driver and has gotten into more than a dozen fender benders. I encourage him to take the train whenever—"

Turns out Susan and her brother have a lot in common when it comes to talking. "Susan, can we cut to the chase?"

Closing her Coach bag, she furrows her brow and offers a less than enthusiastic smile. "I'm not sure what you mean by that."

"Are you interested in Justice?"

She nervously toys with a button on her cardigan, and just when she's about to reply, Aris's door opens.

He sticks his head out and looks down the hall. "There you are! You're never late, and I was starting to worry. Hi, Cane Kallevik. Hey, I made some coffee and bought some more triple-chocolate doughnuts."

"I brought some maple nut coffee cake!" exclaims Susan. "I left it in the car. I'll have to go get it."

"Homemade?" her brother asks.

She gives a light, tinkling laugh. "I don't serve anything but."

Aris steps out into the hall. "Cane, you have to try that coffee cake. It could win awards. It's that amazing." He points at me. "Don't move, I'll be right back. I want to bring you some coffee." He ducks into his apartment.

"The coffee cake is honestly amazing. One of my favorites." Susan presses her palm against her flat stomach. "But I'm off all baked goods.

194

Have been for a year now."

How kind of her. She's preserving her body mass index while trying to sabotage everyone else's. "So it's your goal to make everyone insulin-dependent and obese?"

She laughs. "You're hilarious!"

"Yeah, I'm a big old riot," I mumble.

"I'm going to go help him get that coffee. Nice seeing you." Susan turns slightly.

"You haven't answered my question."

She raises her brown eyes to mine. "I understand that you have a lot of history with Justice, but as to whether or not I'm interested, it's not your business," she replies without an ounce of nastiness.

Clearly, confrontation isn't her style, but it's mine. "A simple yes or no would suffice."

"I prefer to keep matters of the heart private," she says in a ladylike, demure tone.

I don't know why I bothered asking. She doesn't have to spell it out in words when she's been making it plain as day with actions. Smiling like a fool every time he's in the room. Offering him a ride to the hospital. Helping him paint. Bringing him baked goods. Touching him whenever she has the chance—and she'll have plenty of chances now that she's going to Iowa.

I'll bet it's only a matter of hours before she sets up house in her hotel room. She's such a homemaker, she'll probably pack an Easy-Bake oven and start whipping up delectable treats for him. She'll feed him pastries for breakfast, dessert after dinner. Then, in the morning, she'll iron his shirts and offer to remove any stubborn stains.

Justice is going to Iowa with the perfect woman, and there isn't a thing I can do about it. He isn't mine anymore. I can't forbid her to stay away from him. I can't threaten her. I can't tell her to keep her hands to herself. What I want to do is the same thing that Justice did to Nikeo. I want to deliver a right hook to her cheekbone, which is highlighted with the perfect amount of blush. For a fleeting moment, I entertain the thought—what it would be like to execute this move, what it might look like to see Susan flying through the air, her pretty flats clear off the ground.

I won't go through with it, of course. I can't justify such an act of violence. Unfortunately, she's sweet through and through, a true sugar cube of a person—no one can help but love her. I, on the other hand, evoke more extreme emotion—people either love me or despise me. I'm not a sugar cube. I'm more like a Sour Patch Kids candy, so strong I cause an intense pucker, but stick around long enough, and a burst of sweet comes.

Aris emerges from his apartment, balancing a big steaming mug of coffee in his hands. He starts hustling our way, his head bobbing right and then left.

This could end badly. Third-degree burns. Another bloody nose and split lip. I'd have to hand over my scarf again. More stains for Susan to remove.

"Careful!" Susan and I shout simultaneously.

We look at each other, surprised at the timing of our words.

Slowing, he approaches cautiously. "I didn't get the doughnuts. Couldn't carry everything," he says apologetically as he hands me the mug.

I wind my clean-as-a-whistle scarf around my neck and take the mug. "I don't need any. I still have some left from yesterday, and besides, it's past noon."

"I'll run out to the car and get that coffee cake," Susan announces, making a hasty exit.

Taking a gigantic step forward, Aris invades my personal space. He's so close that I don't know if I'm feeling steam from the coffee or his hot breath.

"You went biking. You haven't changed yet," he observes.

Confirmed. It's not the coffee—it's his breath, which smells like rancid milk. I retreat, stepping backward into my apartment, and inadvertently land on the tip of Lenny's tail. He emits a yowl and sprints for the kitchen, running smack into the island.

Aris winces. "Think he's hurt?"

Lenny, swaying slightly, regains his balance and then gives me the cat version of the middle finger—he closes his eyes, disdainfully raises his chin, and does an about-face, turning his butt to me. "He's fine."

I turn back around, planning to tell Aris to get lost, but I guess he has other plans, because he's only four inches from my face, looking at my lips.

"I'm going to kiss you now."

I gently push him until there's a safe arm's length between us. "That's out of the question."

"But why?"

"You know why."

"Who was that guy at your place? He spent the night. Where did you meet him? Are you interested in him? What does he do for a living? Do you like him more than me?" He frowns. "I can't believe you've moved on so quickly. Are you sure you won't change your mind about us?"

How did I end up with two guys chasing me, and the one guy I love running away from me? "I'm sorry, I won't change my mind about us."

"How about another date? Do you like Italian food? French?"

"Remember that girl I mentioned? I'm setting you up with her."

He regards me as if I'm speaking a foreign language. "On a date?"

"Be at my place this coming Wednesday. Six thirty sharp."

CHAPTER FOURTEEN

J ustice opens the refrigerator. I spy condiments, a carton of milk, a gnarly pizza box—the contents of which probably look like a science project, but I'm not about to look—a bag of apples, bottled water, and beer. He might as well unscrew the appliance light bulb and plug in flashing neon sign that reads "Bachelorhood."

It would seem like a harmless thing—peering into his refrigerator—but it isn't. My heart pops like a balloon. It's an up-close-and-personal look into his life without me.

When it comes to planning meals and cooking, he's self-admittedly helpless. Up until this summer, I'd routinely taken Justice to the grocery store on weekends to restock his pantry and freezer and to buy ingredients for simple meals.

The only thing that makes me feel better as I scope out his naked shelves is that there aren't any baked goods in sight. At least Homemaker hasn't gained access to this part of his life.

Justice holds up a Corona in one hand and bottled water in the other. "What's your poison?"

Still reeling from my drinking escapade last night, I prudently choose the water. Justice tosses it to me like a football. I catch it and twist the cap. After drinking half the bottle in seconds, I place it on the soapstone countertop. Lenny, who I've brought along for my dinner date, curiously sniffs it, hoping for a gin and tonic. Sorely disappointed, he awkwardly slides off my lap and wanders over to Justice.

"He looks thirsty," notes Justice. "What should I give him?"

"He likes lime and tonic water, but I bet he would love a Corona."

"Sorry, buddy." He pats Lenny's head. "I'm running low." Justice reaches for the milk carton. Let's hope it's still in liquid form. He pours some into a bowl and sets it on the ground. "I've always pictured us with a dog, not a cat. Guess we could have both."

Here we go again. Mixed message mania! Does he still picture us ending up together and getting a dog? Is this general commentary on our past relationship, on what could have been if I hadn't fled to Colorado and ended up getting all tangled up with Nikeo, literally and figuratively?

Justice takes a drink of his Corona and studies Lenny. "I like him, though. I'm glad you brought him."

"Wasn't really my choice." I haven't become some weird cat lady who has to take her beloved animal everywhere. I only brought Lenny because at some point during the late afternoon, he climbed into my oversize navy-and-white canvas handbag and fell asleep. I tried to rouse him and get him out, but he wouldn't budge. He hunkered down and looked up at me, ready to do battle with his claws. I was forced to bring him, along with his many accoutrements: litter box, food, and his favorite toy, the feather duster.

Purring now, Lenny sticks his nose close to the bowl of milk, taste-tests it with his tongue, and jerks back, teeth bared, shaking his head as if he's been forced to drink vinegar.

Lenny wanders away from his milk to inspect the house. It seems like he approves, and why wouldn't he? The place is gorgeous, a true Craftsman gem. Despite the tenuous state of our relationship, Justice asked me to help select the finishes for the house. Overwhelmed with the monumental task and feeling pressure to do everything right, I checked out design books at the library, frequented home improvement stores after work and on the weekends, and consulted Grandma Betty via phone. In a matter of weeks I'd become a design maven and put together a cohesive, attractive plan for every room in the house.

Justice approved all my selections without once complaining about the price of any of my choices. Inlaid espresso maple flooring in all the living areas. Slate tile in all the bathrooms. Beefy off-white crown molding and baseboards throughout. A coffered ceiling in the master suite and family room. Six paneled wood doors painted off-white to match the crown and baseboards. Simple, modern light fixtures. Brushed nickel knobs and faucets.

Seeing as how Justice was so adamant about seeking my input on every minuscule aspect, even as trivial as what brand of primer to use, I'd been more than convinced that he was planning for our life together. Why else would he have gone through such trouble?

However, things change. Breakups happen. Well-endowed hourglass Home Wreckers toting baked goods and stain-removal secrets arrive on the scene.

I'm not sure if this place is currently mine or will be mine, but Lenny doesn't have any trouble taking ownership of the place. He trots around with his nose in the air.

Justice sets his beer down. "About last night and what happened—"

"Here we go—the reason you invited me over."

"That isn't why I invited you, but I do want to talk about it."

I crinkle the water bottle in my hand, applying pressure and then releasing it, filling the kitchen with the noise of collapsing plastic. "Are you going to offer an explanation? Because"—I lock my eyes on his—"it wasn't fair what you did to him, or what you said to me. It's like you were accusing me of something."

"I saw him, and I snapped. I picture you and him together, his hands on—" Justice pauses and sighs harshly. "Why was he there?"

"Why is that any of your business? We're broken up."

Drawing up his shoulders, Justice sticks his hands in the front pockets of his frayed Gap jeans, the pair with a heart-shaped ink stain on the butt. I drew it there last February.

After a long afternoon of cross-country skiing, Justice had taken a nap, falling asleep facedown on the bed. I sat next to him, reading a snore-worthy article about Renaissance literature and taking notes. Pen poised in the air, I glanced over and looked at his cute, muscular butt. He was constantly connecting the freckles on my body with ink, spelling out words, drawing pictures. I thought I should return the favor. Quietly lowering my textbook, I reached over and proceeded to draw a heart, filling it in with ink, repeating the process until I was certain it bled through the denim to his underwear.

We went to Savage Suds that night for drinks with friends, and he unknowingly walked around with a three-inch heart on his butt. His friends razzed him for half the night, referring to him as Lover Boy and Cupid. I kept a straight face, and Justice remained oblivious. Jeremy, taking pity on his older cousin, finally told him that he might want to take a look at his Valentine's Ass. Craning his neck, Justice had a look. Cracking a goofy smile, he looked at me and said, "Got me good, didn't you?"

I expected him never to wear the jeans again, but they became his favorite. This is the first time I've seen him wear them since last spring. Deliberate? Or is it just that he hasn't done laundry in a while, another sign of bachelorhood?

Justice ponders my statement about the breakup. "I take it you're not going to be patient about this. Not that I expected it."

"Why should I be, because clearly you—" Pausing, I take a deep breath, hold it between pursed lips, and then make a popping nose. "Nope, I'm not doing this." Standing, I walk over to the stereo and flip through the CDs.

"Not doing what?"

"I'm not going to argue. Fight. Pick at each other until there's nothing left. That's what we've been spending most of our time doing lately, and I'm tired of it. I had fun yesterday during the photo shoot, didn't you?"

Setting his beer down, he plants his palms on the countertops. "I did."

"Then let's have fun before you leave town. Let's play a game."

"What did you have in mind?"

Waggling my brows, I hold up the party music tape that I made a few years back, a compilation of my favorite booty-shaking songs. "Surfer dance." In preparation, I'm already stepping out of my sparkly flat shoes and shedding my tight cashmere cardigan, the one that Justice bought me last Christmas, the one I deliberately wore tonight to impress him.

"No, please don't do that to me." He lets his head drop forward. "Anything but that."

Not a dancer, Justice hates this game, whereas I love it. Two years ago, shortly after New Year's, we went up to Cable, Wisconsin, to stay in a friend's cabin for three days. We'd planned to snowmobile, cross-country ski, build a snow family, and ice fish. I was excited about all of these activities except for the one that included a hook, bait, and hours sitting in a shanty, losing sensation in my butt. As it turned out, a blizzard came out of nowhere and trapped us inside for two out of the three days, and we were forced to find other activities to amuse ourselves. We watched movies, played card games, board games, and other games of the rated-R category, and even exercised to an old Jane Fonda workout video in our underwear. By the second night in captivity, we'd run out of things to do, and that's when I put on some music and invented the surfer dance game.

I pull my hair back into a high ponytail, fastening it with the rubber band that I've been wearing as a bracelet. "Oh, yeah. We're doing this." I pop in the tape, crank up the volume, and hop up on the coffee table. Pointing at him, I remind him of the most important rules of the game. "No touching the ground at all—you have to surf the furniture. You must invent at least two new dance moves. And you have to keep moving for the entire tape—"

"There's at least thirty minutes' worth of music," he grumbles.

Stretching my arms over my head, I do a side bend to warm up. "Deal with it."

"I'm going to get thirsty." He dives into the fridge and pops open another Corona.

"The music is going to start." I wave him over. "Hurry up!"

Less than enthusiastic about the idea, he ambles over and steps onto his very bachelor black leather couch, the one that I've been dying to take out to the curb since the day he bought it. If we do end up together forever, first on the list is a ceremonial dumping of his couch and mine.

"If my friends saw me doing this, I would have to turn in my man card."

"I think you already lost it, buddy." I point at the ink heart on his butt.

MC Hammer's "U Can't Touch This" starts playing, and Justice and I start dancing like maniacs. I have rhythm, Justice not so much. The best part of this game is watching his jerky, strange movements. We dance alone for the first song, but when Sir Mix-a-Lot's "Baby Got Back" comes on, I spring onto the couch for a couples performance. Justice and I do a sad version of a dirty dance, disgracing the standard set by Patrick Swayze and Jennifer Grey, though it does feel amazing to have our hands all over each other. I jiggle my less-than-ample bootie, and Justice moves that ink heart all over the place.

When "Good Vibrations" by Marky Mark starts playing, we switch it up. I leap over to the love seat, and Justice jumps onto the fireplace hearth. By this time Lenny has ventured into the room. Unsure of our strange behavior, he crouches, maintaining a spring-loaded position. When he realizes we're just behaving like idiots and not a threat, he gradually relaxes, sits down on his haunches, spreads his legs, and starts bathing his privates, pausing at intervals to regard us with disdain.

Justice looks at him and then me. "Deliberate?"

I laugh, regarding my cat's splayed hindquarters. "Lenny tells it like it is."

For the next half hour we laugh, invent dance moves, sing out of key, and surf the furniture. We have the most amazing time, and when the last song finishes, I'm totally relaxed and completely euphoric.

Justice jumps off the couch and walks over to where I'm standing, which is on the large kitchen island. He wraps his arms around my lower legs and lifts me in the air. I'm so high that another few inches and my head would hit the ceiling. I slide down the front of him in increments. He controls my movement by holding tightly and then relaxing. When we're eye to eye, he stops. My heart pounds so hard that I'm afraid my dark navy camisole, the one that reveals what little cleavage I have, might bust open.

I can feel his heart as well, and I don't think it has anything to do with our impromptu dance session.

"I've missed us. I've missed this."

His words scrape the bottom of my heart and soul, and I'm mortally wounded by hope. To anchor myself to him, I wrap my legs around him, and he slides his hands under my butt, holding me there. I stroke the sides of his face with my hands. Resting my fingers on his bottom lip, I make an admission. "What you did to Nikeo? I liked it when you hit him. I never thought you would fight for me."

"How could you think that?"

I make another admission, one that I've often thought but never spoken. "I've always thought that if I walked away from you, you wouldn't notice, and that when you finally did, you wouldn't care. That you wouldn't miss me. You would be fine. Maybe even better without me."

His brow collapses in the middle. His eyes go all soft. He takes half a breath. "I was destroyed when you left this past spring. Things wouldn't be better without you. They would be worse. Unbearable."

Do I believe him? Would they be that unbearable, or would Susie Homemaker swoop in and save the day? Wouldn't she love that? I bet she would love to get her hands on Justice's ink-stained jeans and life, and get rid of all signs of me. She probably has an emergency stain-fighting kit all ready, and knowing her, she's packed it for the trip to Iowa, right next to a nine-by-thirteen pan of brownies.

My hazel eyes, still a sickly shade of olive, fill with tears. "But you are without me. You broke up with me. And you seem fine."

"Cane, it's only because I need—"

"Time."

"That's the only reason," he insists with a pliable sadness that makes me ache for him.

My breathing goes all shallow, and my mouth waters. I'm ravenous for him, starved for his touch and for the intimacy and love we share.

By the way his body reacts, I know that he's hungry for me as well. Our mutual wanting makes us crazed with desire. He moves one hand up under the front of my camisole, his fingers slipping under my bra, the pad of his thumb brushing my nipple. This one stroke starts a fire in my body, and it blazes out of control. My hands dive into his hair.

Our lips meet, and we skip the light and playful and go right for the down and dirty. We don't kiss as much as attack each other with lips and tongues. Justice makes a sound in the back of his throat, a purely male sound that makes me want him even more.

I'm not one to stop things once they get started; it's not my style. Act first, think later—which is why I'm surprised to discover that I'm acting and thinking simultaneously.

Is this wise? Will I regret this? Will I get what I want and need out of this? With our relationship in a perpetual state of confusion and his impending departure to Iowa, this probably isn't the—

Before I can finish this thought, the stereo pops loudly in the background as the cassette, having run out of tape, stops abruptly.

Lenny, startled by the sound, tears around the room like he's been shot. Nothing has been killed but the moment.

I pull away from Justice. "We—I—wait."

"Why?" Not easily deterred, he kisses a trail up the side of my neck and glides his tongue over my jawline.

Trying to ignore those delicious shivers of pleasure that are skating up my neck and skating around other places on my body, I take my hands out of his hair and grip the front of his shoulders. "I can't. Not until I know for sure where this—where we are going. We should stop."

Confused, he meets my eyes. This is unprecedented for us; I've never put on the brakes. When we first met, and the age difference made it impossible for us to be together, Justice spent most of his time hitting the brakes. Frequently, and with a lot of pressure. A champion of common sense, doing the right thing, and making sure things were thought through, he constantly monitored his actions, and mine as well.

I've done his job, and I've put us in foreign territory.

"I guess you're right."

He loosens his grip on me. The second my feet hit the hardwood floors, I regret opening my mouth. The thing about doing the right thing and controlling impulses—impulses that would lead to fun and delightful experiences—is that I feel like I've cheated myself out of something. In this case, I've denied myself amazing sex with the man I love. The man who loves me. How could sex possibly be wrong?

Grandma Betty, who's deeply embedded in my conscience, comes back to haunt me. Plain as day, I hear her say, "You shouldn't have had sex with Justice before you got married! That's where you went wrong."

I would never admit this to her, and I surely don't want to admit it to myself, but this may be exactly where things went haywire. Had we waited until we were married as God's law and Grandma Betty's law decrees, I wouldn't have left this past June after he popped the question, because I would have been too focused on the fact that he would finally be able to pop my cherry. Sorry for the crude pun, but if Justice and I had managed to keep our hands off each other for the past four years of dating, which would have taken iron-clad restraint and a very big chastity belt, I might be standing at the altar this very minute with him lifting the veil off my virginal face and kissing me senseless.

Had we waited, would I have hightailed it to Colorado and gotten caught up in Nikeo?

"That was . . . fun," he says, smiling grimly and looking as frustrated as I feel.

I can't help but laugh at him. "You hate dancing."

"Not when it's with you," he responds sweetly.

Before I change my mind about the sex thing, I pull my camisole back into place and reach for my sweater. "I'm starving."

Walking into the kitchen, I open the fridge and smile wryly. "So, what are we having, ketchup?"

"That wouldn't be the worst thing, would it?" Justice flips on the gas fireplace.

Like we need any more heat in this place. Turning on the air conditioning might be a better idea. Better yet, a cold shower. Then again, maybe he's not as hot and bothered as I am. I stick my head into the refrigerator, cooling myself down. Scanning the empty shelves, I sigh. How is he ever going to survive without me?

"I didn't think that far ahead," he says, staring into the gas flames.

"You invited me for dinner, and you didn't think that far ahead?"

"I had other things on my mind—like you. I wanted you here, and I thought a good way to get you here would be to invite you to dinner. Mikayla was sure giving me a hard time, telling me how pissed off you were, how—"

"She was playing games with you. You know that's her style."

"Only I didn't think she was playing. I thought you might stand me up." He walks around the large kitchen island and joins me at the refrigerator.

"I wouldn't do that to you."

He pulls open the freezer drawer. "Frozen pizzas?"

We cook the pizzas and keep the mood light by engaging in playful and flirtatious conversation. We avoid any and all things pertaining to our relationship, including the two people who have wormed their way between us: Susan and Nikeo.

When we finish eating, Justice challenges me to a game of one-on-one basketball. We walk into the garage, and he grabs the ball and heads for the small court that was paved last week.

I'm dribbling and getting ready for a warm-up shot when I decide that it's about time I inform Justice of Caprice's job offer.

"Caprice wants me to move back and work for Maid Hot."

"You're not considering it, are you?"

I launch the ball into the air; it bounces off the rim. Justice grabs the rebound and looks at me, waiting for a response.

"I like Colorado."

He levels me with a look. "You like the people in Colorado."

"This isn't about him. I loved living in the mountains. I don't know." I shrug. "Don't you ever get tired of Savage? Of the cornfields and cows?"

"I've never thought about living somewhere else."

"I hadn't either. Not until this summer, but I kind of fell in love with the Rockies."

He forcefully pushes air out his nostrils and twists his mouth into a smirk. "Sounds like you've already made up your mind."

"I haven't, not by a long shot. But this is a big opportunity for me. Caprice's company is going places, and it would be incredible to be in on the ground floor."

"I don't get a say in this?"

"Do you want a say in it?" I ask leadingly.

Shaking his head, he dribbles the ball and walks to the perimeter of the court. I want him to declare, "Yes, I want a say in it! You can't leave. Our life is here. Together!" If he got down on bended knee and begged while making that declaration, that would be even better.

But what I want is not what I get. He remains mute.

"I just wanted you to know about it."

"Now I do. Thanks for that." His response has a hard edge. He takes a jump shot, and the ball hits dead center, the net not moving at all. This time, I grab the rebound.

"I'm sorry if—"

"Samson told me what happened with Jocelyn. That's why I came over last night," he interrupts, abruptly switching topics. "I wanted to talk."

Pulling the ball back to my body, I rest it against my hip. I keep my eyes trained on the hoop. "What happened . . . it's horrible."

"It's worse than that," he muses.

I look over at him and meet his eyes. "I would have loved to talk to you last night. Things never seem quite right until we talk. You've been my best friend for six years."

"When I showed up at your place and he was there—it feels like I've been replaced. In more ways than one."

"You haven't been. I didn't invite him over."

Justice shakes his head curtly. "You can't tell me he was in the neighborhood, not when he lives in Colorado, which I'm sure makes Caprice's offer more interesting."

"The offer has nothing to do with him. He's not even living in Colorado anymore."

"Regardless of where he's living, he has an agenda."

I raise my brow. "If we're going to talk about agendas, I know someone who has one when it comes to you."

Turning toward the basket, I perform a neat jump shot, again missing. I don't even have to move for the rebound; the ball bounces and returns to my hands.

He walks over, positions himself closely behind me, and places his hands on top of mine. I'm holding the ball, and Justice is holding me.

He kisses the back of my neck and moves one of his hands to my hip. I drop the ball, and it rolls off the concrete and gets wedged under my car. His fingers work their way under my coat, up under the bottom of my sweater, and find a sliver of bare skin just above my jeans. His fingertips move back and forth until my skin hums with pleasure. Blood rushes to the most sensitive spots in my body, and my mind goes all fuzzy and vapid. I want his hands to dive below my waistband.

"It doesn't matter what her agenda is. What I care about, what I've always cared about, is you and your agenda," he says.

His words prompt my heart to go all gooey, like a piece of melted caramel. I spin around in his arms. Our eyes lock, but that isn't the only thing I want locked together. I know what Grandma Betty said about everything going wrong because of sex, but I have to believe that the opposite is also true. Everything can go right because of sex, can't it? Because all I want right now is to throw Justice down on this basketball court and demonstrate my agenda in detail.

His lips work aggressively over my jaw and then down my neck. He fixes his hands on my hipbones and pushes himself against me. Sensors go off all over my body, and his sensors, with which I'm well acquainted, are lighting up as well. It never felt like this with Nikeo. It didn't even come close. Being with Justice, it feels like coming home. It's the strongest sense of right in my world.

He takes my face in his hands and has moved in for another kiss when my cell phone inconveniently chirps, vibrating in the pocket of my coat.

Sighing impatiently, I reach into my pocket. I flip open the phone. "Hello."

"Ca-Cane. Something horrible—"

Choking on her sobs, Jocelyn's unable to finish the sentence.

"Oh, Jocelyn, sweetie." Her doctor's appointment was this afternoon. This can't be good. She's pregnant. Or she's contracted a disease from that weasel. "I'm here. What's wrong? What is it?"

"There aren't just pictures. There's something worse."

Justice and I pull into the Schaeffer driveway. Samson sits on the back bumper of his vintage yellow pickup truck, the one that he, Justice, and Jeremy spent eight months restoring last year. He stares off into the distance, his eyes fixed on a cow pasture. A bottle of Maker's Mark and a shot glass sit on the ground next to him.

Justice turns off the ignition and unbuckles his seat belt. He sits up straight, pushing his back against the leather seat as he studies his uncle. "He's destroyed."

I regard Samson's defeated pose. "The whole family is."

The October air, infused with pungent odor of manure and freshly cut hay, has gone from warm to cold in a matter of hours. It's so chilly this evening that it blisters the inside of my sinuses.

Turning slightly, Samson nods a greeting, but his ever-present, easy smile, the one that reveals his chipped front tooth, is absent.

Justice and I get out of the truck and walk over. The three of us regard each other briefly. The quiet night, brittle with cold and tension, seems dangerously close to cracking. Words. Movement. A gesture. Anything might cause catastrophic damage.

I remain perfectly still, respecting the frailty of the situation.

Samson swings his eyes back out to the pasture. I'm surprised when he starts speaking.

"Just got back from the office," he says in a detached tone. "I looked at all the proofs today. They turned out great. I picked one out, so we're ready to go. The campaign will be a success. We'll roll out production in a week, and then we're going to test-market the product in a few prime locations."

"That's great." Justice sits down next to his uncle.

"I'm going inside," I announce softly.

"Cane—" Samson clears his throat and reaches for his shot glass and whiskey. "I want to thank you for being there for Jocelyn. Justice told me what you did at the game last night after I left with Jocelyn and how you tried to help."

In light of the new developments, what I said over that loudspeaker last night probably made things worse. The only thing I succeeded in doing was making myself and Jocelyn look like a pair of lying fools. "I would do anything for her."

With shaking hands, Samson pours himself a shot, but instead of drinking it himself, he hands it to his nephew and then looks at me. "I'm glad you came over, because I don't know what to do for her. I don't know how to make this better."

Justice drinks the shot like medicine, and I leave the two of them and walk toward the house. I enter through the back door that leads into the family room. The youngest Schaeffer boys are watching a movie and eating popcorn.

Jade stuffs popcorn in his mouth and looks at me. "Jocelyn's in her room. She's crying about something again."

"Knock it off!" His older brother, Jonas, throws a pillow at him. "You don't know what you're talking about."

"Could you hold on a second," Jenny says into the phone. Decked out in sparkly black pajamas, she stands in the kitchen, phone pinned to her chest, a tightly wound dish towel bunched in her right hand like she's ready to whip anyone who crosses her. "No fighting, or I'm turning off the movie!" she warns.

She puts the phone back to her ear. "I apologize for the interruption. As I was saying, unless this is resolved in a timely manner and in a way that we see fit, Samson and I will no longer donate any money to the school."

She pauses. "No, I don't think we can come to an understanding. Suspension isn't enough. Those three students need to be kicked out of the district. If they aren't expelled, I will be hiring a lawyer and pressing criminal charges. You don't want the school to show up on the Chicago news, do you? Call me when you've reached a decision," she says severely and disconnects, tossing the phone onto the counter.

She glances at me, a nasty look on her face. If I were any closer, she might scourge me with the towel that she's busy twisting in her hands.

Narrowing her eyes, she regards me critically, as if I can't be trusted. "She told you what they did?"

"Yes."

Her cheeks slacken, and she releases the cotton towel; wrinkled and dejected, it hangs by her side. "I'm trying to fix things."

"I know." I make my way toward the staircase. Jenny rushes over to me. Believing she's going to assault me in some fashion, my first reaction is to duck and cover. As it turns out, she's not attacking. I can't quite believe what she's doing. It's unexpected. Shocking. No-nonsense, bitter, sharp-tongued Jenny is crying.

Though her expression is frozen, fat misshapen tears roll down her face, revealing a vulnerability that I didn't think she possessed.

"When you talk to her, make sure she knows that whatever she wants to do, I'm behind her. No matter what."

"I'll tell her."

"That might not be good enough." Jenny presses the towel to her eyes and wipes roughly. The towel was never intended as a weapon but as a substitute for tissues. It's damp with her tears. "Make her believe you," she pleads.

Nodding in understanding, I climb the staircase and knock gently on Jocelyn's door. I enter slowly, expecting to find her facedown on her pink carpeting, nearly drowned in a lake of tears.

Instead, she's sitting on her bed, arms crossed, a jaded look on her face. Suitcases and random grocery bags packed with all of her belongings surround her.

Jocelyn is stoic and angry. Jenny is openly emotional. I said *no* to sex with Justice. The world has officially flipped upside down, and if I don't grab on to something, and quickly, I might fall off.

"How are you?" I ask, closing the door.

Looking to the side, she fixes her eyes on the far wall and shrugs. "Who was my mom talking to?"

"Someone from the school."

She laughs mirthlessly. "Like that's going to do any good. She's getting the school board involved. She wants to go to the police and press charges against all of them. She wants to get a lawyer. The list is endless."

"What does your dad say about all of this?"

"Hasn't said a word since we left for the doctor. It feels like he hates me."

"But he doesn't," I state emphatically. "He loves you so much that—"

"That's the problem. He loves me so much that he can't handle this."

"He can handle anything." Remembering my promise to Jenny, I add, "So can your mom. They'll do whatever you need. They're both behind you."

"Maybe. But it feels like I'm alone."

"How did the doctor go?"

"Clean bill of health, except for the slut title I've earned. I'm sure they put that on my medical chart."

"I'm not going to let you beat yourself up. Don't say that about yourself, because it's not true."

"That's not how I see it."

I pull out her desk chair and sit. "What can I do?"

She shifts her gaze to me. "Destroy the evidence. Destroy Deanna. And Taryn and Colin," she says weakly.

I thought the larger-than-life poster of a Jocelyn in lingerie was bad, but snapshots are the least of her problems. One of the younger varsity cheerleaders, a junior named Elise, was so disgusted with Deanna and how she'd embarrassed Jocelyn that she betrayed her squad captain and called Jocelyn a few hours ago, telling her the whole gruesome tale.

Colin had not only taken still shots of the rendezvous with his Nikon, but he'd also picked up Taryn's video camera off the dresser and recorded the event.

Once the boys had developed the film and watched the sex video, Colin bragged to Deanna about the illicit escapade and invited her over for a private viewing session. Deanna convinced Colin to make copies of everything. Even before she had the evidence in hand, she started spreading the word about what Jocelyn had done at Taryn's party through the high school underground.

When Deanna's word wasn't good enough to convince her peers, she hosted her own film festival at her home for twenty of her closest friends, where she took immense pleasure in proving that she'd been telling the truth.

Wanting to exploit the situation for all it was worth and boost her popularity, Deanna distributed the evidence to some disreputable characters at the school. Unfortunately, Elise doesn't know who Deanna gave them to, or how many copies have been made.

When Jocelyn tearfully relayed the story on the phone, I was ready to buy a machine gun and play vigilante. So was Justice.

"I'm still not ruling out going above the law, and if I can't go above it, I'll limbo below it," I tell her now.

Despite her bravado, her despondency is palpable. I attempt to lighten the mood. "I'll have you know that no one can beat me at limbo. I'm low to the ground as it is. Virtually undetectable. What do you want me to do? I could call the news stations; see if I can get the media to take them down. How about we kidnap them? Justice and Jeremy could help us. We'll make them strip naked and tie them to the trees in front of the school. Or we could go the Middle Ages route and tar and feather them. Maybe take them to the gravel pit and give them a good stoning."

"That's just it. It doesn't matter what happens to them. Even if they're kicked out of school, it won't matter. I'm stuck with what happened. It will never go away."

I'm the first to admit that I'm not always a nice person. More often than not, my thoughts have horns and a spiked tail, and my tongue is like a medieval flail. Over the years I've left carnage in my wake with my cutting words. However, I'm baffled by what Taryn and Colin did and even more disturbed by Deanna's premeditated cruelty. All for what? To shame and humiliate? To ruin another person's life for the sheer fun of it?

As far as I'm concerned, those three are missing brains and hearts. Forget expulsion or even incarceration; their parents should donate their bodies to a lab so that scientists can assess how they live without vital organs.

I watch Jocelyn studying the contents of her room. The tall four-poster bed. The frilly pink. The canopy above her. The plush mauve carpeting below her. "Look at this place," she says with disdain. "Isn't it obvious? I don't belong here anymore."

"If you want to leave, we could go to Florida and stay with Grandma Betty and Frank. Or how about Colorado? I'm sure Caprice would be thrilled if we came for a visit."

"I need to get out of here."

More than willing to whisk her away from this nightmare, I stand. "Then let's do it. I can talk to your parents, see if they would be willing to let you leave—"

"No. That's not what I meant. There's something I need to do." She surveys the surface of her bed. "But first I need to put all this stuff away."

If I were placing monetary bets on what people, including myself, would say or do this evening, I'd be in the red. "You want to stay?"

Squaring her shoulders and raising her chin, Jocelyn stands. "As soon as Elise told me what had happened, I lined up the suitcases and started packing."

"I would have done the same thing." Actually, if I'd been humiliated in the way that Jocelyn was and then discovered that there was a sex tape of me circulating around my high school, I would have skipped the packing and gone straight to the leaving. If I were her, I'd be on another continent by now.

"That's what they want—right? Me to run away with my tail between my legs. If I did that—if I went to Florida or Colorado, if I dropped out of school, if I did any of those things—they would win. I'm not going to let that happen. I'm not going to let them intimidate me or bully me. I'm staying. I'm winning."

Who is this girl and what has she done with Jocelyn? I know firsthand that she doesn't like to stick around and deal with her problems. When the going gets tough, Jocelyn usually gets going, and the faster the better. "You're sure about this?"

"More sure than I've ever been. About anything." She unzips a suitcase and dumps out her clothes. "I'm not an idiot. It's going to be hard. Next to impossible, even. I know that people are going to laugh in my face. Talk behind my back. Say horrible, disgusting things about me. Make fun of me. I'm going to want to change my mind every single second, but I'm not going to."

Opening her dresser, Jocelyn neatly folds her shirts and places them in stacks. "Can you help me?" she asks.

"Of course."

Twenty minutes later, everything is back in its place. Suitcase shells are scattered around the floor. Jocelyn stands by her bed, one foot crossed over the other, her hand wrapped around the curvy white post of her bed.

"We can go now. I'm ready," she announces with pluck.

I'm not sure where we're going, but I have no doubt that she's ready for whatever comes next.

CHAPTER FIFTEEN

What is she doing here?

Turning off the ignition, I climb out of my dusty, dirty, hasn't-been-properly-cleaned-in-a-year Cavalier and glare at her shiny, waxed, I-could-check-my-reflection-in-it Solara convertible. If it's filthy on the inside, I'll feel better. Hands cupped in front of my face, I peer in through the driver's-side window and examine the immaculate buff leather interior. Perfection. Does she have a magic stain removal formula for cars as well? Because if so, I could use her expertise on removing the large coffee stain on the ceiling directly above my steering wheel.

The disparity in the state of our cars discloses the disparity in our personalities. She's tidy and pulled together, outside and inside, and I'm a hot mess, in the process of coming undone on multiple levels. It would take a magic trick and a miracle, possibly a reincarnation, for me to be anything like her.

Doing some investigative work, I place my hand on the hood of her car. Cold, no hint of activity. She's been here for some time. Seeing as how there's nothing in the car, no oversize Coach handbag, no pan of goodies, she's probably inside, getting comfortable and hoping she's in it for the long haul.

Not if I can haul her out of there first. Frustrated, annoyed, and pissed as hell, I flip off her car and growl.

It's not like Justice doesn't know I'm coming over to pick up my recovering alcoholic cat and spend time with him before he leaves for Iowa tomorrow morning. We've talked three separate times today, engaging in long, not-so-innocent conversations where the subject of sex kept coming up.

During our last conversation, I told him about the comment Grandma Betty made about everything going wrong because we'd had sex.

"No wonder you fell on your face that day." He laughed.

"Do you think if we'd waited, things would be okay right now?"

"I don't necessarily think things would be any different. We would have still gone through growing pains. Given how we feel about each other, I think what she said is shortsighted. Although I know why she said it. Sex complicates things in the best of circumstances."

And in the worst of circumstances, sex can ruin a person and leave scars of regret and shame that will last a lifetime. Case in point: Jocelyn. After what I witnessed last night, though, I'm not that concerned about Jocelyn's scars lasting too long. "That's why I stopped us last night. It would have messed everything up," I told him.

"You did the right thing, but if I'm being honest, I wish you hadn't. It's been too long."

I performed some quick math in my head. Justice and I hadn't slept together in four months, sixteen days, and eight hours. Give me enough time, and I could calculate the minutes and seconds. "What if sex wasn't an option anymore?"

"You're not going celibate on me?"

"Not forever," I responded. "Don't get me wrong—I want to have sex, and lots of it. I want to rip your clothes off and attack—"

"I've already taken one cold shower today. I don't want to take another. Not unless you're in the shower with me, which would make it totally worthwhile."

"This conversation is headed for an X rating."

He lowered his voice, making it all naughty and sexy. "You wouldn't like that?"

Just talking to him about sex got me all hot and bothered. "Have mercy on me please. I was thinking—what if we waited to have sex until we get married?" I hastened to add, "I realize that might not happen, that we might not be together—"

He immediately interjected. "Don't say things like that."

"I'm being realistic. Would you want to wait?"

"*Want* is a strong word. I wouldn't want to wait, but I would. For you, I would do anything."

Justice would do anything for me? He'll have a chance to prove it when I ask him to kick Susan out of the house, but it's likely I'll beat him to the punch. I mean that in the most literal way. Glowering, I hoist my navy-and-white-striped bag over my shoulder and stomp toward the house, intending to make a grand, obnoxious entrance.

By the time I step onto the slate-tiled porch, my blood is at a rapid boil. My brain feels all bubbly and hot. My vision has gone fuzzy. I'm wired with a powerful dose of adrenaline. As I'm reaching for the doorknob, I spot Lenny. He's sitting directly in front of the long vertical window to the right of the solid fir front door—another one of my selections. Tail twitching, eyes half closed, he looks right at me and then swings his head once to the right and then way over to the left.

Is this a sign?

It's like Lenny is trying to tell me that what I'm about to do is a bad idea. I'm sure it must be, but I can't confidently make that judgment, since I'm pretty sure my head might explode. If that happens, I'll be forced to mop up the mess with my red knitted scarf, the same one that Susan diligently cleaned and returned to me yesterday, the one that smells faintly of her citrusy perfume.

In a very un–Cane Kallevik move, I force myself to stop, take a moment to fill my lungs with oxygen, and consider my situation calmly. It isn't just Lenny who's getting to me. Although he's continuing to stare at me and adamantly shake his head, I realize it has nothing to do with me and everything to do with the fat squirrel running back and forth on a branch behind me.

The person who's really gotten to me and made me think about how to handle tricky and unpleasant situations is Jocelyn.

Behaving with maturity far beyond her years—and mine—Jocelyn had me drive her to Deanna's house and then pardoned her for all of her sins.

I'm ashamed to say that I was rooting for a different outcome—not a public hanging or anything that drastic, but definitely an ending that included some ridicule and humiliation. I wanted Deanna to feel some of the pain that she'd inflicted on Jocelyn. On the ride over to Deanna's, I encouraged Jocelyn to take the low road and to take it fast, no matter the consequence.

"We have to think of something, and quick. We're in this together, Jocelyn. Your mom can focus on trying to get her expelled, and we'll focus on revenge. It's not like we won't have an army of people to help. Jeremy, Justice, and Mikayla would pitch in. I know I mentioned tarring and feathering and stoning earlier, and just so you know, I was only half kidding. We can get creative and find a way to torture her."

Jocelyn pulled her knit cap off and flung it onto the seat beside me. "I need to handle this on my own."

"I got it!" I slammed my fist against the steering wheel. "Frank has all this video equipment, and I wouldn't be surprised if some of that included high-tech surveillance stuff. I'm going down to Florida soon, and I could bring it back. Better yet, I could call and have him ship it up here. We could plant cameras and microphones all over her house and even in the girl's locker room at school. We'll collect all the material, edit accordingly, and make our very own Deanna video." I glanced at Jocelyn, hoping for a reaction, but she kept her eyes trained out the front window.

"How about we hire a couple of strippers, being sure to use her name when we book them, then have them show up in one of her classes. That would get her expelled." I looked over at her. "What do you think?"

She pushed her palms down the length of her thighs and looked at me. Her eyelids were puffy from crying. "No."

"There's always the good old-fashioned framing," I said cheerily. "We could plant some liquor and marijuana in her locker. But that might get her in too much trouble. We don't want to slap her with a felony or get caught doing it. So, we could just put some grass clippings in a baggie, or—"

"That's her house. Right up there. The last one on the left." Jocelyn pointed to a dilapidated, wonky farmhouse.

Peeling paint. Rotting wood. A porch that was barely attached and looked more like a lawn ornament. Cracked windowpanes held in place by duct tape. I was caught off guard. Deanna was a beautiful girl, and she behaved with such a fierce sense of entitlement, I expected something much more upscale than this. "I was picturing a *Gone with the Wind* kind of house," I remarked as I turned into a driveway so pitted and muddy I wasn't sure if I could get my Cavalier back out. "But I suspect that it might be gone with the wind if we get a strong enough storm."

"It's probably why she hates me so much," Jocelyn said. "She thinks I have everything."

I turned off the engine and unbuckled my seat belt. "Does she know you're coming?"

"I called her. She knows." Jocelyn opened her door and then carefully pushed it shut.

I got out of the vehicle, and at the same time Deanna, wearing shorts so tiny they could have been underwear and an Abercrombie sweatshirt, appeared on the crumbling cement steps. I expected Jocelyn to swing her eyes my direction with a help-me-I-don't-know-what-to-do look, but she marched confidently forward.

Deanna, contemptuous to the core, sneered at us. "Why the hell is that bitch here?" She pointed at me. "You didn't say anything about her coming."

I was about to make an unforgettable, witty retort, something like "Someone has to dispose of your body," when Jocelyn turned and shot me a warning look, shaking her head slightly.

Keeping quiet wasn't my strong suit, but if that was what she wanted, then I would do it. Even if it killed me, and it just might.

Jocelyn faced her enemy. "She drove. She's a friend."

"What's your point in coming here? Because I already know that your parents are trying to get me kicked out of school. They can't. I didn't make the video, and"—she paused and emitted a high-pitched you're-an-idiot kind of laugh—"I'm not the one who got high, screwed Taryn, and was dumb enough to be caught on pictures and video."

The old Jocelyn would have cowered, cried, and run away, but the new Jocelyn squared her shoulders and boldly stepped forward. I adored this confident new girl.

"I'm not going to ask why you did what you did, because it doesn't matter anymore," she said. "But I want to know, did it get you what you wanted?"

Deanna walked down the steps and came face-to-face with Jocelyn. "Why are you here? Are you here to warn me that your rich mommy and daddy are going to make my life hell?"

"My being here has nothing to do with my parents. I'm here because I wanted to know if what you did—if it made you happy." Jocelyn briefly studied Deanna's face. "But I think I already know that it didn't."

Taking a noticeable step backward, Deanna blindly reached behind her for the rusted wrought-iron railing. "You don't know anything."

"I'm okay," Jocelyn said softly. "Better than okay, actually. But I don't think you are. Just know that I don't hold this against you. I forgive you."

Deanna's face went in four different directions at once. Eyebrows up, then down. Lips twisted, then flatlining. Jaw protruding, then going slack. "Get the hell out of here."

"If that's what you want." Jocelyn turned around and started walking. "I'm finished here. Let's go," she said, addressing me.

"You sure?" I asked quietly.

"Positive."

Jocelyn opened the passenger door, and Deanna was determined to get the last word. "There are so many copies, you're never going to live this down," she proclaimed loudly.

Jocelyn's smile was blasé. "Probably, but you know what? I don't care." With that declaration made, she climbed into the car and slammed the door.

Twenty-some hours later, I'm in a position where I can take the high road or the low road. God knows I love the low road. I know it like the back of my hand. All those fun turns, twists, and dips that make for an exciting ride. But I know that the low road doesn't always lead to the best destination; sometimes it causes a catastrophic crash.

Last night, Jocelyn set the bar high and handled herself with dignity. As an adult, shouldn't I do the same?

The answer, of course, is yes. It's time to time to forgo the limbo and leap over the high bar. Even if Justice isn't sure he wants to spend the rest of his life with me, I know that he loves me. He's told me time and again that Susan's a friend, and I'm going to trust him. He's innocent until proven guilty, and I'm not going to indict him and cause a scene. Susan, on the other hand . . . she's never been innocent. It's obvious what her intentions are, and I'm going to make sure she's more than aware of mine.

I'm about to open the door when Lenny backs up and lowers himself to the ground, preparing to attack the chattering squirrel that's now running on the grass behind me. Only poor Lenny has forgotten that there's a glass barrier between him and the outside. Before I can shout a warning, he launches himself in the air, slams into the glass, and topples over. It takes a long moment for him to recover, and when he does, he shakily rights himself and looks up at me, all dazed and confused.

"You're not the only one who feels like knocking his head against the glass," I inform him.

He meows in response. Plastering a smile on my face, I open the door.

Dropping my bag on the floor, I console my rattled cat, stroking his head softly and scratching under his chin. "If you're not careful, one of these days you're going to really hurt yourself."

He glances up at me and then hops into my bag, curls up, and closes his eyes.

Justice walks into the entryway. He has a caught-red-handed look on his face. He walks over to me, pushes my hair off my shoulders, and leans in close. "I swear, I didn't know she was coming. I didn't invite her," he whispers urgently.

He may not have invited her. He may not even want her to be here, but it's clear that he's taking advantage of her presence and even enjoying it. There's evidence of this enjoyment on his face, in the form not of a smile but of the powdered sugar smeared at the corner of his mouth. There's even some on his jeans, which are the same ones he was wearing yesterday. Powdered sugar on the front of the jeans I can handle, but if he's gotten anything on that heart I drew, or if Susan has gotten anywhere near that heart, I'm not sure if I'll be able to pull off the maturity act.

Before I can get riled up again, I inhale and exhale with the concentration of a devoted yogi. In with the good, out with the bad. "No big deal."

Kneeling next to my bag, I inspect Lenny more closely. He has already fallen asleep and is snoring. "He just crashed into the window. Do you think a cat can have a concussion? Should I try to rouse him at regular intervals?"

Justice gives Lenny a brief once-over and then looks at me. "You're okay with her being here?"

"Why do you look so surprised? It's fine."

He regards me warily. "It is?"

I give Lenny one last pat; he throws open one eye, letting me know that I've disturbed his slumber. I stand up and shrug. "I left all the weapons at the door. I'm not going to start throwing punches like someone else I know." I can't resist that one little dig.

"Is Cane finally here?" Susan asks from the other room.

Sliding my arms around Justice, I rest the side of my face against his chest. His heart is racing. "I'm sorry about this. I wanted it to be just us," he says.

"It still could be. Ask her to leave."

"You know I don't like to be—"

He isn't able to finish telling me what I already know—that he can't possibly kick anyone out of his house, because he can't be rude—because Susan walks around the corner. She spies Justice and me in an embrace, and before she can put her princess smile in place, her lips pucker as if she's tasted something bitter.

Relaxing my hold on Justice, I force my face into an expression that doesn't scream "I hate you." Justice's beautiful aquamarine eyes dart from me to Susan and back again. His brow creases with worry.

"Great to see you!" she gushes.

Sorry I can't say the same, because it's so horrible to see you! Thanks for being the home wrecker that you are and ambushing my last night with Justice before he leaves!

The old Cane would have said these things. The new Cane, or at least the one who's temporarily filling in for the evening, or for the minute, or for the second, or for however long I can keep up the dignified behavior, settles for a simple, "Hi."

Susan's wearing a ruby-red wrap shirt that reveals her ample, beautiful cleavage, cream wool trousers pressed within an inch of their life, and dark brown high-heeled boots. Her hair is arranged in an artful French twist. Her makeup is simple. Mascara. Blush. Red lipstick. Even from five feet away I can smell her signature perfume, a citrusy scent that reminds me of an overripe orange.

I don't match up in the least. I'm wearing jeans that Mikayla and I shot up with a BB gun last fall; we'd been trying out new methods of distressing. Unlike Susan's displayed cleavage, I'm hiding mine underneath an oversize navy wool ski sweater that belonged to Frank before Grandma Betty shrunk it. As for a bra? I'm not wearing one. If loose, long, and wavy is a hairstyle, then I have that going for me. Other than the Carmex I smeared on my lips after I got out of the shower, my face is naked. I never wear perfume, unless powder-fresh-scent deodorant counts.

"I thought I would swing by with dinner and dessert—you know, a sort of going-away celebration for Justice and me. I figured he wouldn't have anything in his refrigerator. You know how bachelors are, right?" Susan winks conspiratorially. "I looked in the fridge a few weeks ago when I was here painting, and I was appalled! I don't know how he survives. Anyway, he mentioned that you were coming over tonight, and I say, the more the merrier!"

I proffer a tolerant smile and parrot Susan's words, spicing it up with a dash of sarcasm. "The more the merrier!"

"Could I interest you in a glass of wine? I brought red or white. I also have some delicious appetizers, and of course some baked goods for dessert. Justice got into those already."

"You must have come with a pretty big picnic basket."

Laughing, she replies, "It was pretty big, actually. Come in, come in!" She waves me into my own house.

She's acting like she owns the place. Act all you want, Susie Home Wrecker, but this house, this man, and this life aren't yours.

When Susan's out of earshot, Justice's lips brush against my ear. "I didn't expect you to be okay with this."

"If there's one lesson I've learned over the last few weeks, it's never to have any expectations."

"Thank you for handling this so well."

I draw one corner of my mouth up into a sharp smile. "Don't thank me just yet."

I play mature Cane very well. I make it through appetizers (olive tapenade on crackers), dinner (pecan-crusted chicken breasts), and dessert (brownies sprinkled with powdered sugar) without making one nasty remark. This is mostly due to the fact that I rarely have an opportunity to open my mouth. Susan does all the talking. While she tells Justice and me all about her scrapbooking and card-making hobby, I eat and fall asleep with my eyes open.

The three of us find common ground in work and discuss the ad campaign for Farmer and the Belle, the new Iowa location, and the increase of online sales thanks to the slick new website.

Talk of marketing leads to a discussion about dead weight in the department. "Trina drives me crazy. I'm carrying the workload, and it isn't fun," I complain.

"She's such a nice girl," Susan remarks diplomatically.

Good to know Susan likes her, since I'm about to set Trina up with her brother. I just hope Trina is on board with it.

"Nice doesn't mean anything if she isn't doing her job," comments Justice.

When we're finished eating, Susan insists on cleaning up and doing the dishes. Justice and I sit idly by and watch her whistle while she works (she actually does whistle), and when she's finished, she announces that she's brought movies.

"*Pretty Woman* or *Jerry Maguire*. Which one do you guys want to watch?"

Perfect. Two romantic movies to choose from. I'm sure Susan anticipated a cozy, I-want-to-jump-your-bones evening with bachelor Justice, only to have me crash her party.

"Cane loves *Jerry Maguire*," Justice announces.

I don't want to sit here and watch a stupid movie with stupid Susan. I glare at him, shrieking Kick her out! with my eyes, but he's blind and deaf to my eye screams. The perpetual nice guy, he walks over to the entertainment center and turns on the system.

Susan opens the DVD case and hands the movie to Justice. "*Jerry*

Maguire it is, then."

Justice picks up the remote and settles himself in the middle of the couch. He pats the cushion next to him. I assume the invitation is meant for me, only he doesn't look at me when he does this. He's staring at the television, leaving the hand pat open for interpretation. Susan seizes the opportunity and sits down next to him, less than three inches from his thigh. She demurely crosses her legs and angles her body toward him.

Next she'll be sliding her arm around his shoulder and nuzzling his ear.

"Are you going to join us?" she asks politely.

Absolutely! Because I can't wait to sit down on the other side of him and make a Justice sandwich. Why not share!

"Sugar Cane, would you grab me a beer?" Justice asks, looking completely comfortable with this awkward situation.

I could get you a beer, but what I really want to give you is a giant knuckle sandwich. As I'm contemplating speaking these very words aloud, Lenny, who's purring in my lap, moves his paw up my chest and places it directly over my mouth. Even though he simply wants more attention, I interpret it as a warning. He's been my personal Jiminy Cricket this evening.

At the rate things are going, I'm going to need more than a paw on my mouth. Does Justice actually believe that I'm okay with all of this? Does he think that the three of us hanging out and watching a romantic comedy together is no big deal? He has to realize that it's disastrous. The equivalent would be me having Nikeo and Justice over for dinner and a movie.

In his defense, I told him it was okay that she was here. I've been doing a pretty good job of acting like everything is just super, so good in fact that if the Academy of Motion Pictures were present, I'd be getting an Oscar nomination. It's not like I expect Justice to read the fine print in my mind, but after six years together, and given all the issues I've had with Susan over the past few weeks, he should know that the last thing I want is for her to be the third wheel on a night that was supposed to have been all about us as a couple. Something like this isn't in the fine print. It's in enormous bold font, and if Justice remains illiterate, then I can't handle staying here a second longer. I'm going to end up saying and doing something that I'll regret.

"I'm wiped. It's going to be a long day at work tomorrow, and I want to get some sleep," I announce. I'm already on my feet, gathering Lenny's food and water bowl.

"You're leaving?" Susan asks, much too pleasantly.

"Obviously I'm not staying, am I?" Oops. I just open-hand-slapped her with sarcasm. If I have any hope of winning that Academy Award, I'm going to have to keep it together for a few more minutes.

Justice pauses the DVD player. "You can't leave," he says, his tone revealing disappointment.

Let him be disappointed. "I can, and I am. Thanks for dinner, Susan. It was great."

"My pleasure," she replies.

Screw the award. Sarcasm can't be stopped, not when it's part of my everyday vernacular. "Have a spectacular time in Iowa. I'm sure you guys will find lots of things to keep you busy."

I head into the mudroom and pick up the litter box. Lenny circles my feet, meowing.

"Go get in my bag." He obediently trots toward the front door.

I turn, intending to follow him, but Justice is blocking the exit.

"Why are you leaving?"

"Because I can't stay here a second longer."

"You're not okay with this, are you?"

"Ding, ding, ding. Congratulations." I push the edge of the litter box into his stomach. "Can you move, please? I want to get home."

Holding his ground, he frowns. "Why did you say that you were okay in the first place?"

"Because I was trying to emulate Jocelyn and be a mature adult, but it backfired."

This confuses him. "What does Jocelyn have to do with this?"

I planned on telling him about Jocelyn's visit with Deanna and what transpired last night, but I'm not about to do that in front of Home Wrecker.

"If you ask her to leave"—I look over his shoulder and then meet his eyes again—"I'll stay."

He rubs the spot between his eyebrows, a sure indication that he's uncomfortable with my request. "I'm not good at being rude."

"Say something like, 'I really want to spend some time alone with Cane tonight.' I think she's perceptive enough to figure that out."

He sighs. "I guess I could do that."

I stick my head forward, drop my chin, and narrow my eyes. "You guess? Don't put yourself out. Move."

He steps aside, and I walk past him.

"Cane, I wanted to spend time with you before I left."

"Ditto, but I didn't picture a threesome." I hoist my navy bag onto my shoulder, and Lenny, who's curled up inside, peeks out at Justice.

"We still could."

He's clueless. "Snuggling with you and Susan on the couch! That would be great fun." I nod at the door. "Could you open it?"

"I'll carry all of this stuff out for you." He reaches for the litter box.

He's going to help me leave, but he refuses to make her leave? "No. Thanks. I got this."

He opens the door and follows me out to my car. "I don't know what you're expecting me to say or do."

I set the litter box in the bottom of the trunk, slam it shut, and then place Lenny and the bag in the back seat. "I think I made it pretty clear, didn't I?"

"Yes, but she was nice enough to bring us dinner and a movie—"

"But nothing." I climb in my car. "If you're that clueless, let me paint the picture for you. Let's say you showed up at my place, only to discover Nikeo in an apron, cooking me dinner."

"That's not the same at all."

"Please." I slam my door and buckle my seat belt. Justice taps on the window, and I begrudgingly roll it down.

"What?"

"It's not the same," he insists.

"Double standard in full effect tonight, huh?"

"You and Nikeo have history. Nothing has happened between Susan and me."

"Yet, but she wants it to, and it seems like she's pretty good at getting her way."

Crouching down so that he's at eye level with me, he rests his hands on the windowsill. "Cane, this isn't how I imagined the night going—"

"Have fun watching *Jerry Maguire*."

"I'm not going to watch. I'm going to ask her to leave."

Perfect. Impeccable timing. "You couldn't have done that two hours ago? Call me when you get to Iowa." Before either of us can say or do anything else, I drive away.

I'm angry with Justice and with Susan, but mostly I'm angry with myself. In trying to be someone that I'm not cut out to be, I've made things worse. I attempted to let everything roll off my shoulders, and it did. But once it was off my shoulders, it slid down my back and bit me in the ass. Now I have a gigantic pain in my butt.

I don't know how to get rid of the pain, but I know what would make me feel better.

I roll up to a stop sign and sit for a long moment, drumming my fingers on the steering wheel. I could go home to my apartment, get on my raggedy old sweatpants, go to bed mad as hell, and probably not get a wink of sleep. Or I could drive out to a derelict old farmhouse and pay someone a visit.

Lenny emerges from my bag and hops onto the front seat. He places his front paws up on the dashboard and looks at me, waiting for me to decide what direction to take.

Unquestionably, my silver compass would come in handy in a situation like this, but what would better serve me is a strong moral compass. Too bad both of those compasses are lost and broken.

Instead of turning left, which would take me back to my quiet apartment, I take a hard right, squealing the tires. Jocelyn may have said her piece to Deanna, but I haven't found any sort of peace just yet.

CHAPTER SIXTEEN

Peter Frawley stares into his compact mirror and applies bright blue mascara to his lashes; no wonder he and Trina have become fast best friends. With their love of all things eighties, they're soul mates.

Peter emits a high-pitched groan. "This music is atrocious. Dave Matthews Band? Talk about cliché adult alternative rock turned mainstream garbage. Don't you have any Madonna in that collection?" he asks, glancing over at the CDs that Mikayla spread out across my living room floor when she arrived earlier.

"I'm not changing it. It's not my goal to entertain you. I'm playing this to entertain myself and Lenny." I've recently discovered that Lenny is a huge Dave Matthews fan. Sunday night, after Justice picked me up from the police station (the result of me visiting a derelict old farmhouse), we'd come back to my apartment, put a Dave Matthews CD on, and chilled. As soon as the first song, "Satellite," came on, Lenny sprinted into the room, stood in front of the speaker, and meowed with loud contentment. Eyes closed in rapture, he sank to the floor and rolled onto his back. He repeatedly licked his lips and looked at me expectantly. Was he expecting a drink? A joint? Both? I suspected that DMB had been on the playlist quite frequently at Zeke's house in Colorado.

"You would have a black cat." Peter bats his lashes and admires his handiwork in the mirror.

"Do you have a problem with that? Are you a cat racist?"

"Is that supposed to be funny?"

"Why did you come along?" I ask, not that I expect a response.

Peter isn't paying attention to me; he's concentrating on applying frosted white lip liner. You would think he was the one going on the date. From the moment he and Trina arrived an hour ago, he began applying makeup with intense concentration.

He isn't the only makeup artist in this joint. Mikayla is using her mad makeup skills to transform Trina. Makeup, however, is only part of the process. When I told Mikayla about Trina's blind date with Aris, she insisted on Trina having a head-to-toe makeover. Taking the task very seriously, Mikayla came to the office to take candid shots of Trina and get her measurements so that she could create a cohesive, hip look for a girl stuck in the eighties.

Finished applying a generous slathering of frosty pink lipstick, Peter blots his lips on a tissue and then looks at me. "I like to prescreen men before I let my friends go out with them."

"No need. I know the guy. He's my neighbor, and Trina already knows his sister."

Crossing his legs, which is a struggle since he's wearing skintight leather pants that display his less-than-manly physique, he gives me a once-over. "Like that's good enough?"

"I'm an excellent judge of character."

He scoffs. "That may be, but from what you've said about this Aris guy, he sounds like a character right out of *Revenge of the Nerds*."

"He is a nerd. That's how I convinced her to go out with Aris in the first place."

I'd proposed the idea of the blind date to Trina on Monday morning, after Samson lectured her in his office for showing up four hours late with a monster-size hangover.

"Remember that guy I had in mind for you? He wants to go on a date this Wednesday night," I announced, fudging the truth. She didn't need to know that the date was my idea. "His name is Aris. He's Susan's brother, actually."

Raising her cheek off her desk, she propped her face up with her hand. "I don't know."

"What do you mean, you don't know? He likes to spoil his woman. He's gainfully employed. And brilliant."

Not sold on the idea, Trina rolled her head back onto the desk, her forehead snug against the laminate counter. "What's he look like? Ugly?"

"Geeky cute. Amazing eyes."

This piqued her interest, and she assumed an upright position. "Huh. Would you say he's a nerd?"

"If you have to label him, then yes, he's definitely a nerd."

"I've never been out with a nerd. Nerds rule the world, you know. It would be nice to be with someone who rules."

"As opposed to someone who drools," I quipped.

"Sure I'll go. You know, Stinky, the garbage man I dated? Whenever he watched television, he would keep his mouth open and drool like a baby."

Peter stands up, claps his hands feverishly two times, and then flings them to the side. "Voilà!" He turns his head to the right and left to give me the full view. "Stunning, no?"

"Sure."

"I should give up photography and go into makeup artistry."

"Considering you look like Ozzy Osborne's personal hooker, don't quit your day job."

Sticking out his bony hip, he puts all of his weight on the heels of his red stilettos. Snapping his fingers, he gives me an all-attitude look. "Honey, you need to filter."

"I tried that the other day, and by the end of the night, it landed me in jail."

He smiles coyly. "Now that makes you a tad more interesting."

Mikayla throws open the bathroom door victoriously. "Aside from the fact that I need to get her to the salon for an updated cut and color, she's a new woman. I performed a miracle."

Trina steps forward, and I don't even recognize her. She's gorgeous. Her frizzy permed hair has been straightened and artfully styled; it falls softly past her shoulders to frame her oval face. Her bushy brows have been tamed into delicate arches, and there's not a trace of blue makeup anywhere on her face. Dark brown eyeliner, bronze shadow, and only one coat of mascara accent her green eyes. Her tanned face, bare of foundation, has a dewy glow. She's wearing a trendy burnt-orange wrap dress with three-quarter-length sleeves, tight in the middle and flaring out at the bottom. The cut of the dress accentuates her small waist and disguises her generous hips and butt.

"Wow—you look amazing."

Trina smiles shyly. "It's different, isn't it?" Reaching up, she tentatively touches her hair as if it doesn't belong to her.

Mikayla puts her hands on Trina's shoulders and pushes her forward. "It's updated and amazing."

Peter pretends to swoon. "Brilliant."

"You think so?"

"No doubt," he says nodding. "You look like Amanda on *Melrose Place.*"

She rushes over and takes Peter's hands in hers. "Do you really think so?" she inquires, batting her eyelashes.

"Please, better than that tramp! You're fierce, and I'm getting some wild and hot ideas for photos!" Peter prances over to the front door and retrieves his camera bag.

An impromptu photo session follows. Peter proceeds to direct Trina in a sexually suggestive photo shoot. He has her straddle a chair, holding her hands to her crotch Michael Jackson style. When he tires of this position, he has her bend over, stick out her rear end, and put her finger to her mouth, which is hanging open with her tongue peeking out.

"Obnoxious," I remark to Mikayla, who stands next to me, watching.

"Keep an open mind—his photos are genius."

"I saw his portfolio. Genius isn't the word that comes to mind."

"You just have a problem with his work because you're an uptight prude."

"I like it that way," I remark defiantly.

As Peter's photo shoot progresses, he requests several props, such as a leather belt, a butcher knife, a curling iron (I don't even want to know what he was going to do with that), and some rope. Despite Mikayla trying to coerce me into retrieving said items, I refuse each of his requests.

Pouting at my lack of cooperation in the props department, he lowers the camera and scowls. "Then turn off Dave Matthews, because his voice is grating on my nerves."

Traitor that she is, Mikayla stalks over and hits the power button. "He needs to concentrate."

Annoyed with her and Peter, I'm ready to have my apartment back to myself. "When is Jeremy coming to get you?"

"He'll be here soon."

"And things are still okay with you two?"

She averts her eyes and shrugs. "For now, yes."

This qualifier alerts me to the fact that she still hasn't told him everything, though she had broken the news about her debt. On Monday evening, Jeremy happened to come home from work at the exact moment that her precious Corvette was being repossessed. When Jeremy pressed for an explanation as to how that could possibly be happening, Mikayla pulled out the stacks of envelopes from creditors that she'd been hiding. She admitted her debt and told him the rest of her sordid tale, from her thievery of petty cash to being terminated by the agency and blackballed in the industry.

Although Jeremy was disappointed and angry that she hadn't confided in him sooner, he promised that they would face this obstacle together.

"Have you told him about the other thing?" I ask.

Mikayla picks up one of Peter's lipsticks, testing the color on the inside of her wrist. "It's not easy hiding this from him. I'm scared I might lose everything if I tell him."

There's a knock at the door. "Cane Kallevik, it's Aris. I'm here for my date with Trina Kelhuzen."

Peter stops shooting. "What's with using the last name?"

"It's one of his endearing traits," Mikayla responds.

Trina gingerly steps off the couch. "I think it's cute."

I open the door. When Aris enters, he takes one look at Trina and flushes a deep crimson.

"Trina Kelhuzen, you're beautiful." He steps forward and hands her the biggest bouquet of daisies that I've ever seen, along with a large wrapped taffy apple.

Trina, smiling and blushing, stares in awe at the gifts that she's holding. "Thank you."

"Do you like Italian food? How about martinis? Because I made reservations at an Italian restaurant in downtown Chicago, and after dinner I thought we could go to this martini bar where they have live music. Since I don't approve of drinking and driving, I thought we could take the train. Do you like trains?"

Trina, though stone cold sober, looks tipsy. She smiles foolishly. "I love flowers and taffy apples. I love Italian food and martinis, and I love trains. I have a train set."

Aris looks at me as if I've performed a miracle. "You honestly have a train set?" he asks Trina.

"Yes, it's a Lionel set. It belonged to my father. Would you like to see it sometime?"

"I most certainly would," Aris replies earnestly.

They stare into each other's eyes. Who knew I was so adept at matchmaking? "You can leave the flowers and taffy apple here if you want and pick them up later tonight," I offer.

Trina hands over the daisies and apple, and Mikayla retrieves Trina's chocolate brown wool coat from the kitchen, another planned wardrobe accessory.

"Let me." Aris takes the coat from Mikayla and helps Trina put it on.

Pleased with the attention, Trina blushes. "Thank you."

"Aren't you two adorable!" Peter snaps several photos. When he finishes, he grins and lowers his camera. "Now please—do me a favor. Don't behave yourself. Good is boring."

Trina air-kisses Peter, and then she and Aris, already holding hands like lovebirds, are out the door.

"They're perfect for each other," concludes Mikayla.

"Who would have thought? The only reason I set them up was to get Aris off my back."

"He is a hunky nerd, isn't he?" Peter fixes the lens cap on his camera. "I have some great shots of the two of them together."

I arrange the daisies in a vase, and Lenny comes over to inspect. He starts batting the petals furiously. I put the arrangement on top of the refrigerator to save it.

Peter places all his cosmetics back in his bag and then goes into the bathroom to retrieve the ones that Mikayla borrowed. When he's nearly finished packing, he pauses and looks at Mikayla. "Honey, I heard about what happened," he says, lowering his voice and dropping his ever-present lisp.

Mikayla wets a paper towel and scrubs off the lipstick stain on her wrist. "I dug my own grave."

"I want to offer you a gratis photo shoot to help you out. The photos will be brilliant. We'll pass them around, see if we can't reinvent you or something. But honey"—he peeks at Mikayla's breasts and then butt—"you better start hitting the gym. What have you been eating?"

"Carbs and sugar," she responds aggressively. "Why?"

"It's no big deal. You can lose it in a week. I know this great new diet pill, or you could do water and laxatives for three days straight and you'll be golden."

"Thanks for the offer, but I'm not going to pursue the model thing anymore."

"You can't deny the world your beauty. Don't let Sutton Beckworth win this."

"I haven't. I'll work when I can. I have a good thing going with Schaeffer Dairy—I'm going to be their ad girl for a new product, and I've found a new career path. Cane's going to help me."

244

I'm turning the stereo on when Mikayla makes this announcement. "I'm going to help you with what?"

"I'm starting a makeover/stylist business. I've been thinking about it for a couple years now. I'm great at transforming people. You're going to help me come up with a business and marketing plan."

Thrilled that she's found something besides modeling, I smile. "I could do that for you. I think you would be great at it."

"So brilliant!" gushes Peter. He pulls on his neon-yellow leather coat and winds a neon-green scarf around his neck. "I already have a few people I can refer to you."

"You could be her first client," I suggest boldly.

Pursing his lips, he raises his middle finger. "Filter it, honey. I'll have them call you," he says, directing this last statement at Mikayla.

"That would be fantastic."

"I'm out of here." Peter sashays out the door.

Soon after, Jeremy arrives to pick up Mikayla. They invite me to join them for dinner, but needing time alone, I turn down their offer.

When they leave, Lenny walks over, rubs his head against my ankle, and meows loudly. "I'm hungry, too. I'll make us dinner."

I turn up the volume on the stereo and sing along to Dave Matthews while I chop up some chicken and vegetables and prepare a pan with olive oil.

I find myself once again ruminating about Sunday night. Though I was revved up for a showdown when I arrived at Deanna's house, I knew initial civility would be advantageous and necessary. As opposed to hurling a boulder through her bedroom window, which had been my original plan, I rang the doorbell in a civilized manner and waited.

The porch light came on, and a woman wearing a short robe with a cigarette dangling out of her mouth—a much older, more weathered version of Deanna—emerged. "Who are you?"

"I'm here for Deanna."

Taking a leisurely drag on her cigarette, she regarded me. When she finished inhaling, she flicked ash on the ground. "It's a school night, and late. Get out of here."

"This will only take a minute."

"That's what you goddamn kids always say." She stuck the cigarette back in her mouth and slammed the door in my face.

Nothing was going as planned for this evening, not with Justice and certainly not with this. Guess I wouldn't have a chance to get the last word. I was about to walk back to my car when the door opened again and Deanna stepped outside.

"What the hell are you doing back here?" She peered around me. "Where's Jocelyn?"

"I'm here alone. Jocelyn may have played nice last night, but I'm not nearly as mature."

She scowled at me. "That goes without saying, doesn't it? The stunt you pulled at the parade—"

"Believe me. That's only a taste of things to come," I interrupt her. "Here's the deal. If you don't find a way to gather every last photo and videotape that's circulating—and I mean every last one, even the originals—I'm going to find a million and one ways to make your life a living hell. I will embarrass you. Mortify you. Disgrace you. Humiliate you. If I were you, I would be terrified, because I'm sickly creative, highly motivated, and am willing to go above and beyond to make your life miserable if you don't cooperate."

Deanna lifted her foot a few inches off the concrete step and shook it. "I'm shaking in my boots here."

"That's good." I looked down. "But you might want to shake the other one as well."

She stomped her foot back down. "You're a bitch."

"Name calling won't get you anywhere."

"Why do you care about her so much?"

"Why do you hate her so much?"

"She's a spoiled brat. A millionaire princess. She has everything handed to her on a silver platter."

"You don't know her at all, and the thing is, people can't help what situation they were born into"—I meaningfully scan her house and the surroundings and then look her in the eye—"can they?"

"Are you calling me white trash?"

"I didn't say a word."

In the distance, I heard the blare of sirens.

She sneered at me. "You're a bitch, and you're going to get what's coming to you."

A threat? Could those sirens be for me?

I didn't have time to process this, because as soon as these words were out of her mouth, she pounced on me. I lost my footing, stumbled backward, and fell onto the ground.

She clawed, scratched, and slapped. Scrambling on my hands and knees, I managed to escape her. I stood up just in time to dodge a slap. As she prepared to hit again, I curled up my fist and socked her in the gut. She doubled over right as the squad car pulled into the driveway.

At that point, retreat was the wisest option. I headed toward my car but was impeded by Joe Radtke, one of Frank's good friends. I'd known Joe for years. He'd even been at the party at Sorrento's back in June when Justice proposed.

Joe hooked his fingers on his belt and shook his head at me. "What have you gotten yourself into now?"

I raised my hands. "The punch was self-defense. I only came here to talk."

"She attacked me, and she's trespassing! I want her out of here!" Deanna screamed.

Deanna's mother popped her head out of the door. "I called you for a reason!" she yelled to Joe. "My daughter said this girl was trouble, so I expect you to read that bitch her rights."

I'd been set up—I had to hand it to Deanna. She looked so proud of herself for planning ahead.

To make Joe's life easier and my own for that matter, I willingly followed him to his car.

When we arrived at the station, he handed me his cell phone. "I doubt they'll press charges, and if they do, it won't hold water. Call Justice to come get you."

Justice came to the police station immediately. When he saw me sitting at Joe's desk, he smiled. "I don't have to pony up any bail money, do I?"

"Not a red cent."

When we were walking outside the station toward his car, he said, "I kicked her out right after you left."

"I wish you would have done it sooner."

"Me, too." He glanced behind him, briefly looking at the police station sign. "I didn't think the night would end here."

"Lately, I never know where the night is going to end."

"I give you credit."

I smiled drolly. "For ending up in jail?"

"For doing what everyone else wanted to do. You're bolder than anyone else I know."

"I just have a deficit of common sense," I quip.

Laughing, he opened the car door for me. I looked up at him. He leaned down and kissed me on the lips. "That, too."

We drove out to Deanna's house to pick up my car—and Lenny, who wasn't happy about being left alone for an hour—and then Justice followed me back to my apartment. He stayed until two in the morning. On account of our lips being stuck together, we didn't talk much, but that was fine by me. Actions are sometimes louder and more effective than words.

When he was leaving, he said, "I ruined things tonight. I should have asked her to leave right away, and I didn't. I'm sorry if I didn't make you feel important, because you are."

Confronting Deanna may not have been the best idea, but it had certainly done wonders for my relationship with Justice. It's just too bad he's in Iowa right now.

After Lenny and I have our fill of chicken, rice, and vegetables, we enjoy a postmeal gin and tonic. Lenny turns his nose up at his virgin drink and keeps trying to dunk his paw in my glass.

My cell phone rings. I run into the other room and answer.

"Holy. Balls. I can't believe that Justice gave Nikeo a black eye, there are sex tapes of Jocelyn, Susan crashes your going-away night with Justice, and then you get arrested? With all the crap you've been going through, you're going to need a shrink."

I smile. I've been expecting her call all day. Since she's never home, I left her a voice mail last night, highlighting all the drama that had been happening over the past week. "I have Rhonda Riddle for that."

I wander back into the kitchen, where Lenny is greedily slurping up my cocktail. Snatching it away from him, I dump it in the sink.

Caprice groans. "Come on, don't tell me you're still calling her!"

Not that I would admit this to Caprice, or anyone else for that matter, but I have Rhonda Riddle's number programmed into my cell phone.

Before I can explain my friendship with Rhonda and my dependency on her, Caprice says, "I want to hear about everything."

I recap the last several days, realizing that my life lately would make a deliciously trashy segment on a daytime talk show. When I finish, she's all business.

"What about the offer? Have you been thinking about it?"

"Ultimately my decision hinges on one factor: how Justice and I fare over the next few weeks."

She groans impatiently. "If I were there, I would kick you in the butt. Seriously, I'm fed up. Make this about yourself and about what you want to do. What do you want, Cane?"

Honestly, I want both. I loved living in Colorado this summer, and more than that, I loved helping Caprice build her business. I want Justice as well. But the two are mutually exclusive. If I have to sacrifice career or the love of my life, career will get the ax every time.

"Hold on a second. The other line is beeping," I tell her.

"You're trying to brush me off."

"I'm not. I'm serious." I glance down at the screen and am immediately filled with dread. She must have gotten my voice mail from last night, and I'm sure she's not happy about me having a run-in with the law. "I can't dodge this call, Caprice. It's Grandma. I'll call you later."

"You better, or I'm going to make good on my promise to kick your butt."

"Deal." I switch over to the other line.

"Sugar Cane," she says, her voice sounding ancient and a thousand times more fragile than I can ever remember.

"I can explain. I wasn't actually arrested, it was more like a ride in Joe's squad car because—"

"Frank's dead. He died this afternoon. We were on the boat. A massive heart attack," she explains calmly.

My body automatically folds in half, chest touching knees. I sink awkwardly to the floor. It can't be true. Dead? It's impossible, ludicrous. A laugh crawls its way up the back of my throat, but I hold it there.

"Cane, I don't even know what to do," she says, her voice cracking in half.

"You don't have to do a thing."

"It wasn't supposed to happen like this."

Death is never supposed to happen, but it always does. When you're busy living an exceptional life, death crashes the party. "I'm on my way," I manage to say.

When I hang up the phone, I discover that it's not a laugh that I'm holding back. It's a sharp, painful sob.

My throat swells, blisters, and splits with it, but I hold it there and then cram it down. Under no circumstances will I allow it to escape. No way am I going to be weak—not when Grandma Betty needs me to be strong for her.

CHAPTER SEVENTEEN

The world rips apart at the seams. Atlantic waves foam at my feet. Shards of lightning fracture the sky and illuminate the clouds. Thunder sends vibrations through the ground. The warmest raindrops I've ever felt, drops that feels like tears, fall onto us. Is Frank orchestrating this from heaven?

I train the video camera on the sky and hit the record button.

"This is what you wanted, isn't it, Frank? Forget the hymns and the sermons, this is more your style. Are you seeing this from up there? It's incredible. I want you to know that you don't have to worry about a thing. I'll take care of Grandma Betty."

My hair whips around in all directions. In my haste to get down here, I forgot my hair ties, not to mention underwear. Also: socks, bras (not that those are a huge necessity for me), my toothbrush, and tampons. Needless to say, I've made several trips to Target—and I've still managed to forget to buy stupid rubber bands every single time.

Despite the crashing of the waves, the howling wind, the rumble of thunder, I hear him approach—though it's not hearing him as much as sensing his presence. He brings with him a quiet comfort that no one else can provide. What would I do if I lost him as unexpectedly as Grandma Betty lost Frank? Or have I already lost him?

I expect him to pull me into the circle of his arms, so when he gathers my hair in his hands instead and puts a hair tie in for me, a simple and kind act of love that gets me every time, I nearly lose control.

Even though I've wanted to bawl my eyes out from the moment Grandma Betty called me, I've kept them firmly in their sockets. I didn't cry when Grandma Betty picked me up from the airport, when we met with the pastor and funeral director to plan Frank's small Florida memorial, or when Justice arrived yesterday afternoon. And even though today, when I saw Frank in his casket and could have cried enough to raise the Atlantic Ocean by at least an inch, I didn't.

My eye sockets are killing me from holding back the tears, and my throat is raw as hell. I've practically gone hoarse from the effort of containing the sobs. My voice is all deep and gravelly, like a smoker or a woman doped up on testosterone, going through a sex change.

"I stopped at a drugstore," he says. "I figured you hadn't packed any."

"Thank you," I whisper in my manly voice.

"Maybe he's the one who's responsible for the storm."

"I thought the same thing. Do you think that's possible? That maybe God is giving Frank some control over the weather? He would love to cook up some storms up from scratch—that would be his heaven." I stop recording and shove the camera into the backpack.

Justice studies the sky. "I don't see why not."

Justice and I make our way back to the condo. We sit on the patio chairs beneath an awning and watch the storm wreak havoc.

Inside, I hear Grandma Betty intermittently singing along to Frank

Sinatra's greatest hits. Frank was the biggest Sinatra fan. Whenever Savage Suds had karaoke night, he would take Grandma Betty there for dinner, drink a martini, get up onstage, and sing "I've Got You Under My Skin" or "My Funny Valentine" to her

"We should skip 'Amazing Grace' at the end of Frank's funeral on Wednesday and have the organist play a Sinatra song," I muse. "Maybe 'Fly Me to the Moon'? Everyone could sing along."

Justice cracks a smile. "I was in the room when you were on the phone with the pastor this morning and made the suggestion. I seem to recall that it didn't go over so well. It wasn't—what did he say, 'traditional enough'?"

"Screw tradition."

Justice's cell phone beeps, indicating that he has a voice mail. He flips it open and frowns as he listens.

"Don't tell me she called you again?" Susan has called four times since he arrived yesterday. The calls were supposedly about business, but I've been less than thrilled at the constant interference. At risk of sounding paranoid and insanely jealous, which I'll admit that I am, I can't ask him for transcripts of their conversations. However, I'm not above asking him to put her on speakerphone next time.

Unfortunately, there's no escaping Susan. She's a constant in Justice's life and mine. To make matters worse, she's planning on attending Frank's funeral back in Savage, as well as the after-party. Knowing Irish Frank wouldn't approve of anything somber like a church basement meal after his service, Grandma and I planned a celebration at Savage Suds, complete with alcohol and karaoke.

"It wasn't Susan. It was Samson," Justice says. "He was just asking if there was anything that he could do to help. Speaking of phone calls, what about Nikeo?" he asks pointedly. "Have you heard from him again?"

Touché. I squirm in my seat. "He only called to offer condolences."

"He's called twice, and the second time wasn't to offer condolences."

Two times is less than four, but I wisely hold my tongue. Shortly after I called Caprice to let her know what happened, Nikeo called to say that he was sorry. Then he called again this morning to find out details about the funeral and to let me know that he and Caprice would be attending. His motivations weren't entirely pure; it was Nikeo, after all. He wanted something out of it, that something being me. He hinted at spending a couple of days in my apartment. I refused, but the call made things a little sour between Justice and me.

I meet Justice's eyes. "You know where I stand with Nikeo."

I wait for him to say, "You know where I stand with Susan," but he doesn't. He regards me for a moment, and I can tell by the injured look in his eyes that he still hasn't moved past this.

Will he ever?

Although the heartbreak of Frank's death has united us and even highlighted some of the strengths of our relationship, it has also brought us to a pivotal point. Although neither of us have dared to say this aloud, we are nearing a do-or-die moment for us as a couple.

"The car will be here soon." Justice stands. "I'm going to go pack my things."

Justice has arranged for a taxi to take him to the airport. "I don't know why you just didn't let me drive you."

He glances inside. Grandma Betty sits at the kitchen table, paging through photo albums, removing pictures that will be used for Frank's memory board. She glances up and waves me inside.

"Because she needs you here."

While Justice packs and makes another phone call to Susie Homemaker, letting her know what time he'll be at the airport (did I mention she drove him to the airport in Iowa City and is picking him up?),

I join Grandma. We hunt through albums for the next hour, gathering all the best pictures of Frank, of which there are many.

"Look at you and him in this one," she says. "It's your sixteenth birthday." Her fingertips rest on her lips. "He loved you so much, Cane."

"He loved you so much too. You were his world."

She takes a tissue and presses it between her eyes, using so much force she might split her skull. I'm not the only one who has been keeping a stiff upper lip. Grandma Betty must be applying superglue to hers. I've seen her cry a total of two times since arriving. She wept when she had to select the suit and tie Frank would wear for the service today. Then she cried again after the service this afternoon.

"He was my world," she murmurs sadly. "I'm not sure what I'm going to do without him. I've been through this before, but it was so long ago. So long." She shakes her head. "I was much younger then. I had more strength."

The Sinatra CD comes to an end. I'm about to go put on another when she puts her hand on my arm. "Old Blue Eyes is making me misty eyed. I've had about all I can take."

"You'll make it through this."

"Oh, Sugar Cane, I know. I know." She crumples up the tissue and closes the last album. "But that doesn't mean that I want to, or that it's going to be easy. I forgot"—briefly shutting her eyes, she presses her hand to her heart—"how much it hurts. I want to find my way out of this place, but I don't know what direction to take. I don't. I'm not sure I ever will."

When I finally find Frank's compass, I'm going to have it repaired and make it into a necklace for Grandma Betty. She can wear it close to her heart, and whenever she's feeling lost, she can look down and find her way.

I watch as one tear sneaks out the corner of Grandma's eyes It goes slowly at first, then races off her cheek and splashes onto the photograph, landing right in Frank's hand.

My nose starts dripping and oozing—a sure sign that my face is about to dissolve into a million tears. With eye sockets on the brink of shattering, I grit my teeth and smile. I point at the photo. "Even now he's catching your tears."

Grandma Betty, confused at first by my observation, fixes her eyes on the photo. When she realizes where her tear has landed, she finds my remark uproariously funny and laughs until she's doubled over from the effort. Justice comes out of the bedroom and regards her with concern.

She sees him watching her. "Oh, I'm okay!" she says, laughing and waving away his concern.

He sets his suitcases by the door. "The car is out front."

Grandma Betty dabs her eyes. "It's not time for you to leave already, is it?"

"I'm afraid so." He walks over to the table and studies the photographs that we've chosen. "These tell quite the story. He was an impressive man."

"He was." She straightens the photos.

"I'm sorry I couldn't stay longer, but I want to get back to Iowa and finish up some business so that I can be there for you and Cane this coming week."

Grandma Betty stands and gives him a hug. "Thank you for coming. It means the world to me."

Justice kisses her cheek. "See you in a couple days."

I follow him outside and help him load his luggage into the trunk. When we're finished, he pulls me into his arms.

"I love you." He looks into my eyes and pushes my hair off my forehead. His thumb strokes the faint cross-shaped birthmark on my forehead.

It's not a proclamation of undying devotion or a promise to be by my side forever, but for now, it's enough. "I love you too."

Justice waves from the back of the taxi, and just before the car turns right and disappears, I see him hold his phone up to his ear.

I'm not sure why—perhaps it's the fear that it may be Susan calling him again, or perhaps it has to do with the fact that much of his life lately has nothing to do with me—but the mere sight of this pushes me over the edge.

My eye sockets endure a nuclear blast of epic proportions. I stumble to the beach, sit at the edge of the ocean, and do my part to increase the depth of the Atlantic by a few centimeters with my own salt water.

When I've finally composed myself, I go back inside the condo, hoping that Grandma Betty doesn't notice my tear-streaked face. I find her sleeping on the couch, clutching one of the photo albums to her chest.

On the coffee table lies one photo she's removed—it's of Justice and me, taken more than six years ago, on the night that she wed Frank. It's similar to the one that I found in my nightstand weeks ago, a side profile of Justice and me, standing on the dance floor. I'm gazing up into his eyes with a true lovesick, desperate-to-be-with-you look.

Picking it up, I examine it more closely. His arms are draped casually around my back, whereas my arms are wrapped around him like a vise. I'm holding on for dear life.

Has it been like that since the start of our relationship? Have I been holding on so fiercely for the past six years that he's fed up? Did my leaving this past June give him the taste of freedom he desperately needed, and now he's not so sure he wants to come back to my straitjacket embrace?

I slip the picture into my back pocket and drape a blanket over Grandma Betty. I go into the guest bedroom and close the door. Unplugging my cell phone from the charger, I dial Rhonda's number.

"It's Cane," I say when she answers.

"I've been waiting for your call. How was the service?"

"Awful."

She clucks her tongue. "I figured as much. How's Grandma holding up?"

"She's fine, but her heart isn't. She's lost in grief."

"It will be a long time before she finds her way out. Poor, poor lady. What about you? How's your heart?"

Her inquiry catches me off guard. No one has asked me about the condition of my heart, not even Justice. I haven't even thought to stop and ask myself this question. The focus has been on Grandma Betty—as well it should be. Her suffering outweighs mine, but I can't trivialize my loss. He belonged to me as well.

I'm going to miss his watery brown eyes, his quick smile and beautifully weathered face, his appreciation of my sarcastic wit, his adoration for my grandmother, his fondness for spoiling both of us rotten, and his compulsion to record every aspect of life.

I once asked him why he wanted to capture everything on film.

"Think of how many things happen in one day, in one hour," he replied. "For that matter, think of how much happens within a matter of seconds. We only remember a fraction of it, and we can never relive it. Once it's gone, it's gone. Photographs and film, that's as close as we can get to a time machine. I want all those moments at my fingertips, so that if I want to or need to, I can go back."

He left behind many time machines, but what good is a time machine if it can take you back to a memory but not the actual person?

How is my heart? "It's shattered."

"I'm so sorry that you're going through this. If you want to, we could skip the drink."

"No, I would like to meet. It would be nice to get out of here for a bit."

Twenty minutes later I enter the Flamingo Bay bar, only a short walk from Grandma's condo. The place is decorated with thousands of pink flamingos. Even the barstools resemble the creatures. A group of overserved patrons are on the bird-shaped dance floor, swaying back and forth to the music of Jimmy Buffet.

Rhonda told me that she'd be sitting at the curved bar closest to the beach. Tentatively walking forward, I scope out my surroundings and spot a thin older woman with a perfectly smooth blond bob, wearing dark denim jeans and a crisp white button-down blouse. She turns, sees me, and slides off the flamingo barstool. "Cane? Is that you?"

She's so different from what I envisioned. I pictured Rhonda as a Mrs. Roper kind of character: flowing housedress, wild hair, and a few layers of costume jewelry. I now realize that I conjured up this mental image because of the ridiculous psychic infomercial.

"That would be me." I smile awkwardly and walk up to her, and she gives me a big hug.

When we separate, she smiles. "It's good to finally put a face to the voice."

I take the stool next to hers, and Rhonda immediately orders up a Tanqueray and tonic.

"You remember my favorite cocktail?"

"We're friends! Of course I remember!"

I shrug off my jean jacket. "It's quite embarrassing how much you know about me. All I do is blab about myself. You must think I'm the most ridiculous, self-centered woman on the face of the earth."

Rhonda takes a drink of her white wine and winks at me. "Honey, I don't think that at all. If I did, I wouldn't be taking your phone calls."

"I appreciate you talking to me. These last few months haven't been easy."

"But that's the beauty of it!" she exclaims. "Enjoy this time in your life, because it's a ride you'll never forget. Easy is overrated." She leans in closer and deadpans, "Easy is boring."

I laugh in a series of short bursts and put my head in my hands. "I can't believe you just said 'Easy is boring.' Do you know who shares that sentiment?" I pause. She raises her brow expectantly. "Nikeo."

She hoots with laughter and slaps the bar. "I would really like to meet that character. Sounds like my kind of man."

"You can have him. I'll give you his number."

"I might take you up on that. Now tell me what's been going on these last few days."

"No." I shake my head firmly. "I refuse to talk about myself tonight. I want to know something about you."

"Well, since I've been alive for sixty-three years"—Rhonda tucks a strand of hair behind her ear and bunches up her lips—"there are so many stories, I don't know where to begin."

The bartender serves me the gin and tonic in a flamingo-shaped glass. I grab the leg and hold it up for closer inspection. "They take this theme seriously, don't they?"

Rhonda smiles. "That they do."

I take a long drink, letting the gin work its magic. Maybe it's just the current crappy conditions in my life, or maybe it's the atmosphere of the bar, or the fact that I'm meeting my not-psychic friend, Rhonda Riddle, but it's the most delicious drink I've ever had. If Lenny were here, I might let him have one. I look over at Rhonda. "You know where every story starts and ends."

"Always with a man," she says.

I nod.

"Isn't that the sad truth? I've sworn off men, but I might make an exception for this Nikeo character. I've been married six times," she announces. "Which husband do you want me to start on?"

"Start at the beginning."

While I drink my fabulous cocktail and then have another, Rhonda summarizes her marriages. She starts with her high school sweetheart, whom she married at nineteen, and finishes with husband number six, a deep-sea charter fisherman who hooked her heart and then threw her overboard two years ago. By the time she's finished regaling me with the finer details of her six marriages and four divorces (two of her husbands died unexpectedly), I've crossed the line from buzzed to drunk. My high blood alcohol level causes me to go all maudlin, and those eye sockets of mine are getting ready for another epic explosion.

Fighting off the catastrophic emotional display coming on, I focus on Rhonda. "Don't you want to find love again?"

She blows a stream of air out the side of her mouth and takes hold of her wineglass. "Phooey. I'm not going to find anything, let alone anyone. The hunt is exhausting. I'm going to do my own thing. I figure love will find me if it wants, but I'm not wasting my life looking or waiting around and twiddling my thumbs. I've done too much of that."

Something about this resonates with me. I've been twiddling my thumbs these last few months, waiting to see how everything plays out with Justice. How much more time am I willing to sacrifice? What if I continue to wait, and nothing comes of it?

I pick up my jean jacket and pull the photo of Justice and me—the one from Grandma Betty and Frank's wedding—out of my pocket. I slide it toward Rhonda.

She picks it up and whistles. "He's gorgeous." She raises her eyes to mine. "But then again, so are you my dear."

"What if I'm looking too hard for love? What if I always have been?" I press my fingertip to the picture. "Look at my arms. I've been suffocating the poor guy from the moment I met him."

"I may have only known you for a few weeks, but you aren't the clingy type. You wouldn't hold anyone down—and I think you'd be damned if anyone tried to hold you down."

"But what if that's not true? I'm so used to holding on to Justice that if it comes down to it, if I need to let him go, I'm not sure I can."

Rhonda tucks the picture back into my pocket and looks me in the eye. "If there's one thing I know for absolute certain, it's that you can do anything. With or without him, you'll be better than fine."

CHAPTER EIGHTEEN

Mikayla, Jocelyn, and I finish arranging the photo albums and memory boards on the table near the small stage in Savage Suds. The collage of Frank's greatest storm photos is missing. Over his years as a storm chaser, Frank captured every atmospheric mood and temperament, from blizzards and ice storms to tornados and heat waves.

"Where's the one with all the weather pictures?" I ask no one in particular.

"Shlop!" Grandma Betty shouts, this word being her version of the expletive *shit*. She surveys our work, her eyes all glassy—not because she's going to cry, but because she just finished the last of her dirty martini. Popping the leftover olive into her mouth, she chews thoughtfully. "I must have left it at the church. We have to have that one. Frank would be upset if we didn't."

"He took some cool pictures. Some of them are kind of scary, too," comments Jocelyn, who has been flipping through the albums and giggling at the pictures of me as a gawky teen.

"Tell me about it! He risked his life to get some of those pictures! You don't know how many times I thought Mother Nature would end up killing him. I used to scold him all the time." Grandma Betty sets her empty glass on the table, her hand trembling slightly. "The storm he missed last night? He would have been right out in the middle of it with all his equipment and gadgets, recording it and filling up his digital camera."

Weather events have been following us, and I don't think the drastic barometric pressure changes are coincidental. Every day since Frank's death, the weather has been changing on a dime. In Florida there would be sun one minute and wicked thunderstorms the next. Last night a crew of us went to Sorrento's for dinner. When we'd entered the restaurant it was a calm and starry night, but when we emerged two hours later, we were greeted with nearly freezing temperatures, lightning, brutal thunder, blinding rain, and the kind of wind that makes every pedestrian a hunchback.

"I'm convinced he's responsible for the atmospheric disturbances," I remark.

"I don't doubt it," Grandma agrees.

"I'll run back to the church and get those pictures," offers Jeremy, already zipping his coat.

"I think I left my cell phone there." Jocelyn pats her pockets. "Check in the fellowship hall, would you?"

Her older brother nods.

Mikayla smiles tremulously at her husband and takes his hand. "I'll go with you."

She casts a quick glance at me, and I shoot her a warning look. Don't tell him today, I plead with my eyes.

Yesterday, when Mikayla and I had lunch at McDonald's (she can't get enough of their shakes), she'd told me that she would be telling Jeremy very soon. She couldn't take the secrecy any longer; it was making her life infinitely harder.

I suspect, though, that once she comes clean, it's going to solve one problem and create dozens more. Once she tells the whole truth and nothing but the truth so help her God, I wonder if she'll end up being my roommate again. Seeing as how Grandma Betty is staying with me for a bit and needs my undivided attention and love, I've begged Mikayla to wait for full disclosure until Grandma returns to Florida in a few days.

"Not today. Promise," she whispers as she passes.

Shortly after Jeremy and Mikayla leave, some close friends of Grandma Betty's arrive. Jocelyn and I insist that the group of ladies sit down in a booth and enjoy appetizers and drinks. Meanwhile Jocelyn and I finish setting up and decorating the joint and make sure the kitchen is on schedule with the food preparation. When we're satisfied that everything is smooth sailing, we test out the karaoke machine, singing a mean rendition of Sinatra's "New York." Our overly theatrical and slightly off-key performance earns a standing ovation from Grandma Betty and her friends.

Jeremy and Mikayla return mid-applause with the collage of weather photos, and Jeremy informs Jocelyn that her cell phone wasn't at the church.

She sighs in frustration. "Dad's going to kill me if I lose it." Suddenly panicked, she grabs my arm. "What if I left it at school yesterday? If someone gets a hold of it . . . all my contacts are on there. Who knows what they'll do with that information."

Although Deanna, Taryn, and Colin are not around to torment Jocelyn because they've been suspended for three weeks, things aren't easy for Jocelyn, who's being mercilessly harassed. She's maintained her brave, blasé attitude at school, but when she returns home for the evening, emotionally exhausted, she calls me for pep talks. "You didn't leave it there. You had it at Sorrento's last night, remember?"

She snaps her fingers. "I know where it is. I left it on your desk last night at the office."

"Call Justice. He's still there, working on the video," says Jeremy. "He can grab it on his way out."

Justice and Jeremy, technological wizards and computer geeks that they are, want to surprise Grandma Betty with a video montage of Frank's life. For the past twenty-four hours they've been holed up in the Schaeffer Dairy offices, using the computer and audiovisual equipment to make the short film. After dinner at Sorrento's last night, Justice and Jeremy took Jocelyn, Mikayla, and me to the office for a sneak preview of the video. Although I thought it perfect as it was, Justice claimed it still needed tweaking, so he and Jeremy had worked on it at the office until late into the night. Then, after the short funeral at Grace Lutheran this morning, Justice returned to the office to put the finishing touches on it and also to make a few copies of the tape for Frank's family.

"I'll call him." I pull my cell phone out of my navy-and-white-striped bag, waking Lenny from his nap.

When Lenny sits up and yawns, Mikayla rolls her eyes. "You're turning into a scary cat lady."

"Not a cat lady." I dial Justice's number. "He's taken up residence in this bag. I tried to take him out before coming, but he bit, scratched, and wouldn't budge. Take him home for me, will you?" Holding my phone between my ear and shoulder, I pass off the bag to Mikayla, but she refuses to take it.

"No way." Holding up her hands, she backs away and plops down on a chair. "I'm exhausted."

"It's right down the block," I say between rings. "A few hundred feet. I think you can make it."

"Too bad." Putting her feet up on the chair, she groans. "I have the worst gut ache."

"Because you inhaled half the appetizers," Jocelyn points out.

"I sampled them."

"Like a Hoover vacuum," quips Jocelyn.

Jeremy shoots his sister a dirty look. "Don't," he says.

She folds her arms and glares. "What? I speak the truth."

Concerned for his wife's well-being, Jeremy places a hand on her shoulder. "Anything I can do for you?"

She shakes her head. "I'm fine."

"I'll take the cat back, Cane." Jeremy takes the bag from me.

Lenny, not pleased about the transfer, pops his head out of the bag and glares accusingly at me. I know that he was looking forward to a party with alcohol.

One of the servers spots Lenny and looks horrified. Setting down a tray of cocktails, he rushes over. "There are no animals allowed. If my boss sees a cat in here—"

Jeremy smiles agreeably. "It won't be a problem—I'm leaving now."

Thank you, I mouth to Jeremy.

Justice's phone goes to voice mail. I close my phone and shrug. "He's not answering."

Jocelyn nibbles the tip of her thumb. "I have to get the phone back."

I hand her my cell. "You try and call. Leave a message."

"I'm going to puke," announces Mikayla. Her forehead breaks out into a sweat. She leans forward and then emits a startlingly loud fart, though only Jocelyn and I are privy to the sound; the music in the room is too loud.

"Disgusting," comments Jocelyn as she backs away and pinches her nose. "It reeks."

Mikayla sits up and smiles in ecstasy. "Much better. Just a little gas."

Astounded at the sounds that have been coming out of her body, I shake my head in exasperation. "There's not much that's little about you lately."

Grandma Betty waves me over to the table. "Do you need any help, Sugar Cane?" She anxiously glances at the clock and wrings her hands. "People are going to start arriving soon. I feel like I should be doing something. I have to do something."

"You don't have to do a thing but sit here and relax."

Her friends echo my sentiments.

"Yes, Betty. Listen to your granddaughter."

"Have another martini!" exclaims Erma, my grandmother's oldest and dearest friend from Grace Lutheran.

Grandma Betty looks scandalized by the suggestion. "Another one? I would get quite drunk."

Erma winks. "Well, now—isn't that the point?"

I kiss Grandma Betty's cheek. "The only thing Frank would have wanted is for you to have a good time."

Erma slaps the table and signals for the server. "Exactly why I'm ordering us another round, gals."

I walk back over to where Mikayla is sitting. She waves the air with her hand. "This area may or may not be contaminated with methane. Enter at your own risk."

"I'll breathe through my mouth."

"Might be best."

Still pinching her nostrils with her fingertips, Jocelyn hands me my cell phone. "He's not answering."

"Did you leave a message?"

"Yeah, two of them—but what if he doesn't get them?"

"He will."

Looking paranoid, she gnaws on her bottom lip. "You know that Justice never checks his messages. He's not going to bring it. I need to get it back. What if my dad finds it? Or my mom? I don't want them picking it up and checking my messages. I don't want them hearing those," she says quietly.

Some of the senior boys on the football team have been harassing Jocelyn by calling her cell and leaving disgusting sexual messages. Though I've urged her to tell her parents and the school, she's made a decision to keep quiet about it, delete the messages, and go about her business as if everything is normal, even though it's far from that.

"Why don't we run to the office?" I say, wanting to make her life as stress-free as possible. "I'm sure Justice is going to need help loading up the television and all the equipment, anyway."

"You'll do that for me?"

"Absolutely. We just have to hurry." I glance at the clock. We have twenty-five minutes until the official party kickoff, barely enough time to make it to Clinton and back. "I'll go get my coat and keys."

I head to the back room to find my coat, and when I return, the entire Schaeffer clan has arrived. Samson gives me a hug. Jenny gives me a withering stare.

"Sinatra and martinis." Samson nods approvingly. "Frank would have loved this."

The rambunctious younger Schaeffer kids ambush the bar and order sodas. Jenny heads over to corral them, and Samson heads over to the display table to look at pictures and albums.

Jocelyn sidles up to me. "Could you go without me? If I try to leave with you, Mom will give me the third degree. That's all she's been doing lately, and I can't handle it."

"Absolutely."

Jocelyn hugs me. "Thank you so much," she whispers in my ear. "If there are any messages on there—"

"I won't listen to them. I promise."

She nods. I'm out the door before anyone realizes I've left. Knowing I have to hurry, I make it to the office in record time and pull up next to Justice's truck in the nearly empty parking lot.

What doesn't thrill me is that the shiny, red, clean-as-a-whistle Toyota is parked on the other side of the truck. A Justice sandwich. Perfect. Knowing Susan and her I'll-pitch-in-and-do-whatever-I-can-to-help nature, she probably called Justice, found out about the video he was making, and rushed over to spend quality time with him.

Spectacular.

Since Samson closed the offices at noon today because of Frank's funeral, the building is locked. I punch in the entry code and hurry inside the lobby. Skipping the slow elevator, I race up the stairs to the second floor and go straight to my cubicle. Sure enough, Jocelyn's phone is on my desk, right next to the glossy photo of Mikayla and Justice that will grace the front of the Farmer and the Belle ice cream carton. It's a fantastic picture; they look like the perfect couple. I'm beginning to wonder if everyone else looks better with him than I do.

Another glossy eight-by-ten photo in a silver frame on Trina's desk catches my eye: Trina and Aris standing in front of a vintage steam train, their arms wrapped around each other. It was probably taken when they visited a train museum this past weekend in Union, Wisconsin. Yesterday, when Trina called to offer condolences and ask about the funeral service, I'd heard every detail of their short courtship, including the fact that they were already talking about marriage.

271

Nothing but full steam ahead for them; after six measly days, they're chugging toward the altar. Six years, and Justice and I can't make it past the gate. At this point, I'm hoping that there's still enough track left to get us somewhere.

Pocketing Jocelyn's cell phone, I walk down the long hallway toward the audiovisual room, where Justice is working on the video, and where Susie Homemaker is probably working on stealing Justice. The door is open slightly, and their backs are to me. They're both staring at the television screen, their heads close together.

I'm about to enter the room when Susan turns toward Justice and puts her hand on his lower arm. I hesitate.

"When are you planning on telling her?" she asks. "Prolonging it is cruel. I don't think you should wait."

Prolonging it is cruel? He shouldn't wait?

My stomach sours and then turns to cement. Slinking backward, I station myself close to the wall, waiting for Justice's response.

"The timing isn't good right now. It's horrible, actually. I should wait a little longer, see how things play out."

"Haven't you waited long enough? There's never a good time for something like this. Regardless of when you do it, she's going to be devastated."

"It's not going to be easy," he admits.

"No, but you can't tell me she didn't know it was coming. Things have been bad for so long now."

He chuckles. "Bad? They've been horrible. You know, we should probably get going. Would you mind helping me load all of this into—"

Turning around, I race down the hallway, down two flights of stairs, and out the front door. I look down the street, wishing I could run and never stop. I momentarily consider this option, but there's no escaping anything. I walk to my car, barely resisting the urge to drag my key across the perfectly waxed surface of Susan's car.

I sit in the driver's seat and flip down the vanity mirror, pulling it low so that I can't see my face but rather my nearly flat chest. Nope. Nothing. I thought for sure that I would find a wooden stake through my heart. The pain is beyond excruciating.

I'm finished with analyzing, deliberating, and waiting. My brain has been operating like a violent spin cycle on a washing machine. I'm putting a stop to it. Obviously Justice has made up his mind, and so have I.

CHAPTER NINETEEN

"He's been giving me dirty looks all night, and I'm at my limit," Nikeo warns.

I glance over at the table where Justice sits with Susie Home Wrecker and the lovebirds, Trina and Aris. Trina, who looks amazing, thanks to Mikayla, who accompanied her to the salon two days ago and also took her shopping for a new wardrobe, has had her hands and lips all over Aris for most of the night. Justice motions me over with his eyes and a subtle wave of his hand.

Sorry, buddy, not going to happen. I'm long gone. Tucking my cocktail close to my body, I look away from him.

"He's jealous of your talent," I respond. Nikeo has just finished singing two Sinatra songs on stage, bringing more than a hundred and fifty people to their feet.

"Jealous? Yes. But not of my talent. If he hits me tonight, all bets are off."

"Absolutely no fighting, Nikeo. Not tonight. Please."

Narrowing his panther-green eyes, he runs his fingers through his unkempt dark rocker hair and gives me his sexiest smile. "I love it when you beg. Will you get on your hands and knees?" he asks playfully.

"You're not going to stop trying, are you?"

"Why would I? There's nothing stopping us anymore." He raises an eyebrow. "Not even Justice. Don't bother denying it. I've been watching you watch him. It's over."

"It's not," I lie convincingly.

He tips his cocktail glass against his lips, captures an ice cube between his front teeth, and chomps down on it, cracking it in half. "I know your face better than you think I do."

Caprice saunters over with a beer in hand and a grin on her face. "This is the best funeral I've ever been to." She knocks her beer against my glass. "I've been dancing, drinking, and—"

"Making friends with Mikayla," Nikeo interjects sarcastically.

Only moments ago, Caprice and Mikayla were arguing about something on the dance floor.

Rolling her eyes, Caprice groans. "Can't stand her. If her husband hadn't come and gotten her, it might not have ended so peacefully. There's a good chance I may kill her by the end of the evening."

"See?" Nikeo smiles at me and sets his empty glass on a nearby table. "I'm not the only one in a fighting mood. I'm going to get another. Do you want anything?"

If I overindulge, there is a definite possibility that I'll be thrown into the back of Joe Radtke's squad car again for assault and battery. Only this time the victim won't be Deanna. I decline Nikeo's offer.

Caprice flips her dark hair over her shoulder and leans in to give me the scoop on the drama between her and Mikayla. "She said I needed to glamorize Maid Hot by hiring her as a model. Like I want her face on all my marketing materials! She bragged all about the Farmer and the Belle shoot and how great she looked in it. Gag. Gag. Gag. I told her I didn't need a skanky ex-model to represent my company. Then she had the nerve to tell me that all my company is doing is selling sex! Shitty. Balls. Like that's even close to what we do. I wanted to punch her in the face. I told her that I didn't trust her anywhere near my—"

While Caprice forges ahead with her rant, I observe Justice and Susan. They are deep in conversation, heads pressed together yet again. Are they planning to humiliate me with a public breakup?

Caprice clues into the fact that I'm not listening and follows my gaze. She gets a disgusted look on her face. "Do you want me to go tell off that conniving bastard? I'd be happy to say a few choice words to her, too. They deserve each other."

Caprice is the only one who knows about the conversation I overheard at the office. When she went outside to smoke a cigarette, she caught me throwing the pity party of the century next to the Dumpster. Tears. Snot. Moaning. Gnashing of teeth. It had been so epic, I should have handed out T-shirts and party hats to commemorate the event.

I hadn't planned on melting down, but my unraveling had begun immediately following the viewing of Jeremy and Justice's beautifully poignant video. Justice had artfully arranged photos and video clips of Frank set to Sinatra music in such a way that I swore Frank was right there in the room with us. Everyone was blown away by the content, including me. Grandma Betty was beside herself with joy, alternately laughing and weeping. When it ended, I looked over at the man I loved, the man who always did the right thing, and could not fathom how he could be duplicitous. How could he be complicit in breaking my heart?

I'd already lost Frank, and soon I would lose the other love of my life. The anguish squirmed around inside me, and I felt my body giving in. Knowing that I was seconds away from the kind of keening that would get me tranquilized and strapped to a gurney, I snuck out the back door.

Seconds later Caprice discovered me hunched over in the alley. Literally pulling me into an upright position, she demanded that I tell her what was wrong.

"I'd be more than happy to go into attack mode," she says to me now, rolling her shoulders and tightening her fists like a heavyweight champion.

"No. It doesn't matter. I've made up my mind." I haven't just revealed Susan and Justice's conversation; I've also told Caprice what I'm planning to do.

"I know, and it's fantastic." She slides her arm around my shoulder. "You and I are going to do great things together."

Up onstage, Grandma Betty wraps her hand around the microphone. The crowd starts chanting for her to sing.

"Oh, no," she says shakily. "That's not why I'm up here. I wanted to play one of Frank's favorites. We danced to it at our wedding. We danced to it quite often." Grandma Betty's eyes find mine. Do you remember? her eyes ask.

I smile at her. How could I forget? On many nights, long after the dishes were done and the ten o'clock news was over, Frank would open the record player, place the needle by memory right at this song, and take Grandma Betty in his arms for a slow dance.

Etta James starts singing "At Last" through the speakers. I'm about to walk over to Grandma Betty so that I can stand in for Frank, but Samson beats me to it. He leads her to the dance floor.

Nikeo appears at my side. "The line at the bar is too long. We're going to dance."

Caprice knocks her beer against Nikeo's arm, causing some to slosh over the side. "Be a gentleman for once in your life and ask instead of order."

"Takes too much time." He yanks me toward the dance floor, puts his arms around me, and pulls me so close I can feel parts of his body that I shouldn't be feeling.

"This isn't a good idea. No need to fan the flames."

He glances at Justice, who looks like his head's about to explode, and spins me around so that I can no longer see Justice.

"I love fanning flames. Back to our earlier discussion. It's over with him, isn't it?" He looks me in the eye, challenging me.

"Maybe, but I don't want to dance right now."

"Yes, you—"

"Get away from her." Arms crossed, stance wide, Justice arrives on the scene. He glares at Nikeo.

Nikeo regards him briefly and sneers. "Absolutely not."

"She said she didn't want to dance."

Nikeo stops swaying to the music. "Buddy, you of all people should know by now that half the time she can't figure out what she wants"—he turns and looks into my eyes—"or *who* she wants."

Justice tenses, and so does Nikeo. Knowing that round one is about to commence, I grip Nikeo's shoulders, squeezing with my fingertips until he drags his eyes away from Justice and back to me. "A funeral isn't a place for a pissing contest. Go to the bar and get me a drink. We'll talk about this later."

Nikeo shrugs me off and gives Justice an I-want-to-kill-you glare before walking toward the bar.

Justice steps in front of me. "I thought it was over between you two. I can't believe you're doing this."

My palms burn with the desire to slap him. I know how satisfying the sting would feel. "Go dance with Susan."

"I want to dance with you, not her."

Incredulous, I shake my head. "Right," I respond caustically. "Maybe the timing isn't right now, but it will be soon, won't it?"

Perplexed, he shakes his head. "What do you mean?"

"It means that soon enough you can dance with her all you like, because I'm taking the job. I'm going to Colorado."

His emotions flip like a coin, from angry to shocked. He searches my face. "You're not—are you serious? But, you can't leave."

I'm not sure why my announcement has this effect on him, when he's holding a knife behind his back so that at the opportune time he and Susan can stab it into mine again. "I don't need your permission."

"But, Cane—"

"But what? Wouldn't it make it more convenient for you if I wasn't around?"

Raising his hands up, he says, "Nikeo was right. You don't know what you want or who you want." With that, he storms off, grabbing his coat off the back of his chair. Susan stands and watches him go out the front door. I'm sure she'll follow him and offer to put homemade salve on his wounds.

Etta James's song has at last ended, and I turn and leave the dance floor. Grandma Betty waves at me from across the room and smiles. I start walking toward her, but I'm distracted by Mikayla and Caprice, who are standing at the bar, near Nikeo, in a heated argument.

Judging from Mikayla's flushed face and Caprice's white-hot Italian temper, I sense that things are about to go too far, and apparently I'm not the only one. Everyone within a ten-foot radius is rubbernecking to get a better look at the two beauties doing battle.

"Give me a break! I have an actual career. And you? Don't kid yourself.

You're not the head of the mob. You're the head of a cleaning company. You're in the business of killing germs, not people. You're a self-righteous, arrogant guido!" Mikayla yells, following this up with a shove.

Caprice loses her balance and stumbles backward, grabbing for the shoulder of Nikeo, who has been watching the exchange with amusement.

It's not Caprice's style to retaliate with words. She's also not the shoving, hair-pulling, scratching, tackling kind of girl. Catfights aren't her style. A natural-born boxer, she fights old-school. She fights like a man.

Caprice's face darkens. Her green eyes zone in on her enemy. Her fist tightens, and her right arm goes back like a trigger. Locked and loaded, she's going to shoot. Her target? Mikayla's face.

If I don't intervene now, there's no telling what damage she'll do. I'm three feet away when I literally throw myself through the air, holding up my hand just as Caprice throws the punch.

"Don't! She's pregnant!" I shout as I'm flying through the air, arms outstretched.

CHAPTER TWENTY

"Thanks." I take the ice pack from Nikeo and gingerly push it against my eye. Lenny sits on the arm of the sofa. He's staring so intently at my face that he sways slightly.

Caprice steadies him. "Careful, Lenny, or you're going to end up with an ice pack too."

"I'm making us drinks," announces Nikeo.

I wince in pain as I readjust the ice pack. "Good idea."

"I'm so sorry." Caprice scrutinizes the bruise that has formed on my cheekbone and jaw, thankfully missing my still-tender nose.

"You've apologized a hundred times."

Caprice sits on the chair across from me. Lenny hops off the couch and crawls into her lap. She strokes him absentmindedly. "I feel awful."

"Not as awful as Mikayla feels. I can't believe I opened my big mouth. I mean, yes, I can believe it. It's me, after all, but it wasn't fair to Mikayla."

It wasn't Caprice's punch that brought the party to a standstill so much as my ear-shattering town-crier broadcast of Mikayla's pregnancy. After Nikeo and Caprice helped me to my feet, I looked over at Mikayla, who had backed herself up against a barstool. Her eyes darted toward the back exit, but it was too late to run.

Caprice scoffs. "Wasn't fair? Come on. She loved the attention. Everyone was fawning over her. Congratulating her. Clapping. Grandma Betty was beside herself with excitement. So were Jenny Ryanne and Samson. And did you see Jeremy's face? He couldn't have been more thrilled. I thought the guy was going to break down and weep with joy. He was over the moon."

"Uh-huh," I say noncommittally.

Later tonight, when Mikayla told him that the baby she was carrying wasn't his but Angelo's, he'd be falling off the moon, entering the fiery ozone layer, and turning to ash. In a last desperate attempt to salvage her modeling career, figure out a way to end her money woes, and win Angelo's affections, she'd slept with him in July after a drunken bash at the studio of Janice Streit, the Sylvia Plath–obsessed photographer. Mikayla banked on the fact that Angelo would remember how much he loved her. Turned out all he remembered was that the sex was good, and that's all he wanted. The ploy hadn't worked, but it had given her much more than she bargained for. She began to see the walk down the aisle as her only way out.

Her savior came in the form of Jeremy, and she went after him hard and fast. She won the man lottery: Jeremy is a for-better-or-worse kind of guy, and he won't take back his vows or his heart. I'm not sure how quickly he'll accept what's happened, but he'll stay by Mikayla's side and raise the baby as his own.

Nikeo returns with a gin and tonic and hands it to me. Dropping the ice pack on the table, I take a long drink. The Dave Matthews Band's "Don't Drink the Water" plays in the background.

I lean into the sofa and close my eyes. Raising my fingertips to my temples, I gently massage. My head throbs; it feels as if Caprice didn't hit my face as much as she smacked my brain. "I should probably go back."

"And go against Grandma Betty's wishes?"

After the excitement had died down, Grandma Betty told me to go take care of myself, and under no circumstances return. "I've gone against them before."

"Don't rock her boat tonight. Besides, Jocelyn, Samson, and Jenny offered to stay and help clean everything up."

I open my eyes. "I don't want to leave her alone, especially not tonight. This is Frank's celebration. I can't miss it."

"I'll be your understudy." Caprice stands up and pulls on her coat.

"You don't have to do that."

"Are you kidding me? I punched my best friend in the face tonight for no good reason. I don't have to go, but I want to."

I'm in too much pain to protest. Once she leaves, Nikeo sits down in her spot and sips his drink. "That was quite a show."

I stretch my legs out in front of me. "It wasn't that big of a deal."

"I'm not talking about the punch. I'm talking about what happened on the dance floor between you and Justice."

I shrug. "Pure entertainment. I aim to please."

"If you hadn't stopped me, it would have gotten more entertaining."

"I have no doubt."

"Tell me what happened between you two."

"I'm moving on out and moving on up to the Rocky Mountains."

"You're not serious."

"I am."

Nikeo studies my face for a moment and then grins. "I didn't think you had it in you to sever the ties that bind."

Technically, Justice is the one severing; I'm just walking away with my head held high.

There's a knock at the door. Nikeo glances over his shoulder but doesn't make a move. Curious, Lenny leaps off the couch and trots over. Too exhausted to move, let alone try to convince Nikeo to do something courteous, I yell, "Come in!"

Aris and Trina open the door and step inside, then stand there awkwardly, exchanging greetings with Nikeo.

"Cane Kallevik, are you okay?" Aris asks, a concerned look on his face.

"We've been totally worried about you. We wanted to stop by to see how you were," Trina chimes in.

"I'm fine. Never been better."

"No blood at least," remarks Aris.

I smile wearily. "No need for a scarf."

"Right, right." Aris chuckles at this inside joke.

"That's something about Mikayla," says Trina. "Isn't it? You know, wouldn't it be cool if we could continue the story line for Farmer and the Belle and have the characters get married and have a baby? I'm sure Samson would love to put his grandchild on the front of an ice cream container."

"Keep thinking along those lines, and you'll be fine without me."

"Without you?" Puzzled, Trina shakes her head.

"I've accepted another job—in Colorado. I'm planning on giving my notice soon. Please don't say anything. I want to talk to Samson first."

"I can't do it without you!" Trina exclaims.

"You're moving!" exclaims Aris. "You can't go, Cane Kallevik! We want you to be in our wedding."

Trina sticks out her left hand and wiggles her ring finger, showing off a two-carat diamond. "He proposed last night!" she squeals.

Proud yet sheepish, Aris shuffles his feet. "I'm just glad she said yes."

"Of course I said yes, you goof!" She kisses him on the lips for a full twenty seconds, prompting him to turn bright red. "The wedding is very soon. We want you to be maid of honor! We wouldn't even have met if not for you."

"Wow." Everyone else is making this relationship thing look easy. "That's great!" I push myself off the couch and hug both of them. I spend an appropriate amount of time gushing over the ring and assuring them that I'll come back for their May wedding.

Once they've gone, the pain in my face seems to have gotten worse. I give Nikeo a nasty look. "You could have at least said congratulations or something."

Now shoeless and making himself at home, he props his feet up on my coffee table and picks up the stereo remote, hitting the forward button until he lands on a Tom Petty CD. "I don't even know them."

"Does it matter?"

"You know where I stand on marriage. I wanted to give them my condolences, not my congratulations, but I didn't think you would have liked that."

"You're a cynic."

"Yes, and so are you."

Lenny climbs onto the back of the couch and drapes himself over my shoulders like a scarf. He's not being friendly; he's buttering me up, trying to get some of my drink. He's been eyeing my gin and tonic longingly ever since I first picked it up. He stares at it and puts his front paw against my bruised face. "Didn't you get a hotel room?" I ask Nikeo.

He smiles. "Yes, but I'm going to cancel my reservation and stay here."

"You can't."

"Because you're a good girl and love your mama?" he asks, mimicking

Petty's "Free Fallin' " lyrics.

"I already have a full house. Grandma Betty and Caprice are staying here."

"That's not a problem. Caprice can take my hotel room, and I'll be in your bed anyway."

"I don't think so."

"Thinking has nothing to do with it."

There's a knock at the door. Nikeo glances over his shoulder. "Great— they're back." He turns toward me. "They want to know if you will be the godmother of their children."

"Hilarious."

"I'm not sticking around for this," he mumbles and makes his way into the bathroom.

"Coming," I yell, and stand. Lenny decides to stay positioned around my neck.

When I open the door, it isn't the happy couple. It's Justice, half of the unhappy couple.

Concern is etched all over his face. He reaches out and strokes my cheek. Lenny regards him with annoyance. "Jeremy called and told me what happened. Are you okay?"

"Just dandy." If I could, I would pack up all my things and leave tonight. No need to draw this out any longer.

"Can I come in?"

If he comes in, there's a good chance I might bust out the nervous-breakdown party hats and T-shirts. I can't risk it. I'm doing this with class and maturity. I stiffen my posture, which earns a protesting meow from Lenny and a frown from Justice. "I'm not sure that's such a good idea."

Behind me, the bathroom door opens. Justice's eyes swing to Nikeo and stay there for a long, uncomfortable moment. Even though my back is to Nikeo, I know that he's giving Justice one of his cocky I-win grins. A tsunami of tension bowls through my apartment.

Finally Justice drags his eyes back to me. He looks lost and hurt.

"Cane."

He's not just saying my name; he's pleading, declaring, and questioning all at once.

Not fair. This is what he wanted, and I gave him the easy way out. Now he's having regrets and second thoughts? Too little, too late. I can't do this anymore. The back-and-forth is ridiculous.

"That's how it's going to be, then? This is what you want?" His voice is just a notch above a whisper.

He's putting this on me?

A righteous indignation makes my pale skin flush purple. I could easily point the finger at him and tell him what I overheard today, that I know what he's planning on doing. But I can't do it. I can't part on bad terms. I'm not going to spout angry and bitter words that, when it comes down to it, I wouldn't really mean.

Because, forever, for always, and no matter what, I love Justice. I can't help myself. I lost my heart to him when I was fifteen years old, and he'll always have it. I'm going to spare him the agony of having to stab me in the back, and spare myself the misery of having him do it. I'm going to walk away once and for all. "This is what I want," I say, pushing the words out of my mouth.

His eyes shrink at the edges, and a deep line forms between them. Shoving his hands in his coat pocket, he turns and leaves.

Closing the door, I rest my forehead against it. Nikeo walks over and removes Lenny from my shoulders. In a comforting gesture, he runs his left hand slowly down my arm and stops at my wrist. With his right hand, he gathers my hair and moves it to the side. He pushes up against me until I feel the thud of his heart in my back, and it's a much better feeling than a knife. With his lips close to my sensitive neck, he sings softly into my ear. "And all the bad boys are standing in the shadows . . . All the good girls are home with broken hearts. And I'm free, I'm free fallin'."

CHAPTER TWENTY-ONE

November 1998

"**B**alls. Stupid wind! Get in, it's freezing out there." Once Caprice has pulled me inside her house and out of the wicked Colorado sleet storm, she kicks the door shut with her bare foot.

"I thought for sure your flight would be delayed."

"I thought for sure the plane would crash."

She grimaces. "That bad?"

I point to my braided head. I look like a redheaded island girl. "I saw at least two women doing Hail Marys, and I'm pretty sure everyone in first class was rip-roaring drunk by the time the plane landed. They held up all of us in coach because they couldn't figure out how to walk off the plane in a straight line. When I fly out on Sunday night, I'm taking a parachute with me."

"We'll buy one for you before you leave."

I drop my bag on the slate entryway, and Caprice gives me a giant hug, momentarily lifting me off the ground. She plants a sloppy kiss on my cheek. "I'm so happy to see you, I could make out with you."

"I think you just did."

"How's Grandma?"

I'm too distracted by Caprice's tight hot-pink Maid Hot bikini to reply. "Most people wear clothes when it's freezing."

"I'm not most people." Shivering and grinning, Caprice struts through the great room and gracefully hops up onto the generous fireplace hearth to warm her backside.

I pry my sore feet out of my soaked ballet flats and wiggle my toes, relishing the freedom. "I thought you were done cleaning."

"I am—this was strictly for a photo shoot," she explains, striking a modeling pose. "That fight with Mikayla got me thinking about marketing. I realized we did need a face for our company, and it wasn't going to be Mikayla. We have plenty of hot girls and guys, so I had a group photo shoot today. Thought it would be helpful for you to have some new brochure and website material."

"Outstanding." I throw my coat over the back of the leather sofa and finally get around to answering her inquiry. "Grandma is fine. Safe and sound back in the sunshine. She's tougher than I am."

Caprice rotates, now warming her front side. She looks at me over her shoulder. "I thought for sure she would move back to Savage."

"She said she wanted to stay down there. She wants to be where Frank was, and besides, since I'm moving here, there's nothing left for her in Savage.

"I guess."

"You don't have any food, do you? I'm starving."

Caprice suddenly spins back around to face me. "Holy. Balls." Leaping off the hearth, she makes her way over to where I'm standing and regards me with horror.

Judging from her expression, she's either going to inform me that someone close to me has died or tell me that I can't have the job. I can't handle either of those things. I've had to say good-bye to Frank, comfort grief-stricken Grandma Betty, and come to terms with the death of Justice and me.

Determined to get out before Justice returns from his Iowa gig and no doubt shacks up with Susie Homemaker in what would have been our dream house, I've been busy strategizing my exit. In the past week I've given Samson my notice, attended my going-away dinner at Sorrento's, thrown by Trina and Aris, rented my apartment to Mikayla and Jeremy, who are desperate to move back to Savage, where it will be better to raise a family, and taped up cardboard boxes in anticipation of the move. Although Samson said he would "take me back in a heartbeat should I ever change my mind," that's not an option. I need a clean break, not the splintering kind that never heals.

Caprice continues to eye me strangely. I can't take the suspense anymore. "What? You're not going to tell me that I can't have the job, are you?"

"That's not it at all." Her lips curled in distaste, she clicks her tongue. "You look disgusting."

I glance down at my emaciated frame. In the three weeks since I've seen her, I've lost eight pounds, an amount the average person could pull off. Me? Not so much. I'm down to ninety-seven pounds of pure skeleton, skin, and freckles. I look like a prepubescent girl. Heartbreak and grief have more side effects than most pharmaceuticals. Nausea, vomiting, headaches, diarrhea, weight loss, heartburn (both the medical and figurative kind), insomnia—you name the symptom, I've had it. "I know I look gross."

"Eat a cheeseburger or ten, would you?" She pokes me in the ribs. "I bet I could grate cheese on you."

I run my hands over my rib cage. "I could make mincemeat out of Parmesan."

Her expression softens in sympathy. "You haven't heard from him yet?"

"Not one word. Not that I thought I would. I made it pretty clear that it was over. And I think Nikeo being on the scene when I broke it off sealed the deal."

"Good riddance." Caprice waves her hands. "He's not worth it."

If only I shared Caprice's attitude. "Jeremy says Justice is really broken up about everything, that he's having a hard time concentrating."

"It's because he's distracted by Susie Home Wrecker."

Feeling like I might gag and burst into tears, I press my hand into the base of my throat. "Next subject."

"Food, then." Caprice hustles into the kitchen and makes me a triple-stacked deli sandwich and then mixes up a bowl of granola, adding extra almonds and raisins.

"Eat all of this, and then I'm making you a triple hot fudge sundae with all the trimmings."

"I'm not going to say no to that." I chomp down on the sandwich.

Caprice closes the refrigerator. "I've got to get out of this bikini. I'm freezing."

Plate and bowl in hand, I follow her down the hall and into her bedroom.

"Hey, fill me in on the Jeremy and Mikayla drama. What happened between them? How did he take the news that the kid isn't his?" she asks.

For the record, I didn't betray Mikayla's confidence. Yes, I announced her pregnancy in the most public of ways, but I didn't tell Caprice—or anyone else, for that matter—that Jeremy hadn't fertilized her egg.

At breakfast the night after Frank's funeral, while I was nursing coffee and pressing ice packs to my two swollen eyes (one bruised from the punch, and both puffy from a long night of weeping for Frank and Justice), Caprice came to that conclusion herself. "I've been trying to figure out why Mikayla wouldn't tell anyone she was pregnant. It doesn't make sense," she said, shoving Froot Loops into her mouth. "Because she loves attention."

I peeked at her from under the ice packs.

She tapped her spoon against the lip of her cereal bowl. "She lives for it. So I'm betting that she was knocked up before she married him. Jeremy isn't the baby daddy, is he?"

Resting my forehead on the table, I sighed.

Holding her spoon in the air in a symbol of victory, she guffawed. "I'm right, aren't I?"

"Pleading the fifth," I mumbled.

"Ha! I am right! The look on her face last night—the absolute terror when you announced it to everyone. I just knew it. I had it all figured out right then and there."

Grandma Betty, wearing Frank's silk black robe that featured lightning bolts all over it, shuffled into the kitchen, her eyes as bruised as mine. "What did you have figured out?" she asked Caprice.

I gave Caprice a sharp look. I didn't want Grandma Betty or anyone else knowing about Mikayla. "Nothing—she had nothing figured out."

Hesitant to talk about the subject even now, I shrug off Caprice's inquiry and focus on gobbling up the sandwich.

Caprice rifles through her dresser, searching for an outfit that's more weather-appropriate. "Come on. I'm dying to know. How did Jeremy handle the news?"

I keep the information to a minimum. "Things are actually okay between them." When Mikayla sat Jeremy down and confessed, he told her that he needed time to think about things. A panicked Mikayla was sure that he would leave her, but I knew better than that. Loyal to the core, Jeremy said that he would stay under the condition that they attend counseling together. They started going two weeks ago, and so far so good.

"Ugh, of course they are. You're not going to give me any specifics, are you?"

"Sorry," I say with my mouth half full.

"That's okay." In true exhibitionist fashion, Caprice rips off her bikini top and steps out of her bottoms.

"Have you no propriety?"

"You belong in the Victorian era." Forgoing undergarments, she pulls on sweatpants and a hooded sweatshirt. "All dressed—you can open your eyes now."

I set the plate and bowl on her dresser, drop down on her bed, and fall onto my back.

"You have to eat more!"

"I lost my appetite when I saw you naked."

"Hilarious."

Turning my head, I stare out at the Rockies. Jagged, immense, and merciless in form, these mountains evoke unsettling emotions. I feel isolated, lonely, and so far from where I should be.

How can this be? Until this very second, I've been if anything overly confident in my decision. Even without Frank's silver compass guiding me, I knew what direction I needed to take, and I took definitive action to make it happen. I've even been a braggart about it, informing Rhonda Riddle, Grandma Betty, Mikayla, Jocelyn, Samson, and anyone else who will listen about my plans to land Maid Hot on the Forbes Top 100 list.

Originally I told Caprice that I needed to come out here this weekend to discuss the direction of the company and set goals for the coming year, so that when I made the official move out here in two weeks, we could hit the ground running. Turns out I've been lying to myself. I came out here to dip my toes in the water, to make sure that I have the guts to take the plunge. Preposterous, considering I've already thrown myself into the water and started swimming for the opposite shore.

Caprice nudges me with her knee. "What's wrong?"

I start working my fingers through my braids, freeing my hair and resisting the urge to start over again. I meet Caprice's eyes. "I'm terrified."

"You're going to be fine without him."

"Am I?"

"When you think about it, officially you haven't been together for six months now."

She's right, but that doesn't mean I like being without him, or that I'm comfortable with it.

Lizzie pops her head into the room. "Hi, Cane. How's Lenny Kravitz?"

"Sober and straight against his will."

She laughs. "He was quite the partier, so I'm guessing he doesn't like it."

"Not one bit. He's constantly hoping to fall off the wagon."

Leaning against the doorframe, Lizzie, who loves sparkly jewelry, shakes her wrist, causing the dozen or so rhinestone bracelets to jingle. "Where's poor Lenny going to go when you move back here?"

"Jocelyn is taking him. She's been spending a lot of time at my place, and they've bonded."

"I heard about what happened with her. How is she?" Lizzie asks.

Caprice gives me a guilty look and kind of shrugs her shoulders. While I'm great at keeping secrets, Caprice has a hard time being discreet.

"It hasn't been easy, but she's keeping her chin up." Things have improved greatly this past week. Three days ago, Deanna showed up at the Schaeffer household out of the blue and apologized to Jocelyn for what she had done. I would like to think that I'd intimidated Deanna enough to prompt her sudden reformation. However, I'm convinced it had more to do with her suspension from school and the fact that Jocelyn had been handling herself with such integrity that Deanna started to feel like a cruel idiot.

"That's good." Lizzie smiles. "Hey, so my friend down the street is having a party tonight. Hot tub. Gorgeous mountain men. A keg. Lots of music—"

"And the all-important illegal substance that you're so fond of," I interrupt.

Lizzie gives me a dirty look. "Nope. Smoking pot got in the way of my strict diet rules."

Caprice grins knowingly. "As in inhaling bags of Doritos, which, as you know, violates her veggies-only-after-five-p.m. rule."

"Right. So I quit." Lizzie steps into the room, checks her sparkly lip gloss in the mirror, and fluffs her hair. She picks up Caprice's vanilla-scented perfume from the top of the dresser, spritzes it on her neck, and squirts a generous amount in our direction. "I'm done with that. Clean and sober, just like Lenny."

Caprice waves her hands. "Knock it off!"

I plug my nose as Lizzie aims the perfume my way and spritzes twice. "You two want to come?"

Caprice glances at me and arches a brow. "What do you think?"

Lizzie puckers her lips. "Make up your mind, because we're already late."

Dragging myself into an upright position, I look at those mountains again. Like it or not, this is my life. Going backward isn't an option, and sitting still isn't my style. I jump off the bed. "Let's go."

I've had enough of the party. Lizzie may be clean, but she isn't exactly sober. This may or may not have factored into her decision to hop up on her friend's bar and start stripping.

"Go for it!" yells a fist-pumping, tank-top-wearing, steroid-addicted guy named Vance who's been stalking me the entire night, grabbing my ass, pushing himself up against me, and flexing his overdeveloped veiny arms. He's repeatedly told me that he's going to follow me home tonight because "Baby, you've got what I need."

Apparently, he's now decided that Lizzie has what he needs. He shoves his way through the crowd and stands in front of the bar for an up-close-and-personal view of Lizzie's crotch, which thankfully is still covered, though I'm not sure for how much longer.

Caprice sidles up to me and tilts her head to the side as she regards Lizzie's impromptu striptease. "Leave it to her to ruin a good time."

"I'm not sure she's ruining their good time." I point to the crowd of men, who are frantically pushing their way to the front for a better view. "The beer from the keg isn't the only thing foaming. Get a load of their mouths."

Caprice and I stand and watch as several guys start pulling dollar bills out of their pockets. Lizzie kneels down, leans over provocatively, and lets them stuff the money into her bra.

Distressed, Caprice places a hand on her forehead. "Please tell me she's not going to take everything off."

Lizzie unfastens her bra and twirls it on her fingers. "Too late. Your cousin missed her calling. She should be a Vegas stripper."

"Shitty balls. I knew I shouldn't have let her have any shots."

I observe Lizzie gyrating. Is this what my life is going to be like? Party-hopping and existing in a girls-gone-wild reality where I'm responsible for babysitting and being the voice of reason? "I can't take this anymore."

Caprice takes my hand. "Neither can I. But hey, at least Lizzie got rid of that Vance guy for you."

"Very true. If that's what I have to choose from"—I glance over my shoulder at the square-jawed idiot—"then shoot me now."

We walk up the stairs together. "There are better guys than that."

"I hope so."

"You'll meet someone soon."

"I have no interest in meeting anyone." I forage through the pile of coats on the living room couch, a plaid monstrosity that looks like a cousin of my bloodstained one back in Savage. I suddenly miss that stupid couch so much, I actually get a dull ache in my stomach.

"What?" Caprice gives me a concerned look.

I realize that I'm pressing my hands to my midsection. "Nothing." After digging some more, I find our coats.

Caprice takes her keys out of her coat pocket and hands them to me. "I can't leave yet. I've got to stay and make sure no guys take advantage of my bimbo cousin."

"I can stay with you," I offer.

"You're going back to my place so that you can eat again." She pinches both of my upper arms. "Put some meat on those bones. Make some microwave popcorn and douse it in butter and ketchup. Then make yourself a pan of brownies."

"I promise to ingest at least ten thousand calories."

"Twenty thousand would make me feel better."

I zip up my coat and pocket the house keys. "How much longer are you going to be?"

"Not long. I'm going to drag her out of here in a half hour or so."

Caprice hugs me.

On the walk home, the vicious wind attacks me, and icy snowflakes slap me in the face. I yank up my hood and tighten the drawstrings. Head down, hands shoved in my pockets, I fight my way down the block, trying not to slip on the icy sidewalk.

Blinded by the elements, I can barely see where I'm headed, but somehow I make it to Caprice's front door. I dig in my pocket and grab the keys, then drop them. As I bend down, my hood flops backward. Great. The entryway of her house is like a wind tunnel. My hair flies every which way, getting stuck in my mouth and plastered against my wet face.

Fumbling with the keys, I drop them again. When I retrieve them for the second time, I can't remember what key it is. I try one, then another. Nothing.

I take another look at the twenty keys, trying to figure out which is which, but my hair makes it impossible to see. If I had scissors right now, I swear I would go butch and hack it off to the scalp. When I get inside, I'm going to do it. I'm going to stand in front of the bathroom mirror and hack away at my beautiful long tresses. Isn't that what a girl is supposed to do when she needs to reinvent herself and start another life? I want to do something so drastic that even I won't recognize myself.

Behind me a car door slams.

I shove a key into the keyhole and it gets jammed. Spectacular. Leaving it dangling there, I cup my hands and blow on them. The wind howls violently in my ears. A piece of gunky sleet falls from the steep roof and smacks me in the forehead. My lungs lose all their air.

Gasping and furious, I take hold of the key and yank so hard that when it releases suddenly, I fly backward at least two feet.

I sense a presence behind me on the walkway and automatically stiffen. My first thought is that it's Vance, but if Lizzie is still stripping, then he's still drooling and foaming at the mouth.

"If you could see, it might be easier to find what you need." He gathers my hair in his hands and puts a rubber band in place. When he's finished with that, he lifts my hood snugly back in place, puts his hands on my shoulders, and turns me to face him.

Confused, overwhelmed, and more relieved than I've ever been in my life, I let the keys fall from my frozen hands, and my face undergoes an immediate nuclear meltdown. I don't cry so much as erupt.

He pulls me against his chest and wraps his arms around my vibrating body. I melt into him. It's so familiar and so right. I want to stay here forever.

He presses his mouth to my ear. "It's all okay."

This makes me cry harder, because it's not all okay. It's all wrong. I shouldn't be in Colorado drinking beer with Caprice and watching Lizzie strip on a bar. I should be back in Savage lying in bed with him, living the life we've been planning for the past six years, dreaming about our future together.

I put my palms on his chest and look up in his eyes. In the shadow of the Rocky Mountains, they are so blue and tranquil, an ocean where I could drift forever. "It's too late."

"It's never too late."

"What if it is?"

Cupping my chin with his hand, he smiles at me. "Let's get out of the cold."

He retrieves the keys from the ground and finds the right one on the first try. I walk through the door. He follows and closes it.

We step out of our wet shoes and shrug off our coats. I'm no longer sobbing uncontrollably, but I'm still weepy and quivery. I don't trust myself to move an inch, because I might collapse or dissolve.

"What are you doing here?" I ask, knowing that it sounds like an accusation. Then something horrible occurs to me. My heart starts pounding so hard my eardrums are close to bursting. "It's not Grandma Betty, is it? Is something wrong?"

"No, everything is fine. I'm here because I called Rhonda Riddle."

This information stuns me. Back on moving day in September, I told him I'd called a psychic, but I hadn't mentioned her name. Nor had I told him that she'd become a good friend of mine. He would have thought I was crazy. "What?"

"I should have known something was off the night of Frank's party. You weren't acting like yourself. I didn't understand why you would just decide to move to Colorado and give up on us. For the past three weeks I've been racking my brain, trying to figure it out, trying to pinpoint what went wrong. I spoke with Grandma Betty, Jocelyn, and Mikayla. I even spoke with Samson about it—not that he was thrilled to have a discussion like that.

"No one seemed to know what had changed your mind about us, or why you would suddenly end things and move to Colorado. I thought maybe the reason you were going to move back here was because of Nikeo—that's what you insinuated when I stopped by your apartment to see if you were—"

"This was never about Nikeo," I interject adamantly.

He runs his hand down across his jawline and sighs. "I know that now. I got a hold of Mikayla early this morning and talked to her, trying to pump her for information again. She said that she honestly didn't know anything."

"Mikayla didn't know why I left." I'd kept the conversation I overheard between Justice and Susan private for two reasons. I did it for self-preservation; let's face it, I didn't want anyone knowing that Justice had chosen Susie Home Wrecker over me. Secondly, I did it to protect Justice. I couldn't stand anyone hating him or thinking less of him simply because he stopped loving me.

He continues explaining. "Just before I was about to hang up, Mikayla said that I might want to talk to Rhonda about it. Obviously, I didn't have a clue who Rhonda was, so Mikayla filled me in and gave me Rhonda Riddle's number. I called her, and we had a very long, very interesting, and very honest conversation. She told me why you left."

Rhonda loves relationship drama, and since I never requested confidentiality, I assume she was an open book when Justice called her. "If that's the case, if you know why I left, then why are you here?"

"That conversation that you happened to overhear between Susan and me—it wasn't about you at all. It was about business."

My heart starts beating so hard that I'm going to be eating slate floor in a second. "No, that can't be right. No, I heard her ask you when you were going to tell me, and she said prolonging it was cruel and that you shouldn't wait. Then you said the timing was horrible, and she said that I would be devastated—"

"That conversation wasn't about you. I swear." He takes my hands in his. "It was about Trina."

"No—wait." I shake my head. "That doesn't make any sense."

"Susan was asking me when I was going to fire Trina. Samson and I had been discussing letting her go for some time, but then you told me about the job offer in Colorado. So the timing wasn't great. I figured I should play it safe and see how things played out before firing her. I didn't want our entire marketing staff gone."

My nose gets clogged with snot, and my tear ducts fill to the brim. "So you don't love her?"

"I love you. It's always been you, just you." He lets go of my hands and fishes in his coat pocket. He removes a velvet box and hands it to me.

302

"Open it."

Flustered, I clumsily pry it open. Inside is Frank's silver compass. "I've been looking all over for this!"

"I took it from your apartment the night I brought you home from the emergency room. I saw it sitting on your nightstand and saw that it was broken. I had it fixed. I'm sorry it took so long. I'm sorry everything took so long."

I carefully remove the compass and flip it open. It's in pristine working condition, and not surprisingly, the arrow spins north quickly, pointing right to Justice. I've taken lots of winding roads over the past six years, and every one of them has led me back to him. "I thought I lost this." I look up at him. "I thought I lost you."

He runs a finger over my cross-shaped birthmark and then pulls me into his arms. "Not possible. How could you lose me when I belong to you?" he asks as he looks into my eyes.

We have our past; we have this moment. And forever, for always, no matter what-we have each other.

ABOUT THE AUTHOR

The Road to Justice is critically acclaimed author Tamara Lyon's fifth novel and the third installment in *The Ugly Tree* series. Released in 2010, *The Ugly Tree* was a Flamingnet Top Choice Award winner, 2011 Next Generation Indie Finalist, Eric Hoffer Finalist, and Midwest Book Award Finalist. She is currently working on her next novel, *Post-Traumatic Brazilian Wax Syndrome*, to be released in late 2014. When she's not writing, Lyon tours the country, delivering her motivational speech "Give Your Dream Wheels." She makes her home in Lake Geneva, Wisconsin with her husband, son, and counter surfing and adorable golden retriever, Macy.